THE KIND
FOLK

THE KIND
FOLK

RAMSEY
CAMPBELL

◤TOR
A Tom Doherty Associates Book
New York

THE KIND FOLK

Copyright © 2012 by Ramsey Campbell

A Tor Book
Published by Tom Doherty Associates, LLC
175 Fifth Avenue
New York, NY 10010

www.tor-forge.com

Tor® is a registered trademark of Tom Doherty Associates, LLC.

The Library of Congress Cataloging-in-Publication Data is available upon request.

ISBN 978-0-7653-8245-0 (hardcover)
ISBN 978-1-4668-8731-2 (e-book)

Our books may be purchased in bulk for promotional, educational, or business use. Please contact your local bookseller or the Macmillan Corporate and Premium Sales Department at 1-800-221-7945, extension 5442, or by e-mail at MacmillanSpecialMarkets@macmillan.com.

Originally published in Great Britain by PS Publishing Ltd.

First U.S. Edition: August 2016

Printed in the United States of America

0 9 8 7 6 5 4 3 2 1

for Billy Martin, with love—

remember Blackpool, Doc!

"Maybe one day you wake up and forget what it was to be human. Maybe that happens, and then it's okay."

Dennis Lehane, *Mystic River*

1

THE SECOND ANSWER

"YOU GIVE ME HONESTY," Jack Brittan says, "and I'll give you hope. When did you start to have doubts that Luke was your son?"

"I've never had any," says Luke's mother.

"He wasn't asking you, Freddy," Luke's father objects. "Maybe I should of had my suspicions before he was born. My brother was a sight too eager to come up with a name. Lucius, he wanted us to call the baby if it was a boy."

"We called him Lucas," Freda says as if this may placate her husband.

"I'd like to know why Terry was so concerned with him. Took him out every chance he got when Luke was little. Always telling him he was special like we didn't think enough of him."

"We could have told Luke how much we thought of him a bit more often, Maurice."

"You weren't so pleased with Terry when the boy started having nightmares," Maurice says and turns to the presenter of the television show. "The doctor sent Luke to a psychiatrist, that's how bad he got. God help Terry if I ever find out he was feeding him drugs."

"I never did," Terence murmurs to Luke.

"I know," Luke says without knowing much at all. He and his uncle are in the green room, an elongated white backstage space containing sofas and a television monitor that sprouts high up on the wall. He's about to put one of several questions to Terence when Brittan says "Let's have him out to answer that."

Perhaps Terence doesn't realise this means him. He stays on the sofa opposite Luke until a hulking man whose black T-shirt is emblazoned **BRITTAN'S RESOLUTIONS** gestures him to follow. Seconds later he's on the monitor, where he's greeted by more booing than applause. There's silence by the time he takes a seat on the far side of Freda from his brother.

She risks a glance at him and a quick smile before she reverts to gazing at Brittan. Luke is sure she views the occasion as a public testimony besides her opportunity to appear on a favourite television show. Though her face has grown plumper since he left home, the features minimised by her cheeks seem clarified by her belief in herself. Her faded eyes have regained their acorn tint, her small nose looks eager for a scent, her wide lips have rediscovered pinkness. She leans forward, betraying the silver roots of the black waves that frame her face, as Brittan says "You ought to be a family if I ever saw one."

Presumably he means the brothers, both of whom have all the Arnold characteristics: large-boned brawny frames, auburn eyes, broad noses, square chins. Luke shares all these, although he has conquered the tendency of the lower lip to droop, and his hair isn't clipped as severely as theirs, which is so short it barely admits to greying. "So, Terence," Brittan says, "what sort of an influence do you think you've had on your nephew?"

"He's a fine young specimen of humanity." Terence's eyes flicker from side to side as though he's searching for Luke. "I'd be proud if that was anything to do with me."

"You were just trying to be an uncle, weren't you?" Freda says and tells the presenter "He never had any children of his own."

"And what kind of uncle was he?" Before Freda can answer, Brittan turns on Terence. "What's this about you using drugs?"

"A lot of us used to have a smoke now and then on the job."

"A lot of us didn't," Luke's father retorts. "Anyone that worked for me that did, they'd be out on their arse."

As Luke wonders if the broadcast will bleep the word out, Brittan says "So why did you trust a druggie with your son?"

Maurice scowls at an explosion of applause, and Luke feels as though he's watching a performance while he waits to go onstage. "He knew not to bring that stuff anywhere near Luke," says his father.

"I never did," Terence assures him.

"You brought whatever it did to you, didn't you?" Far more triumphantly than Luke cares for, Brittan says "Is that why your nephew needed psychiatric help?"

"He told Luke fairy tales, that's all," Freda intervenes. "Maybe Luke was too young for some of them."

"How young was that?"

"Six," Maurice says. "That's when we had to take him to the doctor."

"It doesn't sound too young for fairy tales. Maybe you can tell us what disturbed him, Terence."

"Some of the old tales weren't meant for children."

A memory lights up like a tableau in Luke's head. He's sitting in a sunlit field while his uncle tells him about a little mermaid, a story that seemed to reach deep into Luke. The memory goes out as Maurice demands "Then why'd you tell him at that age?"

"I thought they were his kind of thing. You know what an imagination he had."

"Should have been more careful what you put in it, then. Six is no bloody age to have someone messing about inside your head."

As Luke wonders if this refers to the psychiatrist or Terence, Brittan says "We haven't heard why you've started suspecting your brother."

"Luke's having a child with his partner and the way Terry's been carrying on he might be the grandad. He's like he was when Luke was born."

Having waited for the audience to murmur, Brittan says "After the break we'll meet the man the argument's about and his girlfriend."

Though Sophie has agreed to speak, they've put her in the audience. She can't feel any more distanced from the proceedings than Luke does. The programme is pretending to be live, showing adverts for the sponsor corporation on the monitor—Frugoplan Pensions ("Your super superannuation"), Frugocard ("Pack our plastic in your pocket"), the Frugotel chain ("Check us out and check in") . . . Perhaps they're meant to sell the products to the studio audience, unless someone felt that without them the spectators would feel cheated of part of the experience. Once the commercials come to an end Brittan welcomes viewers back and sums up the story so far, and then he says "Let's meet the man they're quarrelling over."

If there's a quarrel Brittan is happy to exacerbate it; perhaps it mightn't even have happened without his sort of show. Luke marches down the

9

flimsy passage in the wings and onto the stage, where his parents and his uncle join in the applause that meets him. He tries not to let his family's behaviour make the situation even yet more unreal. Sophie is in an aisle seat halfway up the auditorium, and stops clapping long enough to wave as Luke sits beside his father. "So," Brittan says, "what's your take on all this, Luke?"

"I think it's a misunderstanding that's got out of hand. It's as my mother said, my uncle wanted to be involved because he had nobody of his own."

"And what kind of childhood are you telling us you had?"

Luke inspects him before answering. Nobody would know from watching him on television that he's a head shorter than most of his guests, since he never ventures near them when they're on their feet. His close-set features might be called neat, but they strike Luke as pinched together. Below his precisely trimmed black hair his pale forehead bears a faint constant frown. His dark quick eyes want to appear penetrating, and his thin lips are parted by default, either to urge a response or poised to interrupt. "I couldn't have wished for a better one," Luke tells him, "and I'm thanking my uncle as well as my parents. He was why I talked so much, that's what I'm told, before I could even walk."

"You always knew more words," Freda says, "when you came home."

"Maybe he stuffed too much in your little head," Maurice complains. "One more reason we had to haul you to the quack."

"Not too constructive," Brittan tells Terence, "for someone who works in construction."

"He doesn't," Maurice retorts. "He's in demolition."

It occurs to Luke that Brittan takes him to be in his parents' business. If Luke enlightens him, will that stop the show? Surely there's no need; once Brittan has finished melodramatising the situation, the Arnolds can return to normal. His father's doubts can't help making Luke feel as though he has taken his life and his family too much for granted, and he'll be glad when Maurice's suspicions are disproved. The presenter's face closes around a concerned look as he says "Why do you think you needed the psychiatrist, Luke?"

"I don't know if I did need her. It was mostly that my parents didn't want the doctor giving me drugs to help me sleep."

"You should of heard the row you were making in the night," Maurice protests. "Those were never dreams a child should have."

"What do you recall about seeing the psychiatrist?" Brittan wants to hear.

"She kept trying to make me say things about my uncle that weren't true."

"We just want the truth here. What kind of things?"

"That he'd been abusing me, I expect. He never touched me, not like that."

"So you're saying he's completely innocent."

Luke sees that Brittan is frustrated by the lack of conflict and determined to provoke it. "I'm saying," Luke is happy to declare, "we all are."

Brittan doesn't simply look dissatisfied but prolongs it for the camera. "Do we call that honest?"

"Noooo."

To Luke the audience's customary response sounds like the lowing of a herd. He has dealt with many kinds of audience, and he's about to try his skills on this crowd when Freda says "You only wanted Luke to make as much of himself as he could, didn't you, Terry? You were trying to open his mind."

"That's it," Terence says. "That's all."

"I expect you're glad he's creative like you tried to be."

Terence lets out a stammering murmur that goes some way towards agreement. Perhaps he's wary of suggesting that his brother didn't do enough for the boy. Luke thinks Brittan may enquire into the remark, but the presenter turns to the audience. "This can't be much fun for you, Sophie, in your state."

She gives this and him a long look. Though Luke is sure she isn't posing for the camera, he can imagine her features gracing the screen: wide blue eyes, long elegant nose, pink lips poised to smile if they aren't already smiling, all softly framed by cropped red hair. Her face stays amiable, but her eyes have acquired a steely glint. "It shouldn't be much fun for anyone."

"I'm saying you can do without all this."

"I'm certain everybody can." She gives Brittan time to take this as criticism and says "This isn't about me. I'm having an easy time, not like Freda did."

"What are you telling us was hard for her?"

"We thought I'd got too old till I had Luke," Freda says. "We thought he was a gift from God."

Maurice lets his lower lip sag while Terence covers his mouth. Once the audience has finished sighing at Freda's words Brittan says "Shall we do what you asked me to do?"

"About time," says Maurice.

"Let me have the DNA results for Terence Arnold," Brittan says and extends a hand until a technician crowned with a headset brings him an envelope. It puts Luke in mind of a prize on a game show, but he's also recalling a joke of his uncle's—that the initials ought to stand for Do Not Ask. "How certain are you that Terence isn't Luke's father?" Brittan asks Sophie.

"As sure as anyone can be."

"One hundred per cent," Freda vows with a laugh, "and more if you like."

"Another hundred," Terence says, having uncovered his mouth.

"And one from me," Luke contributes.

"Just get the bloody thing done with," says Maurice.

The presenter thrusts his dinky little finger beneath the flap and tears open the envelope. He extracts a card and shields it with the envelope while he takes far too much time for Luke's taste over scrutinising the information. At last he lifts his head and gazes at the family. "Our DNA test shows that . . . "

Luke knows that they're all being filmed. Brittan must be waiting until they've reacted enough to be broadcast, and Luke is on the point of blurting a version of his father's demand when the presenter says "Terence is not Luke's father."

Sophie claps her hands. Though Luke doesn't think she means to cue applause, the audience follows her lead. His father stumbles to his feet and hugs his wife while reaching to grip his brother's hand. "Sorry," he says indistinctly. "Bloody stupid. I'm the one that needs his head examined."

Freda murmurs a demurral as Terence bows his head and shakes it. Luke feels excluded from the proceedings, though he's relieved that the drama is over. Brittan waits for Maurice to resume his seat and enquires "Don't you have anything to say to them?"

"I've said I'm sorry," Luke's father protests but says it again, prompting Freda to stretch out her hands to him while Terence gazes down at his own. Luke is waiting for the presenter to lecture them or wish them luck when Brittan says "We aren't done yet."

Only Maurice seems to understand. "I don't know why I did it," he mumbles. "There's no need."

"It's paid for," Brittan says and gestures for the technician to bring him a second envelope. When he digs his finger beneath the flap Freda cries "You didn't, Maurice."

"They asked if I wanted it. It isn't going to matter now, is it?"

Freda gives him a smile so minute and restrained it barely hints at forgiveness. As Luke understands his father's plea Brittan says "Our DNA test on Maurice shows that . . . "

What does he want the camera to pick up this time? Luke's parents gaze at him with impatient confidence, an expression Luke borrows from them. Only Terence isn't looking at the presenter; he's intent on his own clasped hands. Brittan turns to Luke, and his face is so neutral it's unreadable. Luke can do that too, and he's about to mirror Brittan when the presenter lets sympathy into his eyes. "I'm sorry, Luke," he says. "You aren't Maurice Arnold's son."

2

ONE WAY HOME

IT ISN'T ABOUT HIM, Luke does his best to think. Sophie is stroking the palm of his hand as trees race past both sides of the train. Perhaps she's trying to anchor his sense of himself, but he feels as if Brittan's revelation has yet to take hold of him. He feels shrunk into his own mind, afraid to let the truth in. He's searching for reasons to disbelieve it when Sophie says "Has anybody ever looked into how reliable those tests are?"

Nobody has spoken since they caught the train. Terence is seated opposite her and staring out of the window as if he doesn't feel entitled to face his companions. Across the aisle Freda has kept glancing at Maurice to prompt or provoke him to voice his thoughts, but he seems to think his drooping lip is eloquent enough. Sophie's question rouses him, although he doesn't look at her. "The government uses them," he retorts.

"Maybe the ones Brittan uses aren't as reliable."

"Someone would have sorted them by now if they were getting it wrong."

"Even the official ones are sometimes. There've been cases where they've identified the wrong person. Couldn't it work the other way as well?"

Maurice twitches one shoulder as Freda gives him a hopeful glance. When Brittan read his test result out she looked betrayed, not just by the outcome but, Luke suspects, by the show itself. As she grows aware of his

14

concern for her she turns to him. "You're still our Luke whatever anybody says. That's so, isn't it, Maurice?"

Her husband lifts his head, and his lower lip sags as if to compensate. "Nobody's saying anything against him that I know of."

"I should hope not." Defending Luke has revived more of her spirit. "I ought to have had a test as well," she says. "You should have said."

"Whoever's to blame," Maurice says like a threat, "it's not me."

"It's nobody here, Maurice."

"I thought Luke was supposed to be the comedian of the family." Maurice pauses as though his mind has caught on the last phrase and says "Get on then, tell us who."

"I don't think it was whoever did your test, but thanks for being thoughtful, Sophie." Freda gazes down the carriage at a few scattered passengers. "I'm sorry if I embarrass anyone," she murmurs just loud enough to be audible above the soughing of the train. "Maurice is the only man I've ever had, the absolutely only one. I know most people don't care about saving themselves any more, but I did."

Sophie squeezes Luke's hand. As Maurice twists most of himself around to check that nobody is close enough to have overheard, she says "Then you think . . . "

"If Mr Brittan's people didn't make a mistake," Freda says, "someone must have mixed up the babies at the hospital," and leans across the aisle to grip Luke's arm. "Just don't forget what I said about you, Luke. We ended up with the baby we wanted."

"Nobody's arguing," Maurice says and stares at his brother. "And you're saying bugger all. It's not like you to have nothing to say for yourself."

Terence meets his eyes but withholds his expression. "What do you want me to say?"

"Whatever you're thinking." When Terence doesn't respond his brother mutters "You were always the clever one, that's what ma and dad thought. They never knew half of the stuff you were into or they wouldn't have been so pleased with you."

Luke is dismayed by their hostilities and can't help feeling somehow responsible, but it's Freda who intervenes. "That's not fair, Maurice, and it's got nothing to do—"

"I may not be the brightest but I've got enough upstairs not to waste my time on that crap. You'd better not have put any of it in Luke's head."

15

Before Luke can establish that he doesn't know what his father—no, Maurice—is talking about, Terence raises his lower lip and his head. "I helped him grow up how he has," he says. "I did my best, I'll tell you."

"Are you making out we didn't?"

"I'm sure you all did," Sophie says. "I think you should be proud."

An awkward silence seems to drag at the train, which is slowing as it reaches Runcorn. Terence shoves himself to his feet and avoids touching anyone as he lurches into the aisle. "Be in touch," he mumbles as a promise or a plea if not something else entirely, and hurries to the nearest door.

He doesn't look back from the platform. A few terraced streets on the bank of the Mersey drift past the windows, and then a silent whirring like the flight of a swarm of geometrical creatures closes around the train. The metal lattices that form both sides of the bridge across the river are retreating at speed. "I'll be getting the test," Freda announces, "and then I'll be finding out what the hospital has to say for itself."

The hectic activity comes to an end, revealing that the river has exposed a bank of mud like the ridged glistening back of a colossus about to heave itself out of the murky water. It's the kind of notion Terence might have shared with Luke when he was little, and it leaves Luke feeling painfully nostalgic for his childhood. There are other fancies he will have to live without now—the ideas that Terence was his uncle or Maurice was his father.

— 3 —

NOBODY'S SON

"YOU DID KNOW ALREADY, LUKE. You were as good as theirs, though, weren't you?" Gently and yet with a hint of fierceness Sophie reminds him "That's what you said."

"I wonder how they'd have treated me if they'd known I was an imposter."

"You're nothing of the kind. I expect they'd have wanted to make it up to you, and Terence would."

Hasn't she just contradicted herself? Luke stands up to switch off the television, which is showing him and the Arnolds like a tableau in a waxworks, every face besides his trying to suppress their expressions while he couldn't quite find one. "After the break," Brittan says, "we've a mother who's here to tell her son she'll disown him if he turns into a woman because his wife is now a man . . . " Luke extinguishes him but can't put the words that streamed along the bottom of the screen out of his mind. *After the show was recorded DNA testing proved Freda Arnold wasn't Luke's mother.*

As Sophie said, he already knew. Maurice phoned yesterday, sounding as if he were being required to apologise on his wife's behalf. Luke leaves Sophie on the pudgy leather couch in front of the television and crosses the polished boards to the window. They're in the apartment Freda and Maurice helped him buy when Arnold Building Contractors were converting this Victorian office block. That was early in the renovation of

17

downtown Liverpool, when prices were much lower and the building trade considerably more prosperous, but now he hardly feels entitled to the apartment—the two generous bedrooms, the extensive main room, the fitted kitchen and bathroom that would be at home in a store display. Beyond the window the late April sunlight glints on the edge of the sea across the bay, where the horizon sprouts a windmill that might be fingering the sky for substance. When he moved in Luke had a wide view of the sea, but tall buildings have risen in the way—monolith monsters, Terence calls them. Everything about the apartment brings to mind the family Luke presumed was his own in more ways than it is. He's Sophie's lover and the father of her child, he reminds himself as she joins him at the window and takes his hand to rest it on her ovoid midriff. "Anyway," she murmurs, "we know our baby's ours."

"We know and it will."

"Don't say it, Luke. Parents who call their children that, you'd think they didn't want them to be people."

"He or she," Luke amends, going down on one knee to lift Sophie's voluminous blouse and kiss her just above the navel. "That's you in there if you can hear me."

He presses an ear against her belly and hears the tide of his own blood. When he can't distinguish any movement he gets to his feet, hoping Sophie feels appreciated. Since their encounter with Brittan she has done her best to comfort him with her words and her touch, with favourite meals and singing songs from her repertoire and playing Bach transcriptions on her guitar, but he senses that she thinks she hasn't done enough—that he has lost more than just a blood relationship. Perhaps holding her will reassure more than any protests of Luke's, and he's resting his cheek against hers when his phone breaks the silence.

It's singing "June is busting out all over," which Maurice used to sing on Luke's birthday even though it isn't in that month. Now the ringtone feels like an attempt to cling to his childhood, and so does having listed Freda as mum. Before he can decide what to call her she says "It's only me."

"Hello." This sounds worse than incomplete, and Luke makes haste to say "How are you getting on?"

"I've been to the hospital where you were born." Less defiantly than she offered the last phrase she says "They've looked into their records, but they can't see how there could have been a mistake. Maurice wants to leave it now. I don't know what you think."

"Whatever's best for the family."

"We hoped you'd say that. We can go on as we always have, can't we? And your, and Maurice says to tell you he's sorry if he was a bit abrupt when he spoke to you. He was getting used to it, that's all."

"So long as he has."

"We must get together soon, all of us. Have you heard from, has Terry been in touch?"

"I haven't heard from him since your show," Luke says and feels ashamed of his choice of words.

"We've been trying to contact him but he hasn't answered our calls. Maurice would have gone over but our firm's working on a big job for the council. If you speak to Terry you'll let him know the news, won't you?" Presumably taking Luke's pause for assent, she says "Oh, and Mr Brittan's show rang up."

"What do they want now?"

"She wasn't very pleasant. They've found out what you are."

The words sound even odder when Luke paraphrases them. "What I am."

"Someone who saw the show today knows you're on the stage. The girl thought we should have told them before they had us on."

"If they give you any more trouble, Freda—" The name feels unwieldy in his mouth, and he blunders past it. "You put them straight on to me."

"I did give them your number. Don't be too hard on them. They're only trying to do their best for Mr Brittan."

Luke and Sophie say goodbye to her, and then he opens the address book on the phone screen. He ought to have grown out of some of the things he's written—he ought to prove he can. **Freda Arnold** replaces **mum**, and in another few seconds her husband is listed as **Maurice Arnold**. Terence has always been registered as **Terence**, and so Luke leaves him where he is. He still has all his memories; nothing has changed them or what he is, let alone the people who are still his parents in surely every way that counts. As Sophie reaches for his hand, having watched his actions in wistful silence, the phone rediscovers its voice.

Someone apparently doesn't want to show their number. Luke cuts off the ringtone before it can predict what June will do and enquires "Hello?"

"Mr Arnold?"

The woman's question is sharp enough for a challenge. "That's my name," Luke says and tells himself it's true.

"Luke Arnold the comedian?"

"That's still me."

"This is *Brittan's Resolutions*, Mr Arnold."

"I thought you might be. Have you been talking to my mother? I hear you weren't too pleasant to her."

"We just wanted to know why she didn't tell us what you are when she rang us, Mr Arnold."

Each repetition of his borrowed name makes him feel like an impersonator, but not the kind he is onstage. "She's a fan of yours," he says. "If you want to have a go at anyone, try me."

"Why didn't you mention you were a performer?"

"Nobody asked me."

"That isn't very funny, Mr Arnold. I hope your act's better than that. Jack thinks you came looking for material."

"I didn't, but you can tell him I found plenty."

"Have you nothing better to do than imitate people, Mr Arnold? I was brought up to know it's rude."

This silences Luke but not Sophie, who says "That isn't all Luke does by any means."

As Luke switches the phone to loudspeaker mode Brittan's researcher says "Are you the lady we put in the audience?"

"That's her, Sophie Drew. She's a performer as well. Maybe you know her album *Bach to Folk*. She could have sung you a song."

"I don't think there's any need for that, Mr Arnold." Quite as reprovingly the researcher says "We might have offered you some help in tracking down your parents."

"Don't bother. And a lot more to the point, don't go bothering—" At last he realises what he called Freda, which makes him feel he has been enacting a pretence. "Just leave the Arnolds alone," he says and ends the call.

Sophie watches him pocket the mobile and says "Do you think the net might help you find them?"

"If I wanted to it might." He has very little idea if he does, but her suggestion sends him to the slender metal desk opposite the window in case anybody has been trying to contact his web site.

"Luke Arnold casts a spell with his use of language, physical as well as verbal. You may end up wondering if you're his next character, because you could imagine he has stored up everyone he's ever met . . ." That's a quote from his Edinburgh Fringe review, and he still can't believe how far he has come since university—from putting on a show there and the first time he saw Sophie onstage too. There are emails to demonstrate he must be doing something right, and he beckons her to look. Three of today's emails are from theatres and clubs wanting to book him—more than he generally sees in a week. Sophie rests her hands on his shoulders like a promise of a massage. "They're after you," she murmurs, and too briefly for him to understand why, the words unnerve him.

— 4 —

OUT OF THE AUDIENCE

"WHO'S YOUR DADDY?"

In a moment Luke locates the heckler in the fifth row from the stage of the basement club. He's a man of about Luke's age—thirty—and his stance looks like a challenge. He's sitting with his big hands planted on his knees, his shoulders hunched, his large resolutely bald head lowered and thrust forward. "If you can tell me yours," Luke says, "I'll tell you mine."

The man's shout roused hoots and groans, and so does Luke's response, but he's also rewarded with laughter and applause. More than ever he feels distanced from his audience, as though he's observing them as much as amusing them. He has never really grasped why people find him entertaining; he remembers his bemusement with it when he was a child. Now he could conclude that his impersonations were bids to grow more like the family he'd taken for his own. "Give me honesty," he says, "and I'll give you rope, noooo, hope. You'll hang yourself before you know it if I'm honest . . ."

He judges this to be the kind of humour tonight's crowd likes, and they're roaring before he has said much else. He isn't simply imitating Brittan's pinched quick voice, he's heightening the presenter's traits until the audience finds them hilarious. He keeps raising an admonitory finger like Brittan but just close enough to his nose to seem about to insert it in a nostril. While Brittan often bounces on tiptoe to urge answers and perhaps to add to his stature, Luke adds crossing his legs as if he's

22

desperate to pee. He leans forward with his crossed hands fidgeting behind his back, as Brittan's hands do when he's impatient with his guests, but Luke teeters on the edge of the stage as if he's in danger of toppling off. All this earns him so much mirth that he has to keep waiting to be heard, and he's in the middle of a pause when his phone breaks into song.

It won't be the first time he has built a call into his act. He's had fun with callers purporting to represent the phone company, or insisting that his computer needs treatment, or reading from another script in an effort to sell him insurance—people pretending to be someone other than they were. Now he sees how this applies to him as well, even if he didn't know. Terence's name is on the screen to remind him.

He owes Terence too much to reduce him to a joke, but he can't just cut him off. "Can I call you back?" he says. "I'm onstage."

He isn't ready for the merriment with which the audience greets this, and it makes him feel even less like them. "When?" says Terence.

He might be slowing his voice down to compensate for Luke's haste, but Luke suspects he's had quite a lot to drink. "Now," Luke says. "I'm on now."

This brings another gust of mirth. So long as the audience stays amused, perhaps he doesn't need to terminate the conversation. "Where?" Terence wants to know.

"Over in Rochdale. In a club."

That's apparently hilarious too. Someone at the back is so taken with the situation that they've risen to their feet for a better look. "You mean," Terence says more sluggishly than ever, "you're on right this very moment."

"That's what I said. I'm up here trying to be funny."

The audience lets him know he has succeeded, but he's distracted by the dim figure, which isn't in the back row but behind it, against the wall. How did the watcher slip in unnoticed? "Can't I talk?" Terence says.

He sounds as though he wants to be more serious than Luke can deal with just now. The shadowy intruder couldn't have sneaked in at the back, since the only entrance is beside the stage. "We will," Luke promises. "I'll call you as soon as I'm done."

Not too many people laugh as Terence says "Make it soon." Luke is taking the phone away from his ear when Terence adds "I don't want to be alone with this any more."

23

Luke is dismayed to think that some people might laugh at any response he would make, and so he ends the call. The conversation must have played on his nerves more than he realised; there's nobody behind the back row. Perhaps the stain that resembles someone's shadow on the wall confused him, except that he peers at it he sees there's no such stain. As he puts away his mobile a woman shouts "Who was that supposed to be?"

"He was supposed to be my uncle."

A few titters greet this, but Luke wishes he hadn't been so quick to answer. "Some folk will do anything to get on the box," the woman says.

Luke can't tell whether she means him or Terence or both. At least she has fed him a cue. "Such as . . . " he says and brings back Brittan to interrogate Hamlet and his family, a routine the audience appears to relish along with the rest of Luke's show. Afterwards the manager, a long-haired lanky man with a sprawling ginger moustache, stops him in the backstage corridor. "Brilliant," he says. "We'll have you back."

"Well, thank you. Excuse me if I run out now to make a call."

"That was brilliant too," the manager says, not a comment Luke appreciates. He climbs the stairs between signed posters and emerges beneath the night sky, where a gibbous moon reminds him of pregnancy by lying on its back. The street full of shops is deserted, and he thumbs the key to recall Terence. The distant phone rings in his ear while stars appear to flicker into existence overhead, unless they're so remote that their light has outlived them. At last Terence says "Universal Demolition is open nine to five on weekdays. If it's urgent leave a message . . . "

"I'm returning your call," Luke says. "I couldn't any sooner." He leaves that and waits in case Terence picks up the message. In a few minutes he gives up pacing back and forth past window dummies that look arrested in the act of trying to seem human. He tries calling again, but all he hears is the phone imitating Terence once more. "Don't be alone," Luke says, "let's talk about whatever you wanted to." When the phone stays as silent as the moon he pockets it and makes for his car.

5

THE HOUSE BY THE BRIDGE

AS LUKE DRIVES PAST SPEKE AIRPORT a plane climbs the sky on stilts of vapour. While the stilts lengthen, their lower ends swell and crumble, dissipating into the blue sky. He's on the main road, which is divided by trees like a forest reduced to a single file miles long. Beyond Speke they're supplanted by twin-branched concrete lampposts, on one of which a crow lifts a wing like a black flag raised by a wind. The outermost houses of Liverpool have given way to industrial blocks, and soon the central reservation of the carriageway is bare apart from weeds and grass. It must be the image of a climber in the sky that revives a story Terence told Luke long ago.

Was it called "The Boy who Made Friends with the Clouds"? It involved a mountain so high that the clouds would nest there while they whispered to one another. At those times nobody from the village in the foothills would venture near the mountain, until one day an orphan boy found a hidden path. As he made the final ascent the clouds came down to gather about him. He thought they were about to blind him so that he would lose his way or fall, but they ushered him up to their eyrie and told him secrets they'd learned in their voyages across the sky. After that he climbed the mountain whenever they were there, but failed to realise how they were changing him. If he dreamed even while he was awake he would begin to lose his shape in the manner of a cloud, and soon the villagers noticed how they couldn't see him properly. When they drove

25

him out he fled up the mountain, starving until the clouds returned just in time to raise him up. Once his body dissolved it was free to rove the spaces above the world. Sometimes the villagers would see him striding the mountains on legs composed of cloud and as long as the sky was tall.

Presumably Terence wanted to expand Luke's imagination; Luke seems to remember that the tale made his mind feel enlarged and unfamiliar. Just now he's only interested in learning what Terence wanted to tell him last night. Terence still isn't answering his phone, and Luke wonders if he has had second thoughts—if he's unwilling to respond when he sees Luke's number. That's why Luke is on his way to the Universal Demolition office.

The road is winding towards Runcorn when a Frugoil tanker brakes at the bend ahead of the bridge across the river. The intervening vehicles relay red flares back to Luke as the tanker pulls into the outer lane. Indicator after indicator twitches orange at the bend, and both lanes of traffic slow to the speed of a funeral procession. The obstruction must be on the bridge; Luke sees passengers staring back at it from a train on the elevated track beside the road. If there were a way to leave the road he would use it—he's less than five minutes from Terence's office.

It takes Luke that long to inch to the bend. A white van has broken down halfway across the bridge, and the driver hasn't even switched his hazard lights on. A car races up behind it to sound a disapproving horn and in a bid to overtake at the last moment, which simply helps to impede the traffic. Luke's Lexus is nearly abreast of the obstacle when the bodiless cabin of a lorry speeds past him in the inner lane and pulls out with a token flash of its indicator. It's followed by half a dozen motorcyclists who don't care which side of the Lexus they pass, all of which is so distracting that Luke is past the van before he has a chance to look at it. The motorcyclists veer into the inner lane, blocking his view in the mirror, so that he barely glimpses the driver of the van. He's slumped over the wheel, and he's Terence.

He's staring through the windscreen but doesn't seem to recognise the Lexus. Luke brakes instinctively, and a chorus of horns almost robs him of the ability to think. As soon as he swerves into the inner lane a minibus follows him. It's plain that he won't be able to park on the bridge. He has to drive several hundred yards down the slip road to Runcorn, and even once he switches on the hazard lights cars trumpet at him as they over-

26

take. He slams the door and locks the car and dashes up the narrow pavement to the bridge.

The pavement leads to the single walkway across the bridge. Railings higher than his waist fence off the inner edge of the walkway, and an arm's length from them a taller set of railings borders the road. As Luke sprints along the walkway he can't help observing that the curved girders of the bridge are painted the pallid green of an old hospital interior, perhaps the very colour of the ward where he was born. If he's so alert, how did he fail to recognise Terence's van? Both sides are emblazoned with the Universal Demolition logo, in which the Os are miniature hemispheres. As a taste of petrol invades Luke's breaths he sees that Terence hasn't moved. He's afraid to learn what this may mean, but then Terence lifts a hand.

He has seen Luke. He waves feebly before his left hand grabs the wheel again while he struggles to grin with that side of his face. He sprawls across the passenger seat to wind the window down and then shoves himself shakily upright. "What's wrong, Terence?" Luke shouts.

"That's a bit formal, isn't it?" Terence's voice is as weak as his lopsided grin, so that Luke can barely hear him across the gap between the barriers. "Can't I still be Terry even if I'm not your uncle?"

"You still are." Luke hasn't time to make that clearer while he needs to learn "What's happened?"

"Just the old heart, son. Left my pills. Too much on my mind. Not your fault, so don't think it."

He seems increasingly less able to form complete sentences or perhaps to take the breaths they need. Luke digs in his pocket for his mobile. "I'll call an ambulance."

"Don't bother them. Just get me home."

As Luke hesitates, Terence clutches at the passenger seat with his left hand and begins to haul himself across the van. Luke attempts to vault over both barriers at once, but they must be designed to prevent it. He has to clamber into the gap between them and then scramble over the roadside railings, bruising his midriff. The oncoming traffic has slowed while drivers watch his antics, and a fanfare of horns greets his sprint around the front of the van.

Terence has managed to drag himself into the passenger seat. He dabs his glistening forehead and gives Luke a sluggish wink; at least, that's how his right eye looks. In a voice that strains to sound amused he says "Can you do my belt?"

Luke has to wonder how senile he's suddenly grown until Terence points a shaky thumb in the general direction of the seat belt. Luke leans over to find the metal tag and pull it across him. At first the belt refuses to pay out enough length, and Terence doesn't help by tugging at it like a petulant child jerking at a parent's sleeve. Eventually Luke succeeds in coaxing the tag all the way to its socket, and Terence slumps against the seat, mopping his forehead. "Are you sure you don't want to go to a hospital?" Luke persists.

"I said." Just as fretfully Terence adds "Need to be home."

Luke twists the key, and the engine sputters before spluttering alive. "That's where your medication is, yes?"

"Where a lot is." Terence does his best to lean towards Luke against the seat belt, but his left hand can't reach Luke's arm. "Don't let them see," he mutters.

Luke indicates and sends the van forward, earning a blare of the horn from a driver who was about to swing into the inner lane. "Who?" Luke says. "See what?"

"Forget it, Luke. No point knowing."

"Is it anything to do with why you called me last night?"

"Wish I hadn't." More fiercely than Luke understands Terence says "Fed up with wishing."

Drivers are braking on the slip road as they see Luke's abandoned car and trying to pull out before drivers in the outer lane will let them. Once he's past the car Luke speeds to the junction and heads through the narrow streets towards the railway bridge. "Leave it till you're feeling better," he says, "but I really would like to know why you called."

"Sure about that?" Terence grasps the top of the dashboard one-handed to help him turn to Luke. "Tell you," he says and has to draw an unsteady breath, "one thing."

Luke glances at him, but the eye that's fully open seems as veiled as its twin, and Terence's bottom lip has sagged beyond expressiveness. "They're all you ever needed," Terence pants. "Freddy and my brother. All you'll ever."

"And you," Luke says, but he knows none of this is an answer to his plea about the phone call. The terraced street he's driving down ends opposite the brick arches that lead to the viaduct across the river. They're taller than a house, several of which nestle against them. One house in the two-storey row is Terence's, a few doors away from a spiritualist church. Reflected sunlight makes the two front windows as opaquely pale as the front door with its step on the pavement is black. "You stay in the van," Luke says, "and I'll get your pills. Where do I look?"

"There," Terence gasps—at least, that's what it sounds like. He has raised his hand as though he means to point, but clamps it to the dashboard and cranes forward as his voice gives out. He's gazing at the house so fiercely that he shudders with the effort; certainly he's shivering. Luke drives towards it as fast as he dares, and then he sees what Terence must have seen. Somebody appears to be standing at the upstairs window.

It has to be a reflection from one of the houses opposite. The figure seems not just to be resting its forehead against the pane; the white face looks pressed as flat as the glass, squashed virtually featureless. The rest of the shape is too blurred to be distinguishable. Before Luke can focus on it or tell Terence what it must be, his passenger topples across him and snatches the keys.

The van judders to a halt in front of the house as Luke tramps on the brake. Terence has been thrown against the dashboard, clutching the keys. Luke reaches for them, but they clank along the dashboard as Terence drags them out of reach. Perhaps another spasm is making him do so, because his head lolls sideways, thumping the windscreen. His eyes are still on Luke, but in a moment they're as empty as the windows of the house.

6

THE LAST ROOM

WHEN LUKE'S CAR DRAWS UP OUTSIDE the house a woman turns to watch him from beside the spiritualist church. She looks shy, perhaps about her generous proportions, which she has tried to camouflage with a long white dress that only succeeds in suggesting she's more pregnant than women generally are at her age. She hesitates while he locks the car, but as he makes to unlock the front door of the house she plods along the narrow pavement to him. "Are you one of Mr Arnold's people?" she says and then blinks at his face. "I'm sorry, you're a relative, aren't you?"

By now Luke has concluded that his looking like the Arnolds is one reason why he was misidentified after he was born. "You can tell."

"Do you mind if I ask what took him?"

"A heart attack. Two of them."

"Didn't he know to be careful of himself? I suppose that's men. He'd been drinking a lot, you know."

"I didn't," Luke says and feels inadequate.

"He'd let the whole street know when he came back from the pub. He was carrying on to nobody at all."

Luke feels compelled to ask "What was he saying?"

"From what we could make out he wanted somebody to stay away from someone else. You'd have thought they were there, he was being so fierce with them."

Luke imagines Terence's voice resounding in the darkness of the arch that's taller than his house. "We'll pray for him," the woman says and indicates the church.

As Luke thanks her she glances at the upstairs window. She retreats towards the church while Luke unlocks the mortise lock, and she's gone by the time he turns the Yale. He's remembering a moment from his early childhood, when Terence flung the door open with a cry of "Here's our magic boy" that embarrassed both Luke and Maurice. The door gives a few inches before it's blocked by an obstruction. It has crumpled a bunch of dun official envelopes—bills, which he lays at the foot of the stairs that bisect the hall. A stale smell meets him as he shuts the door: old food and musty paper, a smell he would expect from a house that has been abandoned longer than this one. It makes him feel guilty for not having spent more time with Terence. If he had, mightn't Terence still be alive?

He's heading for the front room when thunder masses overhead. It's closer than the sky and too prolonged for a thunderclap, and he seems to feel the house shudder. A train is rumbling along the line above the roof. Perhaps you can become unaware of anything if you've lived with it long enough, or at any rate take it for granted. It looks as if Terence was growing too used to solitariness, given the state of the front room.

It feels steeped in dusk, no longer lit by Terence's stories or his enthusiasm for them. An inch of stagnant beer is turning murky in a bottle next to an armchair that slumps in front of the television. A worn pair of slippers is splayed on the carpet as if to represent a step in a grotesque dance. A coat Terence sported for many years is draped untidily over half of the back of the chair. The latest issue of the local newspaper is strewn across the floor, and on the television listings page the Brittan show has been marked so fiercely that the inky blotch resembles a black hole. Could all this untidiness have been why Terence didn't want anybody in the house?

Luke advances down the hall, which is decorated with framed images. A painting of a windswept river shows figures in midstream huddled in a boat—the ferry that was rowed across the Mersey centuries before a bridge was built at Runcorn. There's a tattered brownish photograph of the Liverpool waterfront under construction, with one lonely sculptured bird perching on a domed tower to await its avian twin. A fragment of mosaic preserved under glass depicts another winged creature, though it's impossible to guess its species, since it has a jagged gap for a head. All these are souvenirs Terence collected from properties he demolished. They're just some of his attempts to keep the past alive.

His brother never understood why Terence chose to stay here when he could have afforded so much better, and Luke is beginning to wonder; it resembles a hiding-place more than a home. The next room was meant for dining, with a hatchway in the wall giving access to the kitchen, but the unpolished table is bare except for several magazines. Luke wonders if they're Terence's guilty secret until he sees they're devoted to angling, not a pastime Luke associates with him. Was it a bid for distraction? While a rod and tackle occupy a corner of the room, they look not merely new but unused. The house begins to reverberate with the passing of another train, and Luke imagines the vibration is troubling the flimsy doors in the wall; he could almost fancy they're about to be flung wide to reveal a face. Maurice always seemed to think that Terence indulged his own imagination, and at the moment Luke could think he's right that you can have too much.

He finds several days' worth of utensils and plates trying to lie low under the opaque water in the dingy metal sink. He hauls at the unpleasantly slimy chain to clear the plughole, which gurgles as if it's trying to imitate a chuckle without much of a throat while he sluices the unwashed items and consigns them to the draining-board. The window above the sink overlooks the yard, such as it is—a cracked concrete rectangle under the arch, occupied by bins and a few scrawny unsunned plants in boxes of soil. A wall about ten feet high, fanged with broken glass, bricks up the far side of the arch, where a door scaly with old paint is secured with a massive padlock. There's nothing in the kitchen to detain Luke, least of all the sight of an empty tin poking its round mouth out of the pedal bin and drooping the outsize lip of its lid.

Another train goes over as he climbs the stairs, and he thinks the chipped banister trembles under his hand. He hurries upstairs into the insubstantial mass of sound, which feels as if it's accumulating in his brain. As he shoves the bathroom door open, an object with not much of a shape slithers to the floor. It's a ragged towel that he has dislodged from the rail on the wall.

There's another movement, as soundless as it's violent—the struggles of a large black fly in a half-drunk mug of coffee beside the sink. Luke wouldn't bother venturing into the room except to identify the pillbox in the cabinet, which is ajar. When he slides the mirrored door aside, losing his reflection that's infected with a rash of spatters of toothpaste, he's dismayed to see how many medicines Terence was prescribed for high blood pressure and a heart condition. Both shower curtains have been tugged loose from several of their hooks, but Luke needn't imagine Terence wrenching them apart, having fancied that he heard an intruder in the house.

His bedroom does suggest that kind of mental state. The quilt has flopped on the carpet, and the sheet has pulled free of the mattress; it's so crumpled that it could be describing the chaos of a nightmare. Clothes crouch on a chair at the foot of the bed. One door of the wardrobe is open, revealing suits and shirts lined up like images of Terence squashed lifeless, incomplete cut-out representations of him. They remind Luke of a story Terence used to tell, about an orphaned shadow that made its lair among clothes in wardrobes. Only one room is left—the front bedroom— and Luke pushes the door wide.

The curtains are shut tight, which has to mean the figure he saw at the window was indeed a reflection, if he needed any proof. Although what- ever colour they once possessed has faded pale as fear, they still darken the room, and he has to take care not to tread on the objects that clutter the floor. When he takes hold of the curtains the heavy fabric seems to stir in his hands; he could fancy that he has roused handfuls of parasites— encouraged them to hatch, perhaps. In a moment the sensation evaporates like the memory of a dream, and he drags the curtains as far as they will stagger on the rusty rail.

He isn't prepared for the view from the window. Beyond the terrace opposite he can see the road bridge. Cars are racing past and, worse, over the spot where Terence's heart attack halted the van. Luke imagines the tyres rubbing out traces of the man he knew as his uncle, and he feels as though the loss has caught up with him at last, gouging a hollow at the core of him. He can't help hoping to find a keepsake as he turns to the room.

A small desk stands in the nearest corner, hidden from the houses opposite. Perhaps Terence has been keeping secrets in a battered ledger, which is as thick as Luke's forearm and occupies most of the top of the desk. Suppose it means that he was falsifying the accounts for his firm and wanted Luke to hide this from the authorities? Luke would rather not deal with anything like that just yet, and he surveys the rest of the room.

It's full of souvenirs. A broken plaque depicts a rearing horse with its rider missing from the waist up. Beside it on the dusty carpet a jagged section of a stone frieze represents a parade or a dance. Some of the participants are not just leggy but hirsute, and erosion has robbed them all of faces. A fragment of ironwork, perhaps from a gate, contains a rusty smiling moonlike face that's flanked by open hands Luke initially mistakes for wings. An irregular piece of stained glass represents a dark blue sky in which stars form a constellation he doesn't recognise, while below them is either a halo or a ring filched from a planet such as Saturn. A marble hand too incomplete for its gesture to be clear lies next to a portion of a marble face—most of the smooth white brow, which is overlaid by a pallid wisp of hair, and enough beneath the forehead to include a single eye that, despite the absence of a pupil, looks unwaveringly watchful. None of these items means much to Luke, but he draws a sharp breath that tastes of dust and aged paper as he notices an object in a corner where the sunlight doesn't reach. It's a skull.

Or rather it must be a carving of one. The irregular remains of the features suggest that the face looked none too human, and it's crowned with an intricate tangle of branches of its own substance, as if the brain has grown uncontrollably luxuriant and sprouted forth, unless the cranium is burgeoning like coral. The sight revives a memory that feels like starting awake. "Flowers grow up to the sun," Terence told him once, "but some bones grow up to the moon."

If that was part of a story, Luke can't recall the rest. No doubt the sculpture suggested Terence's fantasy. As Luke stoops to examine the item the contents of the hollow sockets swell to meet him—nothing like eyes, just his own shadow. He cradles the skull and is carrying it to the window when he seems to feel movement between his hands, as if he has wakened something inside his burden. Surely it's just a loose fragment, and he takes a firmer grip. He mustn't know his own strength, or the carving is more fragile than it looks. He hasn't reached the window when the skull implodes in his hands without a sound and crumbles into bony shards. As they strike the floor they disintegrate further, and in a moment nothing but pale dust is left—not even the memory of how the object felt for Luke to hold.

He feels like a child who has caused damage somewhere he was trusted to be careful. How could he have been so clumsy with such a delicate item? Rather than risk doing any more harm he turns to the ledger. Above the river beyond the road bridge a bloated moon has crept into view, and as he opens the massive volume he could fancy that a hint of daytime moonlight has settled on the page. The ledger is a journal written entirely in capitals, and it doesn't appear to relate to Terence's firm. The first word Luke sees is his own name.

GRACES FIELD. LUKE SHOWED ANIMALS. The large sprawling letters look no less childish than the grammar, as if they've betrayed the writer's secret self. The entry is dated almost a quarter of a century ago, but Luke thinks he recalls the day when Terence took him walking outside Ormskirk. They'd stood in the middle of a field for so long that Luke had lost all sense of his own body, and at last wild animals had begun to emerge from a wood—squirrels, rabbits, a hare, a fox. Didn't Terence tell him they were putting on a show for him? Presumably they'd acted as wild creatures do when they're unaware of being watched. Luke must have moved eventually and scared them off, because he remembers Terence saying "See what you did."

He leafs through the journal and keeps seeing his name. Other entries record places Terence visited and mention how kind the local people were. Some pages contain stories or notes for them, many of which apparently came to Terence in the night. Quite a few seem unfamiliar; perhaps Terence never told them to Luke. The moon is peering down like a head cocked to spy in the window without much of a face. If Luke reads the entire journal he wouldn't be surprised to find himself still in the house after dark.

He shuts the ledger on a desiccated sprig of vegetation, another souvenir of Terence's travels, which resembles an insect more than a foot long with an irregular arrangement of legs. As he carries the ledger downstairs the treads shudder underfoot; the extra weight must be shaking them, however much it feels like being followed. He lowers the book into the boot of his car and locks the house before glancing up. A pallid object that appears to be doing its best to watch him is pressed against the glass—the reflection of the moon. No matter how fast he drives on the way home, the embryonic mask in the sky stays with him.

— 7 —

WHERE IT BEGAN

"So THAT'S WHY TERRY USED TO CALL it a Johann Christian,"
Freda says and tells Sophie "That was his name for a mechanical dig-
ger."

"Did he teach you about music, Luke?"

"We like good music too," Freda protests. "You've heard Maurice put it
on when you've come for dinner."

"I know you do," Sophie says, having been honoured by movements
from Mozart and Beethoven and more than one Strauss, along with as
many other highlights as the disc had space for. "I was just thinking of
Terence."

They're in the large back garden of the thatched house where Luke
grew up. Other mourners occupy the wrought-iron furniture or congre-
gate beneath the trees. Luke suspects they've brought their buffet portions
outside rather than risk having Freda clear away their paper plates the
instant they're put down anywhere in her house. He used to retreat out
here whenever he sensed that she thought he was playing with too many
toys at once—more than a couple meant he was making a mess. He
might play a game that seemed to shape faces in the spiky depths of the
hedge, or imagine that the murmurs of the village spoke of secrets he
needed to learn, or lie on the close-cropped lawn to see what the sky
would produce for him. He remembers seeing fossils, the remains of
gigantic creatures that must be as old as the stars; perhaps their descen-

dants still lived in the dark the sky hid. A spinal cord the colour of the moon is growing more enormous and losing definition overhead as Freda says above the thunder of the airliner "We're all thinking of him, Sophie, and you helped."

Luke owes at least some of his childhood fancies to Terence. They're a way of remembering him, but Luke feels as if he's fending off the bereavement—as if he's bracing himself for a greater loss. He's nowhere near identifying it when Sophie says "I wouldn't have presumed, but you did ask."

She played Bach fugues on her guitar while the mourners assembled and as they left the crematorium—melodies Terence used to hum, if less tunefully. Now she hesitates and says "I'm only sorry Freda or Maurice won't know him."

Freda blinks and blinks again. "What are you saying, Sophie?"

Sophie rests one hand on her midriff. "We've decided she'll be Freda or he'll be Maurice."

Freda takes her hand and Luke's, calling "Maurice? Maurice? Did you hear?"

"Hang on till I see what's up this time," he says to several workmen Terence employed. "Hear what, chuck?"

"They're going to call their baby after one of us, whichever it turns out to be."

"Good on you both. Give me a few minutes here, will you? I'm just in the middle of talking business."

"He's really pleased but he can't show it when there are a lot of people," Freda murmurs. "You used to take after him, Luke."

"Who says I don't still? Let me get you both chairs, and what else would you like?"

"That's Maurice right enough. He's thoughtful when he remembers to be," Freda says and gives Luke's hand a parting squeeze. "But I'm not, am I? You don't want to be standing round in your condition, Sophie."

"Freda seems to like me on my feet, or Maurice does."

"Why, you've brought it back," Freda says as if remembering a dream. "I was just the same when I was having—"

She visibly wishes she hadn't relinquished Luke's hand. In a moment she says "Do you know what I think Terence would have loved? A bit of Luke's show while Luke was talking about him, and never mind it was a funeral."

She's thinking of Luke's eulogy from the angular unadorned pulpit, where he'd felt as though he was performing an impression of a celebrant. While he hadn't claimed Terence was his uncle, he'd stopped short of saying the opposite, which left him feeling even more like a deceiver. "I wouldn't have wanted to offend anyone," he says.

"You could have said it was for Terry. You could do it now."

"I haven't brought your chair."

"I'll be sitting enough when I'm old."

"Maurice won't want me distracting people while he's in conference."

"Who's saying what I want?" Maurice says and ambles over. "That's settled. Terry's boys are fine to stay on if we merge the firms."

Luke senses Maurice feels he has regained his masculinity, even if Maurice wouldn't put it that way—the masculinity threatened by learning he wasn't Luke's father. Observing this with such detachment makes Luke feel disloyal if not worse, but Freda is saying "Do Terry's favourite. Be the Welsh headmaster."

"He used to ask Luke to do it at Christmas," Maurice tells Sophie. "You remember, son."

While Luke has kept his memories of the festival—the tree that sprouted lights, the doorways festooned with them as though magic places lay beyond, the impression that the house was full of hidden presents, the songs wending their way through the village—he feels as if all this belongs to someone else. "I'd like to see it," Sophie prompts him.

"You reathly would."

She looks puzzled, though not unamused. "Say that again?"

"You'd reathly like to see Mr Futhlalove address the school."

"Do his face," Freda urges.

Luke could fancy that they're willing him to become somebody he's not, but hasn't that turned out to be his life? He lets his chin drop, lengthening the lower portion of his face, and shrinks his mouth, all of which seems to squeeze his voice high and thin. "I'm Mr Thlewethlyn Futhlalove and I'll be patrothling the school to make sure there's no sithly behaviour..."

Several mourners have turned to watch and are hushing their companions. "Do his walk as well," Freda cries.

Luke begins to waddle back and forth as if his legs are shackled. That's how a teacher at his school used to promenade in the classroom, and the face belongs to another one, but the language began with Terence—with his song about Llangollen and pollen, which Luke apparently improved upon. Though it feels like abandoning more of his personality, Luke interlaces his fingers on his stomach and waggles them every time he lingers over mispronouncing a word. "I'm warning you I'll have no buth-lying in my school. Not on your nethly, as they used to say when I was your age. No puthling anybody's hair, that isn't just a peccadithlo, and no name-cathling either. I don't want anybody being told they're smethly for a start. And don't be afraid of spithling the beans, because that's just the height of fothly. If you report bad conduct that isn't tethling tales, so I don't want any shithly-shathlying about it. If I think there's been any scoundrethly behaviour then by gothly I'll have all the suspects in my office for a grithling . . . "

Most of the mourners are laughing. Onstage Luke often feels as if he's yielding up his individuality to the expectations of the audience. Doing so can distract him from self-consciousness, but just now he seems to be hearing himself say "I hope I'll see no apawthling spethling this year. We don't turn out duthlards here. And make sure you conduct yourselves civithly. No mithling about in the corridors and no strowthling along, and no lothling against the walls either. I'll be muthling over what else you can do for the good of the school. You may think I'm a wathly with a swothlen head or even that I'm off my throthley, but if you abide by my rules you should have a jothly good time . . . "

His imagination falters as the headmaster starts addressing pupils by name—Dolly, Molly, Polly, the Halliday twins—and he brings the routine to an end. "Just throw a shithling," he says when the mourners applaud.

One of Terence's demolition team repeats the line with relish, and another says "Terry told us you used to do that. He said we'd not believe how young you were."

"How young was that?" Sophie is eager to learn.

"Too young to know what some of those words meant, I should think," Luke tells her, though he recalls being sufficiently precocious to unnerve his present self. "You were working for him back then," he says to Terence's veteran.

"Since before you were born, lad," the man says and frowns extra wrinkles onto his weathered leathery face. "All right to talk about it, Maurice?"

"Nothing to do with me, Rudy."

"I was going to say Terry was over the moon when your boy came along."

"The whole lot of us were."

"I'm only saying now you know he hadn't anything to do with it, but you'd have thought the babby was his own to hear him. I thought I was nervous when mine were on the way, but I never had the shakes like him."

"Blame the stuff he was putting in himself."

"Smoking doesn't do that to you, Maurice," Rudy says and doesn't pause to add "I gave it up years back."

"Carry on. You've still got a job."

"That's all, mostly." When Maurice holds him with a gaze Luke wouldn't call inviting, Rudy says "He always had a photo with him. Your lad when he was in his crib, and you'd hear Terry talking to it if he didn't know you were about."

"What was he saying?" Freda seems to feel they ought to hear.

"You thought he was praying, didn't you, Dan?"

"Did till I had a listen," Rudy's large slow curly-haired colleague admits. "More like baby talk. Not what I'd call words."

"He was always showing us the photo," Rudy says, "and telling us how much like you two the lad was growing."

As Maurice lets his lip sag while Freda responds with an uncertain smile, Luke thinks it best to intervene. "Did you work away from home a lot for Terence?"

"We never went far," Dan says. "When he went off it was mostly on his own."

"We thought he hired men where he went," Rudy adds, "but Eunice in the office told us not. Maybe he'd got a woman somewhere."

As Luke reflects that many more than one would be needed to account for all the travelling Terence noted in his journal, Maurice says "More like it was another thing he'd got into his head. He was never the same after you pulled that house down in Toxteth."

Perhaps Dan and Rudy feel he's holding them responsible, since they don't answer. "Why," Sophie says, "what happened?"

"Some young scum hid in there from the police," Maurice says, "and the cellar fell in on him."

"They got the body out," Dan risks contributing, "and then the place needed making safe."

"You mean," Luke says, "someone having died there bothered Terence."

"Not that he ever let on," Rudy says. "It was all the faces we dug up in the cellar."

"Don't," Freda protests as though she sees them rearing up from the earth.

"They were only carved on stones," Dan assures her. "All the same feller. Looked like he thought he was some god in a museum."

"One of the lads smashed most of them," Rudy says. "He didn't like the look of them. It's the only time we saw Terry lose his rag. Fired the lad on the spot, and the only stone that wasn't broke he took home with him."

"First I've heard," Maurice says like more than one accusation.

"Do you know what he did with it?" Luke finds he needs to learn.

Dan and Rudy glance at each other and at Maurice. Eventually Dan says "Rudy asked him once."

"Said he slept with it under his pillow."

When nobody else speaks Sophie asks "Why?"

This time the men don't quite look at each other, but Dan appears to have delegated his workmate to mutter "Expect he meant it made him dream. He said things came to him."

Luke remembers an entry in the journal about the stories Terence told him, and blurts "When's all this supposed to have happened?"

"We knocked the house down," Rudy says, "the year before you were born."

Luke can't think what else to say, and the conversation drifts away from him. Soon enough the mourners start to leave, and he and Sophie promise to visit again soon. As they drive home alongside the river, they're paced by a sliver of moon that appears to be waiting for the night to fill some of it in. At the Pier Head he swings the car uphill towards the town and immediately down the ramp under the apartments, where he has an odd sense of hiding from the moon. The electronic door tilts up, and he coasts into the numbered space next to Sophie's Clio in the underground car park.

The converted cellar mimics the slams of his door and Sophie's. As she heads for the stairs in the lobby he retreats to the steps down to the car park. "You start the coffee," he says. "I'm not sure if I locked the car." Once he's certain that she won't be coming after him he opens the boot of the Lexus. The glare of the security lights leaves Terence's journal lying in a trough of darkness like a baby's grave. Luke balances the ledger on the edge of the boot, and every page he turns gives rise to another shadow. The entry he wants is close to the start of the journal, which he shuts and locks away as soon as he has memorised the details. **IT WAS STRONG HOUSE**, the entry says and lists an address in Toxteth.

8

THE REMAINS

As LUKE TURNS THE CAR along Mulgrave Street, Christ leans out from the church on the corner. He's spiky as a bolt of lightning made into a man. He looks poised to dive from perching high up on the concrete wall and start a race along the dual carriageway of Princes Avenue. Luke imagines Terence inviting him to wonder what the lithe metal shape might be chasing or attempting to outdistance, but that doesn't offer any insight into Terence—it just reminds Luke that he has very little idea why he's here or what he's looking for.

The street he's following is no help. Most of the buildings look younger than he is: compacted terraces where the houses seem squeezed thin to fit their boxy gardens, a mosque built of peach-coloured bricks not much bigger than playthings. Above the low roofs a wide blue sky decorated with a few white wisps like shavings of a moon adds to the impression of newness. Luke drives almost to the end before turning along a side road, which brings him to Amberley Street. At least, it does according to the street guide in the glove compartment, but now the location is occupied by a car park.

Terence gave him the guide when Luke bought his first car. So the street has been demolished, not just the house that's mentioned in the journal. Luke finds a space for the Lexus at the far end of a rank of vehicles opposite the car park, which is enclosed by a spiky metal fence. He's beside a pallid pebbly terrace of thin houses, guarded by a wall on which scraps of litter caught by coils of barbed wire flutter like a substitute for foliage. Windows hardly large enough to frame a head and shoulders are visible over the wall. Luke crosses the uneven road and sees that the car park is next to a grassy patch of waste ground, where a path leads from a gateless entrance in the fence. Perhaps the path will let him find a way into the car park, even if he can't see why he should bother. He's heading for the gate when a voice says "I'm watching you."

A woman has emerged from a doorway in the wall. She's at least a head shorter than Luke, but her size appears to have concentrated her fierceness, tugging her small face into sharper relief. A dusty wind flaps her faded black dress like a crow's wings and tousles her greying hair. "What do you see?" Luke retorts.

"Someone pretending, it looks like."

He feels altogether too exposed. Is she another viewer of the Brittan show? "What do you mean?" he blurts.

"Pretending you've got business round here."

"Just looking. No harm in that, surely."

"You look a bit too interested in other people's cars."

"Well, I'm not. There's mine."

When he uses his key to make the Lexus yip and blink she continues staring narrowly at him. He's beginning to feel he has forgotten how to portray an ordinary person by the time she says "Maybe you're the other kind we get round here."

"You'd have to tell me what that is."

"If they're not buying they're selling."

Once her stare makes her meaning clear Luke says "I've got nothing to do with drugs at all."

"You knew what I was talking about, though, didn't you?" Rather less than immediately she says "What are you after, then?"

"I was looking for Amberley Street."

Her stare doesn't relent, but it changes in some way Luke isn't sure of. "What do you want there?" she demands.

"My uncle—" Luke may not feel entitled to say that any more, but to alter it seems disloyal. "He knocked down a house there," he says.

"What one?"

"I think it was owned by somebody called Strong. Apparently the cellar collapsed while someone was in it, and then the house had to be demolished."

43

He hasn't finished speaking when her gaze softens at last. "God bless him," she says. "Tell him that if you see him."

"I wish I could." In some haste Luke adds "Why?"

"The man who had that house was messing with things nobody should. John Strong, they called him or he called himself. Don't ask me what he did, but worse than drugs." With something like defiance she says "There were always people going in like they couldn't stop themselves. Tell me why he'd live anywhere like that if he could do that to people."

Luke isn't even sure what he is being asked. "Can you say where it was?"

"Across there." She raises a hand in the direction of the car park, so briefly and violently that she might be trying to fend off whatever it signifies. As soon as Luke thanks her she retreats through the doorway, and he can't be certain that he hears her mutter "Maybe it needed more than knocking down."

It seems even more pointless for Luke to abandon the search than it does to continue. He advances through the gateway and is halfway across the waste ground when he hears rats squealing in a heap of rubbish beside the path. No, chunks of polystyrene white as headstones are chafing together in a parched breeze that rouses random clumps of grass and weeds to twitch like insect limbs. As the noise subsides and the vegetation reverts to lying low he makes for the end of the path.

This side of the waste ground is overlooked by a block of student flats, juvenile with bright red bricks and relieved only by four storeys of niggardly windows. Opposite the block on Falkner Terrace a row of Georgian houses is fungoid with satellite dishes. Two tiers of indifferent faces spy on Luke from a passing bus. He's alone on the pavement, and the sound of the bus recedes to isolate his footsteps. He tramps past the flats and turns the corner, and lets out a lingering breath.

He's in Amberley Street, all that's left of it—a strip of roadway flanked by pavements, ending at the fence on this side of the car park. It's identifiable by a street sign attached to the railings of a basketball court and covered with graffiti. Opposite the court the multicoloured railings around a windowless brick bungalow show it to be a Caribbean centre. Otherwise the lopped-off road seems to have nothing to offer except the view of parked cars, beyond which a slender pointed spire that appears to be fixing a stray cloud. Luke is back on the path across the waste ground when he falters, remembering what Dan said after the funeral.

"Looked like he thought he was some god in a museum"—that was how Dan described the face on the stone Terence took home. Luke wasn't sure what Dan had in mind, but he knows all too precisely now. High domed forehead without wrinkles, deep staring eyes with no eyebrows, long smooth hollow cheeks, blunt elongated nose, thin lips not quite keeping their amusement to themselves—if he looks behind him he will see that face. He marches a few paces and then, although he's enraged by doing so, swings around. The path and everywhere around it are deserted.

How could he have imagined a face in such detail? He feels as if he's leaving it behind rather than simply putting it out of his head. The Lexus blinks awake, and he's annoyed by a sense of taking refuge. As he starts the car he resists an impulse to glance across the waste ground. At last he does, to see no more than he already saw. The car jerks forward and he drives away, eager to outdistance the impression that made him look towards the student flats: that he was being watched from the dozens of windows—that every window would be occupied by the same pale elongated face.

9

GOING BACK

"COME IN, LUKE," Maurice shouts and flings the door wide. "Come in, son."

His lower lip droops as though it's miming openness, and Luke restrains his own from reflecting the expression. "Seeing you twice in a week now, are we? Not often enough," Maurice declares. "What are you having to drink?"

"I'd better not, thanks. I was on the way to the house."

"Your house, you mean," Maurice says more enthusiastically still. "Yours and Sophie's and somebody else's as well."

It's clear that he has been celebrating, and Luke guesses Terence's will is why. As well as leaving Luke the house in Runcorn it confirms that Maurice and Freda have been left the demolition firm. Before Luke can say any more Maurice strides along the broad timbered hall. "It's Luke, Freddy," he shouts.

Freda bustles out of the metal and marble kitchen. She's wearing an apron like an elongated humbug, which emits a plastic crackle as she hugs Luke. "Won't you stay for dinner? We're having the pasta you like."

"You'll be coming back this way, won't you?" Maurice says. "Better go before it's dark."

"Why are you telling him that, Maurice?"

"The boys were saying Terry had been letting his bills sit for months. Maybe the power's been cut off by now."

46

"He must have had something on his mind." Freda shakes her head as if to jettison the thought and says "I can always add to the pasta, Luke. I don't like to think of you sitting on your own at home."

"Sophie wants to keep touring as long as she can before she has to come off the road."

"I wasn't criticising her. It's who she is just like your career is you. We ought to admire her driving all the way to Devon in her state." Freda hesitates and says "You won't mind if we pray for her, will you? We did for you."

Luke assumes she means when they were trying for a child. "I'm sure we won't," he tells her and Maurice.

"We heard her single on the radio today. The presenter said they'll be queuing when it's in the shops." As if this is related Freda says "So have we managed to tempt you with dinner?"

By now they've all strayed into the lounge. Beyond the conservatory framed by floor-length windows the sky is darkening above the river. Luke imagines lifting the stale pillow on Terence's empty bed to see whether it conceals a face in the gloom. "Maybe I'll let the house rest for today," he says.

"Get it done before he changes his mind." With equal urgency Maurice tells Luke "Now you're going to have that drink with me."

"Just a glass of white, then." Luke sits by an antique table under which three members of its family crouch increasingly low and small, and the vintage sofa gives a discreet upholstered creak. "A small one," he requests-despite knowing Maurice doesn't go in for those.

Maurice watches and then listens to Freda heading for the kitchen. As he steps behind the mahogany bar that five-year-old Luke helped him build by holding tools, he clears his throat. Rather less loudly he says "Have you been looking for your folk at all?"

"My..." Having gathered why Maurice is keeping his voice down, Luke says "I wouldn't know where to start."

"Maybe they'll come looking now we've been on the box."

"Why, do you want to find out who you might have had?"

Maurice all but fills a relatively diminutive glass with Chardonnay and takes tiny steps with it towards Luke. Once he has planted the glass on the table that squats protectively over its brood he says "I was thinking of you, Luke."

"I didn't mean you wanted them instead." As Maurice's lip droops to meet his whisky glass Luke says "Whoever I should have been, I can't help wondering what kind of life they've had."

"You're who you should have been and don't go thinking different."

Luke suspects that some of the fierceness is intended to prevent Maurice from reflecting on his real son's fate. Maurice takes a gulp of whisky and sits forward to mutter "No need to tell Freddy what we've been talking about, all right? If you ever turn anything up, let me know. I ought to be the one that tells her."

He seems both eager and reluctant to learn the truth, which leaves Luke still more uncertain which he is himself. "I won't," he says and is taking more than a sip from his glass when Freda reappears, having hung up her apron to reveal a black and silver dress that might have borrowed its colours from her hair. "Are there two hungry boys in here?" she cries. "Bring your drinks through."

Luke follows her into the dining-room, where a chandelier poises crystal icicles above the elongated oval table draped with lace, and Maurice tramps at his heels, scragging a bottle of wine in either hand. Freda serves salad and then a Bolognese somewhat suffocated by extra pasta. "Tasty," Maurice says as usual, and Luke declares "It is." Freda dabs her lips after a minuscule drink of wine and says "Are we taking you back, Luke?"

"I hope I've never really been away."

She laughs as if he has made a joke instead of failing to grasp her question. "I was just remembering all our family dinners together."

"So do I."

"Go on then," Maurice says. "Remember some."

"Your mother would pass round all the photos they'd taken that year every Christmas, and your father wouldn't let her pass the next one till he told us all the details. You said by the time they'd shown us Istanbul we could have walked through it ourselves."

"Well, I'd forgotten that. You don't miss much."

"Grandmother Laing used to hold her food up to the light with her fork till you told her not to set me an example, Freda. And Grandfather Laing tried to convince me she was a scientist instead of being fussy what she ate."

"He did." Freda wags her head as if she's shaking more of a reminiscent smile onto her face. "What else are you going to bring back to us?"

"Your Aunt Beatrice thought children never ought to eat nuts or they'd choke. She'd even go through all the chocolates at Christmas to make sure I didn't get one with a nut in. She always used to tell me I wasn't a squirrel."

"You aren't a squirrel, Luke." He can hear the hearty voice addressing him in the manner adults often use on children, as if they're sharing a joke with a larger audience. Perhaps he concluded that was how you were supposed to behave, entertaining everyone in the room. He's tempted to reproduce the voice, except this might be more like a séance than a reminiscence. Instead he says "And Uncle Don used to eat anything he dropped on his chair at dinner, and not just that day either."

"We had to see nobody else sat there, didn't we, Maurice? And we hid the chair when he wasn't here and got a new one after he left us."

"You only let him carry on like that because he made out he was deaf. She'd never let us get away with it, would she, Luke?" Maurice says and gazes at him. "But by God, you had a sharp eye even at that age. You weren't three when he snuffed it. Here's hoping you didn't see things about us we'd rather forget."

"Not a solitary one," Luke says and does his best to back it up with memories—Spanish holidays that felt sunlit even after dark, cycling with Freda and Maurice by the river all the way to Liverpool and back, the few days it took them to teach him to drive (Freda applauded everything he did, Maurice grunted encouragement as Luke imitated all the actions he'd observed), the day they'd delivered Luke and an assortment of possessions to university in an Arnold company van, only to keep being mistaken for a firm doing work on the campus. . . He feels as if he's claiming memories that should belong to someone else—telling tales on behalf of the person he's portraying. He continues reminiscing until Maurice starts to nod, by which time it's plain that Luke will have to stay the night.

A folded towel lies on the bed, which has doubled since Luke had the room. A facecloth is arranged on top of the plump towel, all their corners precisely lined up. In the bathroom the bottles and jars and sprays are ranked in terms of height along the tiles above the twin sinks; as a child he thought they might be pieces in a game his parents played. Above reflections of the backs of the entire parade, his face in the elongated mirror looks as if it's searching for a sign that it belongs in the house. A new toothbrush is perched on the edge of the left-hand sink, and he uses it once he succeeds in releasing it from its sarcophagus of celluloid and cardboard. He doesn't loiter in the extensive room next door, though it offers a book called *Tiny Tales for the Smallest Room* and a floral scent that seemed to suffuse his childhood. Another volume—*Thoughts for Sleepy*

People—is provided on the venerable bedside table Luke's room has acquired. Sleepy doesn't sum up how he feels, and he pads barefoot across the springy carpet to the window.

There's no moon. Large soft lumps of dusk stand about the garden, which is boxed in by spiky blackness. The night is silent except for Freda's murmur and then Maurice's in the front bedroom. Beyond the far hedge the river is a thin foreshortened glint, above which the Welsh mountains have been reduced to an ebony frieze as the length of the sky, if a shade darker. He remembers standing at the window to see the mountains garlanded with cloud, and a sun that swelled huge and red before wavering like jelly into the earth, and stars that multiplied in the night sky as if his vision were calling them back from the dead. Now he watches while stars appear, beacons that hint at the vast distances they mark. What else can he be waiting for? When he begins to glimpse figures in the hedges, attempting to take a variety of shapes and then reverting to the dark as night winds enliven the foliage, he draws the velvet curtains and retreats to bed.

He doesn't dream, in spite of remembering a story Terence told him about the children of the moon. People would see them when it was full, because then they were closest to taking form. They waxed with it and waned as well, and merge with the dark when it did. At the new moon you might mistake them for thorn bushes bleached by the light, unless you saw their faces that were thinner and spikier than bone. They would grow flesh as bushes grow leaves, and on nights of the harvest moon their round faces would be wider than their fat white bodies, and anyone they touched would see more by moonlight than they ever did at midday. Luke was never sure how appealing this was, and he doesn't find it attractive now. He's glad when the tale drifts away into the dark that leads to sleep.

A cry wakens him. It's his mother—no, it's Freda. As he strains his ears he hears Maurice grumbling "What's up, woman? It's only a dream." Luke hears an apologetic murmur, and the night settles down once more; at least, his hosts do. He peers about and eventually shuts his eyes, and tries not to feel like a child left alone with no light. When he dozes he's intermittently able to forget Freda's cry. "It's got in."

— 10 —

THE FACE FROM THE DARK

THEY'VE BEEN STOPPED by traffic lights at the edge of Speke when they hear the song from the car that has pulled up beside Luke's car at traffic lights. "That's me," Sophie says. "Luke, it's me."

He switches on the radio and searches for the station. Her voice in both vehicles begins to duet with itself just as the refrain comes up—"A song we all can sing." The presenter fades the record out and sings the line. "Sophie Drew with the Liverpool sound for this century," he says, and so does his twin on the road. "Watch her climb the charts."

The show is on national radio, not local. The lights step down to green, and as the Lexus surges forward Sophie says "I still can't quite believe so many people like me."

"I can't believe anybody wouldn't, so just you believe in yourself."

"I will if you will."

"I'm still trying to decide who I am."

"You're who you made yourself, just like everybody else. The people you've known had something to do with it, but you're the one who had to make the choices." As Luke wonders if it can be so simple for anyone she says "You're Maurice and Freda and Terence and the bits of them you decided not to be."

"Is that how it worked with your parents?"

"I'm sure it was."

He's inclined to agree. He has grown to know them, classical musicians

51

who lecture on the subject and who are even more delighted that their daughter writes songs than by her arranging and performing them. The speed limit on the open road lets the Lexus have its head, and he says "I wish you'd given me a chance to clear up at the house."

"I promise not to be appalled. I saw your place before I moved in, remember."

"That was a shadow. This is the real thing. I just don't want you trying to tidy up when you're what Freda's mother used to call delicate."

"We're sturdy even if we don't look it, the Drew women." When Luke doesn't answer she says "There's nothing I can't see, is there?"

"Terence asked me not to let people into the house, but he can't have meant you. He must have known he was leaving it to us both." Luke hesitates and doesn't know why before blurting "I found his diary last time I was there."

"Did it tell you anything?"

"Not that I noticed. Some of it might as well be in code."

There's a promise of green at the end of the concrete vista ahead— the bridge over the river. As he drives across it Luke can't identify exactly where he found the van, but he vows never to forget all that Terence did for him. A procession of glazed faces is slithering above the house. The train snakes away as Luke halts the car, and Sophie says "How long did he live here?"

"More than all my life."

"It's almost hidden, isn't it?" She clambers out of the car and blinks at the arch. "I think he was quite a private person," she says, "under everything we saw."

Luke finds he doesn't want to be reminded. He's anticipating resistance when he unlocks the front door, but there are no more bills. He tries the light and finds the electricity has indeed been switched off. The stale smell is waiting like a friend that's grown too old. Luke hurries to retrieve the bottle from the front room and empty it into the kitchen sink. "I should think so too," Sophie says and instantly relents. "No, I shouldn't think anything of the kind. I can imagine how you felt when you were here."

She's gazing at the relics in the front room: the gaping slippers, the coat the armchair has shrugged on. As she picks up the scattered pages of the newspaper she sees how Terence dug his pen into the listing for the Brittan show. "He must have been angry," she murmurs. "Maybe he thought Brittan was right."

Luke doesn't have time to examine his own anger. "Right how?"

"I'm not saying he was, just that Terence might have thought so. That's how he looked when Brittan tried to say it was his fault you had medical help."

"Well, it wasn't, and why should he have blamed himself all these years later?"

Suppose Terence was afraid that Luke might revert to the condition, perhaps from going on the Brittan show? As Luke tells himself there was no need for the rear Sophie says "Do you want to talk about it? You never have."

"We can bin that paper. Wait, there's no room." Luke unlocks and unbolts the back door to evict the smelly contents of the kitchen bin. As he dumps the bottle and the scragged bag in the dustbin against the weedy brick wall underneath the arch, a train rumbles overhead and the yard door jitters as though an intruder is fumbling with the latch. He secures the back door while Sophie finishes lining the kitchen bin. "Sorry for the wait," he says. "Hardly worth it. I kept waking Freda up, that was the problem."

Sophie folds the newspaper as small and thin as a book and lets the lid clap shut on it. "Do you remember what you were dreaming?"

"What, when I was six?" He's surprised to be able to say "It was the same thing for however long it lasted. Somebody was watching me and I don't think I wanted to see them."

"Did you, though?"

"They used to be at the window." He's disconcerted by how vivid the memory is growing. "Sometimes they were looking in upside down, more than one of them. And sometimes I thought their necks must be as long as a giraffe's if they were the right way up, or they could stretch that far."

"I'm not surprised you made a noise."

"That wasn't all," Luke says, though he's beginning to wish it had been. "If I didn't they would come in even though the window wasn't open and stand at the foot of the bed."

"They weren't as stretched as you thought, then."

"They could take all sorts of shapes," Luke says, and another memory lights up like a tableau in a ghost train: how the figures silhouetted in the moonlit dimness would lay their hands on the bedrail. They would grasp it as though they were establishing some form of ownership, and then all their hands would adopt another shape. It seems to him now that it resembled a symbol more than any hand ought to be able to do. "I've forgotten how they looked," he says, "before you ask."

"Did you tell anyone at the time?"

"I had to. Freda, Maurice, the doctor, the psychiatrist. Just that I kept dreaming somebody was at the window or in the room."

Sophie lowers herself onto one of the quartet of rickety chairs that loiter around the stained table. "What did they say?"

"Not a word I can remember. Sometimes I thought they hadn't got around to having mouths," Luke says and laughs, though not much. "You're asking me about the people I told, aren't you? The psychiatrist said it was nothing to worry about, so we didn't."

"There must have been more to it, Luke."

"She was the kind even the Arnolds liked. I'd say she thought psychiatry was her last resource after she'd tried everything else, certainly for somebody my age. She said I was highly imaginative and oughtn't to spend so much time on my own, and not to feed me close to bedtime, and keep an eye on what I read and watched. They'd have recommended her to their friends if they hadn't been so embarrassed about taking me to see her. But they did everything she said, and made sure I brought friends home from school, and I stopped waking Freda up."

"So the psychiatrist was all you needed."

"I'm not sure she cured me."

Sophie clasps her hands on her midriff as though she's protecting their child. "Why not, Luke?"

"I think I cured myself." He waits until she parts her hands. "I told you the Arnolds were embarrassed," he says. "I really think that made me feel worse than the dreams or disturbing Freda. I thought I wasn't the kind of son they'd hoped for, and so I did my best to be."

Sophie turns her hands up towards him, and he's put in mind of an opening flower. "What did you do?"

"Whenever the figures showed up I kept my eyes shut, even if they came into the room, and pretty soon they went away for good."

"You managed that when you were six years old, Luke?"

She's expressing admiration, not disbelief, but for an uneasy moment he feels she's implying that he couldn't have overcome his condition—that it's lying low inside him. "I hope they knew how brave you were," she says.

"Nobody needed to know."

"Well, I'm glad I do. They were proud of you, anyway, and they still are," Sophie says and stands up. "Shall we go on with the tour?"

The house stirs in response—at least, Luke imagines that the doors of the serving hatch fidget as the vibrations of a train reverberate through the bricks. He pulls the pair of lightweight doors wide to see Sophie come into the dining-room. With not much more than a glance at the fishing tackle and the magazines she says "Where are his books?"

"In the library," Luke says with some force on Terence's behalf. "He used to say that was how you helped people to read, keeping the libraries open. I expect that's where he found the tales he told me."

"See how many you can remember, then you'll be able to save them up."

Which of them might he tell their child? He remembers Terence saying there were places so remote they weren't on any map and so isolated that they hadn't caught up with the world. They were still in the process of becoming, so that time and space and the tyranny of matter had less of a hold over them, though surely Terence hadn't used those words. He'd talked about a jungle where explorers stumbled on a valley in the mist, where birds of an unknown species flew away at their approach and settled in the trees to wait for them. The explorers wondered if they'd caught some kind of jungle fever, because as the birds flapped into the distance they appeared to grow larger—far too large. This wasn't the reason the party made a wide detour around the valley and never recorded the location; it was the sight of a solitary figure watching from beside a bush as if he was guarding the path into the valley. He wore a mask like the head of a creature too prehistoric to be named, or was it a mask? The explorers retreated into the mist, praying they weren't followed, and one of them risked whispering what they'd all seen: though the shrub hadn't been as tall as the watcher, it was no shrub—it must have been at least fifty feet high. But you didn't have to go into the jungle, according to Terence; if you knew where and how to look you could still find traces of the shaping of the world.

Would Luke ever tell his child anything like that? He doesn't know what effect it might have, which feels like being unsure how it affected him. Before he can decide he sees Sophie making for the hall. "Sorry," he says and manages to reach it first. "Upstairs is worse."

She lingers in front of the pictures and the framed mosaic in the hall. By the time she follows him Luke has picked up the ragged towel and draped it over the chilly metal rail. The dead fly is marinating in the coffee, which he empties down the toilet. He's rinsing the mug when Sophie glances into the bathroom and moves on to Terence's bedroom.

He almost breaks the mug in his haste to put it down, but he's too late. She's tucking the dishevelled sheet under the mattress, and without too much more effort she stoops to drag the quilt onto the bed. "I'm just straightening up for now," she says. "We'll need to make a laundry trip if any of this is worth it." Letting go of the quilt, she takes hold of the solitary pillow.

The house shivers, or Luke's vision does, as a train passes close overhead. The muffled thunder seems to darken the room, unless Luke's apprehension is hindering his senses. Sophie lifts the pillow and begins to tremble—no, she's shaking it into some kind of shape. There was nothing under it, no face lurking like an insect beneath a stone, not even a sculpted face. She lays the pillow to rest and glances at the ceiling as the rumble of wheels mutters into silence. "I suppose you can ignore anything," she says, "if you live with it long enough."

"Maybe he couldn't any more," Luke says and leaves the thought behind as he follows Sophie into the front bedroom.

It smells older than it should, besides dusty and airless. He makes his way to the window, where he has to force the rusty catch out of its groove. He's shoving the sash as high as it will judder when Sophie says "Do you know what I think is in here?"

He swings around to find her gazing at the contents of the room. "What is?"

"A song," she says as if she isn't quite speaking to him. "Maybe a lot of them. Here's a horseman who was so eager to get where he was going he's left half of himself behind. Here's somebody offering us the moon to play with. Here's a ring for a giant to give his girl and stars for her hair. Here's a hand looking for its fingers and an eye to help it look . . . " Stroking her belly, she murmurs "I think someone likes it here."

"Let's decide what to do when we've sorted the place out," Luke finds he's anxious to establish.

"We could make a start if I didn't have a gig tonight. We'll come back very soon."

She could almost be advising her little passenger if not the house itself. Luke shuts the window as she heads for the stairs. He's on the landing when he glimpses something pale in Terence's bedroom. A glance at the object sends him hurrying downstairs. As Sophie climbs into the car he loiters in the hall. "Won't be a moment," he calls, "don't know if I locked the window," and sprints back to the room.

What he saw is under the bed and next to it as well, in the darkest corner of the bedroom. Perhaps it fell from its nest under the pillow, or did Terence try to smash it? The three jagged fragments feel colder than the stone they're composed of and unpleasantly slippery, as if they've just been dredged up from a marsh. Luke fits them together and stares at the result before scrambling to his feet and kicking the remains into the darkness under the bed. He hasn't time to dispose of them now. He'll need to return to the house by himself.

He's running downstairs only so that Sophie won't wonder why he took this long, not because he feels pursued. He locks the house and hurries to the car. "Hard to shut," he says as he starts the engine, after which he does his best to seem too busy driving to speak. He's hoping the task will keep the sight at the house out of his mind until he can set about trying to understand. It was the stone Terence brought home from Amberley Street, the elongated face that looked as though the subject was dreaming he was an ancient god. It was the face Luke imagined he would see watching him from dozens of windows at once. However fanciful that may have been, the image on the shattered plaque is exactly the same face.

A NAME FROM THE BOOK

THE HOTEL ROOM IN NORFOLK smells faintly of lavender. Luke could imagine it's the scent of the chintz that pads the chair beside the bed, and the matching stool that squats bandy-legged at the dressing-table. The bed is laden with a quilt plump enough for winter. The room overlooks a square that's neither regular nor straight-edged, from the middle of which a stone cross extends a narrowed shadow. It might almost be a sundial indicating that it's close to five o'clock by pointing at a butcher's, where headless birds hug themselves as they dangle upside down above a slab. Luke has hours before he goes onstage—hours to spend with Terence's journal.

Downstairs a stone-flagged hallway leads to a cobbled yard behind the inn. A smell of aged paper reminiscent of Terence's house has massed in the boot of the Lexus. As Luke carries the ledger into the hall the manager, an angular woman with shoulders wide enough to hang a doorman's coat on, leans over the sill of the reception alcove. "Heavy work, eh?" she says. "What line are you in, Mr Arnold?"

"They say I'm a comedian. I'm on at the Broadest Broad."

"You must have a lot of jokes in there."

Luke smiles as he supposes he's meant to and tramps up the variously tilted stairs. The ledger is too massive for the dressing-table, and the room isn't equipped with a desk. He dumps the journal on the bed and primes the percolator that's elevated on a shelf. When he sits on the bed the cover of the journal stirs like the lid of a box whose contents have grown restless. "Let's see what you're hiding," he says in the voice of a policeman he used to portray for all the Arnolds, and throws the ledger open.

The smell of stale paper rises to meet him and then settles on underlying the scent of the room. The ledger isn't just a diary, Luke sees now; Terence seems to have used it to record ideas for stories. **HORSEMAN RIDES SO FAST HIS TOP FLYS OFF + HE CANT FIND IT**... **HIGHWYMAN BEING CHASED GETS CHOPED IN HALF BY A TREE**... Luke knows where those came from but prefers Sophie's inspiration, and is disconcerted by the misspellings; could those have been the secret Terence wanted him to keep? **ANGEL LOSES HALO + CHILDREN PLAY WITH IT FOR A HOOP, A DEVIL WHOSE HIS ENEMY TRISE TO STEAL IT FROM THEM**... **SCULPTER FINDS BITS OF GREATEST STATUE EVER MADE + WHEN HE MAKES A STATUE WITH THEM IN**... Apparently Terence couldn't think how to develop this one. **BOY GOES TO HIS FIRST DANCE AT MIDSUMER + HALF THE MEN HAVE LEGS LIKE ANIMALS**... That's more akin to the tales he told Luke. None of the entries identifies the properties where he found the relics; the first one that does refers to John Strong's house.

It was added later than the date on the page, in a different ink that doesn't reappear for several pages. The original entry celebrates the granting of the demolition contract by the city council. After that the diary grows more terse, often with just a few words to a page, and some phrases read as though they were meant for only the writer to understand. **CAME INTO MY HEAD** is followed by **LIKE DREAMS** and then NOT MY DREAMS, possibly suggesting that Terence found he didn't like them after all. The thought is greeted by a choked hiss at Luke's back and an outburst of liquid bubbling. "Coffee for the mister," he says like a waiter at the tapas bar he and Sophie frequented when they were at university, and pours himself a cup somewhat tempered by a packet of powdery cream. A bitter sip sends him back to the journal.

SHOWS WHERE THINGS STAYED... The coffee doesn't help his mind grasp that, but doubtless **BROUGHT MOON IN** refers to the ironwork at the house—the gleeful moon framed by open hands. **GO TO LIBRARY** must have been important, since Terence underlined it thrice, infecting the page with an inky rash. **LEFT PAPERS THERE** may be the explanation, and **COPY DOWN** comes next, followed by **SAYS IT**

BRINGS BLESSING. That seems obscure if not actually secretive, and Luke finds it disconcerting. It's dated less than a year before he was born.

He remembers Terence telling Freda and Maurice they were blessed with Luke, but that needn't mean he helped, even if he thought he did. The jottings in the diary don't prove that: **FEEL FULL MOON** isn't comprehensible, and a few days later **FELT WHEN IT WAS** is as bad. **ONLY WORDS** might be summing itself up as a phrase, and the next one is **JUST LIKE PRAYING**. By the time Terence wrote it Freda knew she was going to have a child.

It wouldn't be Luke, and the thought leaves him feeling hollow. He may have made a virtue of imitation, but he has yet to come to terms with being one. The journal is reminding him with references to the situation: not just **FREDA RADIENT** but presumably **LIT FROM INSIDE** and also **BIGGER AND BRIGHTER**. Months before the birth Terence is thinking up names—**LUCIUS + LUCIA COME FROM LIGHT**—and it occurs to Luke that even the name he calls his own is just a substitute. He turns another page, rousing its introverted smell, and feels as if he has missed the birth. In fact there's no entry for the date, but three days later Terence wrote **LUCAS HERE**.

Perhaps the entry is so brief because he was disappointed that the Arnolds didn't use the name he liked. Surely it can't mean he knew they had the wrong child—Luke. **EVEN BETTER THAN THEY COULDVE WISHED FOR** ought to be heartening, as well as the record of Luke's progress: **LUCAS ON THE MOVE** at two months, **LUCAS WALKING** by Christmas, **HEALTH VISITER NOT SEEN ANYTHING LIKE** the following week, **LUKE TALKS SENTENCES** almost immediately after, **LOST COUNT OF LUKES WORDS** less than a month later... Perhaps Luke should be pleased, but he feels remote from this account of a deception everyone played out without realising. It seems unlikely that this section of the journal will help him find out where he came from, if any of the entries will. As he leafs fast through the diary he feels as though he's trying to leave his childhood behind.

The name of a town catches his attention—Peterborough, which he drove through on his way to Norfolk. The entry is dated almost a quarter of a century ago. **RALPH SANSOM PETERBOROUGH, TOLD ABOUT HIM**. Suppose the person referred to didn't live in Peterborough but had that for his surname? Even if he lives there, what can Luke ask? He's already starting to feel absurd and deluded as he uses his mobile to search online. But there is indeed a Ralph Sansom in Peterborough, and the listing gives his phone number.

Luke thumbs the key to make the call and immediately wants to cancel it. Surely he won't run out of words when his job is improvisation, but is he nervous of what he may learn? As he takes a breath that tastes of lavender and old paper a voice says "Yes?"

It sounds more like a challenge than an invitation. "Yes," Luke says. "Mr Sansom?"

"Yes?"

"Mr Ralph Sansom?"

"Yes?"

The voice has grown thinner and shriller, pinching the word. "I'm sorry to bother you, Mr Sansom," Luke says. "I—"

"Then don't. Whatever you're selling, I'm not in the market."

"I'm not a salesman, Mr Sansom."

"What are you, then?"

Luke doesn't want to answer that, at least not yet. "I found your name in—"

"Wherever you've got it, rub me out. I've signed up not to be pestered by your kind."

"It's nothing like that," Luke says and wonders whether he does indeed sound like a cold caller. "Your name was in a diary, Mr Sansom."

"A diary," Sansom says as if repeating it may cancel the notion. "You do surprise me. Whose?"

"His name was Terence Arnold."

"Arnold." Sansom isn't quite so ready to repeat this, and pauses again before saying "And what is that expected to mean to me?"

"I was hoping you could say."

"I've said it." Presumably in case this is unclear Sansom adds "Not a thing."

"You wouldn't know of another Ralph Sansom in Peterborough."

"There hasn't been one while I've been living here, and that's my entire lifetime." Sansom takes a harsh effortful breath and says "May I ask what you know about this Arnold person?"

For a moment Luke can't understand why Sansom has grown more resentful, and then he thinks he does. The man is wishing he'd said there was somebody else called Ralph Sansom; he feels he has betrayed himself. "He was in demolition," Luke says. "Maybe you hired him."

"I did nothing of the sort." With no diminution of annoyance Sansom adds "You keep saying was."

"He died last month."

"You'll realise why I've no response to that." As if he doesn't think this is a contradiction Sansom says "How, may I ask?"

"A heart attack."

"Common enough. Was there any cause?"

Luke tries not to feel accused. "He didn't have his medication."

"We can be careless as we get older. Now if you'll excuse me—" Sansom interrupts himself with a laborious exhalation and says "Just before I bid you farewell, what is Mr Arnold's diary supposed to have said about me?"

"Either somebody told him about you or one of you told the other about someone."

"Yes?" The word is sharper than ever. "And so?"

"That's all there is. I thought you might be able to fill me in."

"Then your call has been a waste of time," Sansom says, and immediately "One moment. If that was all he wrote about me, what made you seek me out?"

"I'm trying to find people he may have been to see," Luke decides as he speaks.

"Been to see for what purpose?"

"I'm trying to find that out too."

"There's nothing to discover," Sansom says. "And may I enquire who you are that you're prying into his affairs?"

"I'm one of the heirs of his will."

"Then may I suggest you content yourself with that? I assume it didn't authorise you to go through his private papers."

"I want to find out more about myself, that's all."

Sansom draws a breath that rattles in his throat. "Who are you exactly? What do you think you'll uncover?"

"I thought I was Terence Arnold's nephew but I'm—"

Even if Luke knew how to continue, there's no point in voicing it. Whatever noise Sansom makes in response is cut off before Luke can be sure it's a cry, and then the phone is silent except for a hiss of static like a fall of dust or a whisper searching for words. In a moment he finds some of those for himself. "What a joke."

— 12 —

THE SECOND CALL

THE MANAGER KEEPS GLANCING at the ledger Luke has planted on the sill of the reception alcove. As she returns his credit card and hands him the receipt she says "Do you know what I'd do if I had your gift?"

"You'll tell me."

"Find out what makes people happy and do my best to put that on."

"I'm afraid that's what I do already."

"No call to be afraid. I think it would make me happier as well," she says and gives him a doubtful look.

There's no question that he lived up to expectations last night at the Broadest Broad. When someone shouted out for Jack Brittan, the voice and the mannerisms came so readily to Luke that it felt like being possessed by the needs of the audience, and he found himself observing his performance while his mind replayed the conversation with Ralph Sansom—especially the end. He's sure the man recognised Terence's name, but however often Luke echoes Sansom's last sound in his head he can't decide what it may have expressed: dismay or shock or incredulity or even some kind of delight? Suppose Luke's call managed to locate a member of his actual family? The only way to resolve any of this, if it will, is to speak to Sansom or somebody who lives with him.

Luke locks the journal in the boot and drives out of the small town. Fields reach for the horizon under a blue sky parched of clouds, and soon the roadside begins to sprout signs for Peterborough. Each one feels more like a reminder, and when he sees a layby he pulls in. Before any doubts can overtake him he recalls Sansom's number.

"Yes?"

Despite the reminiscence of the last call, it's a woman's voice. "Can I speak to Ralph Sansom?" Luke says.

"I'm afraid you can't, no."

"Do you mind if I ask why?"

"He isn't here."

"Can you say when he will be?"

"I wish I knew."

"Ah," Luke says but can hardly leave it at that. "I'm sorry, what . . . "

"My father has had to be taken into hospital."

"I'm sorry." Luke feels reduced to echoing himself. "What's the trouble, do they know?"

"Somebody upset him very much. He isn't of an age to be able to shrug that sort of thing off."

Luke struggles not to apologise a third time. "Have they said how serious it is?"

"He's already had more than one attack. They've told us not to hope too much."

Luke feels still guiltier for asking "Did he say what upset him?"

"I know someone rang him yesterday but I don't know who or what about. Believe me, I'd like a word or two with them."

Luke opens his mouth, which fills with silence. Eventually Sansom's daughter says "Can I ask why you're calling, Mr . . . "

"It's Luke, but it isn't important. I won't bother you any more."

"Will my father know you if I'm able to give him a message?"

"We've never met. Are you waiting to hear from the hospital? I'd better say goodbye in case they're trying to get through," Luke says and rings off.

He's ashamed to have used the excuse. How responsible is he for Sansom's condition? He already feels to blame for Terence's death. The Lexus shivers as a lorry several houses long speeds past, and he watches the vehicle shrink into the distance until the road is deserted. Can he really justify contacting people Terence mentioned in the journal when the effect on them may be as random as his search? He has no idea how dangerously unpredictable it may be—and then he sees his mistake. He shouldn't abandon the hunt quite so soon, and he gets out of the car to consult the journal.

THE LAST NAME

AS SOON AS HE HAS TURNED along the street Luke parks the car.
It's the only vehicle beside either of the pavements shaded by trees. Cars
are sunning themselves in some of the driveways of the large front
gardens, where pairs of houses too individual to be twins stand together.
He climbs out and shuts the door, not gently enough to avoid rousing the
dog that runs to snarl at him through the bars of a gate. He has barely set
out along the street, which slopes up to a steeper hill that overlooks the
town, when he grows aware that a vehicle is creeping after him.

It swerves sluggishly away from him as he twists around. Its roof sports
a peak emblazoned with a phone number, while its sides display the logo
of the Pass With Patsy driving school. The driver isn't watching Luke—
she's nervously intent on a hesitant three-point turn—but she has helped
him feel like an intruder. He won't be deterred when he has come so far
out of his way, more than twenty miles off the route home and along
roads the map stretched a good deal straighter than they proved to be.
Harold Yancey is the last person named in the journal, and surely this
means he has whatever information Terence was searching for. If Luke
feels as tentative and apprehensive as the driver on the road, that's
because the man may be his father.

A wind sets the trees dabbing the pavement with shadow. A car on a
drive shudders and begins to flutter, or at least its canvas cover does. It
puts Luke in mind of an inflatable castle at a fairground where the

Arnolds took him for a birthday treat—where the sideshow reminded him of a tale of Terence's about a castle that changed shape once you ventured in. He still has all his memories; he's recalling more every day. Meeting his real parents can't change the life he has lived, and he makes himself stride uphill.

He's several houses short of Yancey's when a woman wheels a pushchair out of her garden, and the toddler waves at him. "Hello," Luke says in the kind of voice people seem to use in such a situation.

She gives him a grin that exhibits almost a mouthful of teeth. "Who are you?"

"Luke Yancey." This sounds so odd, even though unspoken, that it comes close to robbing him of words. "I'm nobody in particular," Luke says.

"I'm sure you are," the woman says with a dutiful laugh. "Don't mind Trish. She's asking everyone that, even me."

"Who are you?"

"Now, Trish," the woman says but keeps her gaze on him.

"I'm Luke, Trish. My name's Luke."

"That's just a little name."

"Luke Arnold," he says mostly to the woman and with all the conviction he can summon up. "I'm looking for the Yancey residence."

"It's the one with the lamps," the woman says and points without looking. "Excuse me, we're in a hurry."

She didn't seem to be until just now. "Come along, Trish," she says and speeds the pushchair downhill as the toddler makes to wave to Luke.

The Yancey house is a grey stone building with elongated chimneys crowned by sooty spikes. Four lamps stand beside the gravel drive. They're equipped with sensors, which are so responsive that the lamp nearest to the pavement glares at Luke as he passes through the shadow of a tree. He won't let this make him feel unwelcome, but he could imagine that whoever lives here is anxious for light, as though the lamps are an extension of their nerves. The other lamps stay dormant while he strides along the drive and pokes the bellpush on a pillar of the stone porch. "There's the door," a woman shouts at once.

She sounds harassed and strident, and she could be Luke's mother. He wonders how she'll sound if she learns she is. In a moment he hears weighty footsteps tramping along a hall. As he takes a not entirely steady breath the panelled antique door swings open to reveal the man he has summoned. "What can we do for you?" the man says as though he hopes it's very little if anything at all.

He's quite a few years older than Luke, and might look more like him if his features weren't obesely blurred. Though he's dressed for a race—shorts and singlet—it's unlikely that he could be more than a spectator. He's the colour of a battered fish, and Luke suspects those may figure in his diet. One pudgy forearm is tattooed BELLE above a ruddy heart spiked with an arrow. Is Luke seeing his mother's name? Before he has thought of an answer he can risk giving, the man says "Do we know you?"

"I hope so." Having said that, Luke has to ask "Would you be Harold Yancey?"

"I wouldn't." At first the man seems content to leave it there, and then he says "I'm not the chap he married either."

"Oh, I see." Luke is seeing the reason for his visit disappear like a bubble. "Sorry," he presumes he ought to add.

"We're not prejudiced here." Just as truculently the man says "You're talking about my uncle."

"Ah. Well, good." Luke assumes it is and says "I believe he knew someone connected with me."

"Who was that?"

"Terence Arnold." When Yancey's nephew shakes his head Luke says "He was in demolition but he was into other things as well."

The man meets this with a hint of a grin. Whatever secrets Terence may have had, Luke is sure he wasn't gay, but perhaps he shouldn't make an issue of it when the man's responses are so unpredictable. Instead he says "Does Mr Yancey still live here?"

"He hasn't for a while."

"Could you tell me how I can get in touch with him?"

The implication of a grin reappears and vanishes. "What for?"

"Do you mind if I keep it between me and him?"

"Depends what you're keeping."

"It's to do with my past. I can't tell you any more."

As Yancey's nephew looks dissatisfied the unseen woman shouts "For pity's sake, Donald, send him up."

"That'll make him happy, will it?"

"It'll make him whatever it makes him."

Luke can't tell whether he's still under discussion, since Yancey's nephew has turned away from him. The man faces him to say "She says go up and see Harold. Nineteenth Avenue, number eight."

He's jabbing a stubby finger at the hill to which the street leads. "Thanks for helping," Luke says, but the man only shrugs and shuts the door.

The lamp at the end of the drive lets Luke pass unnoticed and then flares up to celebrate his departure. The blurred restless shadows of the trees mop at his silhouette as if they've resolved to erase it, and the outline of the draped car squirms vigorously enough to be groping for a different shape. The dog scampers to resume its yapping while the gate clangs like a dull bell. Luke starts his car and has to wait for Patsy's learner to execute another tortuous manoeuvre, setting out for the opposite side of the road before backing away with a series of hiccups of the engine and nervous blinks of the brake lights. At last she's facing the right way, and Luke drives uphill.

A row of imposing houses stands along the foot of the slope at the end of the road. A steep unpaved track called Church Lane leads to the top, where a hedge enclosed by railings stands against a scoured blue sky. Luke hears birdsong chipping at the afternoon, the chatter of a magpie that reminds him how the noise would make the air feel splintered when he was a child, somebody urging a dog to be quiet and lie down. A wind is bringing the voice down the hill, and he guesses that the hedge surrounds a park, where treetops have risen into view. "Quiet," the command comes again, "lie still," though Luke can't identify any noise the animal is making or indeed the gender of the speaker. As the car climbs past the highest building on the lane, the tip of a spire appears above the trees. It belongs to a church, and beyond the hedge is a churchyard.

Some distance away a wide road he didn't notice leads uphill to the gates. It isn't Nineteenth or any avenue, and the wide rough track bordering the churchyard is unnamed. There are no other roads to be seen; the one he's looking for must be behind the church. A drive broad enough for hearses extends past the building, and Luke eases the car into the churchyard.

The shadows of memorials don't quite imitate their sources. The silhouettes of headstones are reduced to black squares reminiscent of open trapdoors in the flattened mounds. Winged dwarfs crouch behind angels, and truncated dumpy crosses mark the spot behind each stone cross. Every line of graves is numbered with a plaque set into the drive.

Beyond the church are dozens of new plots and an unused grassy expanse that isolates the stubby shadow of the spire. There are no gates on this side of the churchyard. Having encircled the church, the drive turns back on itself.

Luke parks the car beneath a stained-glass window full of levelled saints and crosses the grass to look for the route to the streets down the hill. He has to drag the foliage apart to be sure of what he sees beyond the hedge. The land slopes gradually away as far as the horizon, and it consists entirely of fields. The town comes to an end at the churchyard.

He can't quite believe the trick Yancey's nephew appears to have played on him, but he trudges back to the drive behind the church. A plaque at the edge of the grass confirms that the newest row of graves is indeed the nineteenth. Most of the stones in the incomplete row are identical apart from their inscriptions. The eighth stone from the drive belongs to Harold Yancey, who died last year aged sixty-eight. The inscription says HE FOLLOWED HIS LOVE.

"I hope you're both happy," Luke mutters, "wherever you are." He can't judge how much of his wistfulness relates to his having no reason to be here. "So you weren't my father," he says. "Why did Terence come to see you, then? Does anybody know?"

He's disconcerted to feel overheard if not watched. He glances around, but the presence at his back is just a sapling, one of several planted on this side of the church. If anyone were observing him they might take him for a relative who is praying for the dead. He doesn't feel like mimicking that role, and raises his voice. "Did you tell Terence anything? I wish you could tell me."

A wind sets the hedge creaking but falls short of him. Otherwise there's silence that he could almost take for a refusal to answer him. He finds himself recalling a day out with Terence—an afternoon they spent at the museum in Liverpool. Terence waited until they were alone with a shrunken head in a glass case, and then he whispered "He's got tales for you, Luke. Just ask him."

Luke can't remember doing so or what he said. Perhaps he didn't even speak aloud. It seems to have felt more like reaching with his imagination—reaching out and deep. He does recall Terence whispering "What can you see, Luke?" and how his imagination responded with a rush of images like a dream he was having while awake: fat vegetation sweaty with rain, firelight hemmed in by dark jungle and a clamour of night cries, an incessant irresistible drumbeat, a ring of virtually naked dancers prancing around the flames as though only exhaustion could end the rite . . . All this must have come from films he'd watched or books he'd read, however vivid it still seems, and yet some aspect of the memory prompts him to lean towards the grave and murmur "Can't you give me an idea? Show me if you can."

The hedge creaks again, although the noise seems closer and the wind doesn't reach him. He still feels watched, and straightens up, perhaps too fast, since his surroundings appear to brighten. He has the odd thought that the moon has risen, though it isn't due for hours. The illumination seems to fill his mind, lighting up a memory of Terence. But it isn't a memory, because he's with somebody Luke has never met, a man with a slumped decrepit face just sufficiently reminiscent of Donald Yancey's for Luke to deduce who he's meant to be. He's showing Terence a gesture or at least trying to demonstrate one, stretching the little finger of his left hand so wide that it's plain he would make a right angle with it if he could and then attempting the same feat with his index finger. Having failed in all this, he uses his right hand to complete the sign, poking fingers out from the palm of the left hand to approximate how it should look.

As soon as Luke recoils a step the impression is extinguished. It felt too much like reaching into the dark under the earth, and he could have imagined that the muffled creaking was there too. His surroundings feel brittle and look pallid, little more than a shell of themselves, presumably because the vision has unnerved him. Of course it drew on his encounter with Yancey's nephew—that was how he was able to visualise how Yancey looked—but for as long as it lasted the image reminded him of how he'd felt when he was so young that his mind wasn't under his control. "Sorry to have troubled you," he murmurs without having intended to speak. He's heading for his car when he hears the voice.

It's somewhere behind him—the voice he heard on his way up the lane. "Stay quiet now," it says. "He's gone." The dog and its owner must be in the field beyond the hedge, even if the command sounded closer, and Luke's soliloquy has been disturbing the animal. If a sapling beyond Yancey's grave appears to have more of a shadow than its girth warrants, that has to be partly a mark on the grass. Luke takes a pace towards it, and at once the illusion vanishes as though the mark has retreated into hiding. He won't let it trouble him any further, and he makes for the car.

— 14 —

A SIGN FROM THE PAST

THE ULTRASOUND TECHNICIAN is a brawny woman whose breasts expand her overall like an emblem of motherhood. As she hands over the photographs she says "He likes an audience."

"We're both performers," Sophie tells her. "I expect it's in his genes."

"I only heard your song once and I bought your album," the technician says and turns to Luke. "And what are you famous for again?"

Luke is gazing at the handful of photographs. He knows this is how scans look—the baby's bones glowing white through blurred grey flesh— but the images seem reminiscent of a vision, of spying into somewhere hidden from the world. "I imitate people," he mumbles.

"Luke's a comedian."

"He's one of those all right," the technician says and relents. "I should think you're looking forward to making your baby laugh."

Luke can't contradict this, but he's still intent on the photographs that reveal he and Sophie have a son now that the evidence is no longer hidden by the cord. "What did you mean about liking an audience?"

"He was just very lively. I don't mean the scan was affecting him."

"I knew that was what you meant," Sophie says.

"You've nothing to worry about that I can see, and you don't need me to tell you that goes for Lukes background as well."

Luke wishes he didn't have a reason to speak. "We don't know that any more."

71

"Pardon me?"

"We've found out the couple who brought Luke up aren't his parents. They didn't even know themselves." More comfortingly than Luke thinks is required Sophie adds "It wasn't here the babies were mixed up."

"I see." The technician spends some time in doing so and then, with an extra blink at Luke, says "Let me just have a word with someone."

As she leaves them alone Luke tries to concentrate on Sophie and the photographs, but he's thinking of Terence's journal. On his way home from the churchyard yesterday he stopped the car to search the ledger for a drawing he was sure he'd glimpsed. It's a perfunctory image of a hand with the little finger and the index pointing directly away from each other while the thumb rests across the palm and the raised middle fingers are pressed together. So Luke had seen it before he had his vision in the churchyard, and he assumes Terence was doing his best to sketch something he'd found, most likely an architectural decoration. He did so opposite the Yancey reference, which dates from when Luke was six and a half, after which all the entries refer to locations rather than to anyone by name. It's the only version of the image in the journal, but Luke is troubled by the notion that he has seen its like somewhere else. He has made no headway with remembering by the time the technician comes back. "Can you speak to Dr Meldrum as you go?" she says.

The doctor meets them at the door of his office. He's tall but stooped, with a forehead so high it comes close to making his face look bisected by his unkempt eyebrows. "Ms Drew, Mr Arnold," he says. "Or is it still?"

"As far as we're concerned it is," Sophie tells him.

"Well, that simplifies matters a little. Will you come in? I have you on the screen." As Luke and Sophie follow him into the white room, where a computer appears to be struggling for space on his cluttered desk, he says "I understand from the lady who conducted the scan that you put on some kind of a show."

"Who did?" Luke demands.

"She remembered seeing you on television. Didn't you go on to learn who your parents were?"

"I suppose that's near enough to it."

"You might think of advising us directly of any alteration in your details." The doctor's faintly reproachful tone dissipates as he says "Do sit down. You're saying you'd prefer to retain the name we have for you."

"It's the only one I've got."

"Capital. Any question mark over your date of birth that you're aware of?" When Luke shakes his head the doctor says "I understand you're blaming some confusion at the hospital."

"Unless you can tell us," Sophie says, "how else the babies could have been swapped."

"There did use to be blunders of the kind once in a blue moon. They're one reason safeguards have been put in place, so please don't feel even slightly apprehensive on your own front." His eyebrows subside, having propped up a stack of wrinkles, as he says "Mr Arnold, your family. Not known, am I to put, or to be confirmed?"

"Whichever you think is best."

"It might be in the interest of your child to discover what you can about your origins."

"But you've seen Luke's history," Sophie protests.

"We have, and most exemplary it is. Be reassured that we've no reason to suspect his family has passed anything undesirable on to him." Dr Meldrum scrolls through the information on the monitor and says "He did see a consultant once when he was a child, but there was nothing amiss to speak of."

"The psychiatrist, you mean." Luke almost doesn't hesitate before asking "What does it say?"

"Nothing to frighten the horses. Your intelligence was well above the average. Your answers were articulate and uncommonly imaginative. You were unusually quick to identify cues and respond to them, that's to say to learn from other people's behaviour. Nothing wrong with any of that, Ms Drew, would you agree?"

"It sounds as if you were already on the way to being what you are, Luke."

"You seem to have had a little trouble with imaginary companions." Dr Meldrum is still intent on the monitor. "Your image of them seems to have been very vivid," he says, "but a few months later you'd completely overcome the problem. It was the main reason you were referred, and you didn't need to be seen again."

"The main reason as well as his dreams, you mean," Sophie says.

"No, those were part of it. The other problem that I'm confident Mr Arnold has left behind was a minor nervous habit, nothing more."

Luke feels absurdly apprehensive, as if his childhood state has been revived. "What habit?"

"Some kind of tic, I believe. Yes, there it is." He's looking not at Luke but at the screen. "The consultant mistook it for a muscular spasm at first," he says. "A minor compulsion to contort your hands. She explored the possibility that you meant to make some form of sign, but since you denied it she concluded the gesture was unconscious."

"Does she describe it?" Sophie says, and when the doctor finds no description "Do you remember, Luke?"

"Why would I want to?" Some of the trouble is that he does. He's hearing Freda protest "Don't do that with your hands, Luke, they'll stick that way" and "What are you trying to do? You'll damage them if you're not careful." Even if he's paraphrasing her words, there's no question of the shape his hands were straining to adopt. He has to assume Terence showed him some version of the sign, but where? If he has forgotten this for so many years, what else may be lying in wait in his mind? "I've no idea what it could have meant," he tells Sophie, which is true enough.

"Perhaps it was your way of fending off whatever you imagined was threatening you," says Dr Meldrum. "I'm sure you both have more immediate concerns, but do appreciate that we've found nothing untoward today."

Luke and Sophie thank him as he ushers them out of his office. Somewhere down the corridor that looks and smells scoured, a baby is wailing. Another one starts a thin imitation, and soon they're joined by a chorus. Sophie gives the clamour a wry smile and says "I'm sorry, Luke."

"What have you got to be sorry for?"

"I was hoping today might make up for not finding your parents when you thought you had."

"Of course it does." At least Luke can persuade her that he has left any disquiet behind. "He'll be bright, little Maurice," he says. "He already is."

The infant wails fade into the distance as the automatic doors let him and Sophie out of the hospital. They turn their phones back on, and Luke's emits a sharp alert. He has missed a call from somebody unidentified who left no message. He's returning the mobile to his pocket, and trying not to wonder vainly how important the call was, when the phone begins to vibrate in his hand. Before it has a chance to ring he says "Hello?"

For some moments he's afraid his urgency has silenced if not scared away the caller, and then a woman blurts "Mr Arnold?"

"Luke Arnold, yes."

"You're the Mr Arnold who was on television."

"I'm one of them. I'm the one who turned out not to be one."

"I know." She sounds apologetic, but she already did, and more so as she adds "How have you been since?"

Sophie is questioning him with her eyes, and he can only wave at her; he would switch on the loudspeaker if it weren't for the noise of traffic on the road outside the hospital. "Why do you ask?" he says, pressing the mobile against his ear.

"I should think a lot of people who saw the show must have felt for you, Mr Arnold."

He doesn't think this is much of an answer; it's more like avoiding one. Before he can say so the woman enquires "Have you done anything about the situation?"

Is she some kind of counsellor? "What would you suggest?" Luke retorts.

"Have you been looking into it, I mean."

"I've been trying to find out where I came from."

"So you want to know."

Sophie is frowning at him, but he waves so fiercely she looks rebuffed. "Why shouldn't I?" he demands.

"That's not for me to say, Mr Arnold."

"True enough, but then why are you calling?"

She's silent, and Luke is afraid he has been too aggressive. He's about to prompt her when he hears her take a long breath. "I was a nurse at the hospital," she says. "I know what happened after you were born."

— 15 —

THE WATCHERS

SHE DIDN'T GIVE LUKE HER SURNAME or a precise time to meet her. She told him to be in the park by eight, and he's still there, sitting at a picnic table that gives him a view of much of Greenbank Park. Ahead of him is an expanse of grass bordered by trees and railings, beyond which it's overlooked by houses on the far side of Greenbank Road. They're on Luke's right, while to his left a concrete path leads alongside a narrow lake almost the length of the park, and behind him is a children's playground. His vision has kept pace with the growing darkness, some of which is brought by clouds; the sky resembles the roof of a coal mine patched with huge wads of soot. Just the same, it's almost nine o'clock.

He keeps telling himself not to call Eunice, even though he managed to persuade her to reveal her mobile number. He doesn't know if she still works as a nurse, but perhaps her job has delayed her. Why does she need to meet him before she'll tell him what she knows? If she's watching him from one of the houses, surely she's had time to be as sure of him as this will make her. Anybody else could take him for a drug dealer or a customer, and perhaps that's why he feels spied upon. He peers at the houses, three-storey buildings with steep gables that each frame single windows, but nobody is visible. A distorted flattened face more than twice the size of his is mouthing silently beneath a gable, and a set of ground-floor curtains pulses with the glow of another television. He hasn't given up attempting to locate a watcher when he sees a light on the path through the park.

It's approaching at no great speed. It's so intensely white that it puts Luke in mind of the essence of the moon. A dull effortful murmur lets him realise that it belongs to a motorised wheelchair, beside which a large dog on a lead is trotting. Perhaps that will help Eunice to feel safe to talk, but as Luke lifts a hand the dog starts to whine and bark. "Good evening," the occupant of the chair says and even more sharply "Hunter."

"Good evening," Luke responds, having sighed at his mistake, because Hunter's owner is a man. The dog is baying now and snarling too, besides emitting a whine like the noise of an unoiled gate. The glare of the headlight clings to Luke's eyes while the chair coasts past the playground. "Hunter," the man commands and yanks at the lead, making the dog yelp, as the wheelchair coasts out of the park. Luke is turning back to the houses when he realises he's no longer alone. Somebody is in the playground.

Perhaps the dog wasn't barking at Luke after all. The newcomer is inside a climbing frame from which his long legs dangle as he pokes his face between the bars. He, if indeed it's a he, isn't on his own. A companion squats on a low seesaw, feet planted on the surface of the playground, and a third figure is sitting at the top of a slide, where his upper half is silhouetted against the dim field across the lake. The outline of his face is at least as starved as those of his fellows—so ill-defined that they're hardly discernible. Their silence and lack of movement suggest they're up to rather less than good. It seems unwise to stay close to them, and Luke rises to his feet, not too deliberately or casually or slowly or hastily, he hopes. When they don't move he retreats along the path.

There's a bench beside it about midway, facing the lake. He sits on it the wrong way round, thrusting his legs through the gap at the back. His view is mostly of the houses now and he has to keep glancing both ways along the deserted path. Whenever he glimpses the playground its occupants haven't perceptibly moved, but suppose they think he's watching them? Their lack of activity feels like a threat he would rather not define, and he doesn't realise how much they've distracted him from consulting his watch until he sees the time is well on its way to ten o'clock.

He takes out his mobile before he sees how this may look. May the loiterers think he's calling someone about them? He shouldn't leave the park in case Eunice shows up, but she has had quite enough time to do so. As he brings the mobile to his ear a dial tone starts to trill, and as it repeats itself a mobile begins to ring in a house. It shrills twice and is cut off, and so is the sound at his ear. In a moment a woman's shadow swells up on the curtain at the window in the gable of the house almost opposite the bench.

The left edge of the curtain stirs as the woman leans towards the meagre gap. The curtain falls into place almost immediately, and the shadow ducks back. As it vanishes Luke jabs the icon to recall Eunice's number. The bell renews its twin trills at his ear, and the phone under the gable responds. It's cut off at once, and the light in the room is extinguished, pasting darkness like an emblem of secrecy against the window. The sight is too much for Luke. "Eunice," he shouts at the top of his voice. "It's Luke Arnold. You know I'm here."

He regrets the outburst at once. He could just have rung her doorbell. He's expecting the loiterers to jeer or otherwise comment, but they don't make a sound. He swings his legs off the bench and is about to make for the house when the curtain in the gable inches back. While he can't see the watcher, he waves as if he has, and the phone goes off in his other hand. Before the mobile can start singing about June he claps it to his ear. "I'm sorry, Mr Arnold," Eunice says almost too low to be heard.

"No need, Eunice. It's all right now." It has to be. "Shall I wait here for you?" Luke says.

"Please don't, Mr Arnold, no."

"Where would you like me to wait? Shall I come over to you?"

"Don't do that, please, no," Eunice mutters urgently, and the curtain edges towards the window frame. "I've said I'm sorry."

She sounds less so than previously. "What for?" Luke is determined to learn.

"I was wrong, Mr Arnold. That's all I can say."

"Wrong about what?"

"I'm afraid I mistook you for someone else."

"It's not the first time that's happened to me," Luke says several times louder than her murmur, "as you know."

"I do, Mr Arnold. I can only ask you to believe I'm sorry if I gave you too much hope."

"I don't know what you've given me yet. I'm not even sure what you're talking about."

"What I said to you this afternoon, I was mistaken. I must have had two other babies in mind."

"At the same hospital? That doesn't say much for the place."

"I think I was thinking of a different hospital."

"Then it doesn't say much for the system, does it?" When Eunice is silent except for an uneven breath Luke demands "So what were you thinking happened to me?"

"Someone must have put another baby's name on you at some stage, Mr Arnold, and yours on the other baby. It almost never happens, but it's been known."

"No." Luke is close to certain she's pretending to misunderstand. "I'm asking," he says, "what you thought when you first got in touch with me."

Eunice works on another breath before whispering "I had it in my head someone swapped you both, whoever the other one was."

"The Arnolds never would have. Whoever did couldn't have wanted me, then."

"Mr Arnold." Eunice sounds unsure, not only of his name. "I told you," she mutters, "it didn't happen."

"If you're saying you're mistaken, how can you know it didn't?"

Luke feels triumphant, though not pleasantly, and apprehensive too. He seems to have robbed Eunice of words, which suggests he has seen through her pretence. He stares at the window, but the sliver of darkness alongside the curtain is as uncommunicative as the phone. "Look, can't we talk face to face?" he says, lowering his voice. "Can't you let me in? I'm not alone down here."

The curtain gapes a few inches and subsides like a nervous blink, and Eunice whispers "I saw them."

The mass of cloud has begun to crumble, wads of it drifting apart to expose a moon that resembles the first line of a sketch on a blackboard. Eunice sounds worse than uneasy, and Luke presumes it's on his behalf. He turns to confront whatever he has to, but the play area is deserted, and so is the park all around him. "All right, they've gone," Luke says, "but just the same—"

"I still can."

She has more of a view of the park than he has. "Where?" he says low.

In a moment he glimpses activity, but it can't be what she means. A shape is just discernible among the leaves in the treetop nearest to her house. If it isn't a bird it's a squirrel, made to appear larger by the surrounding foliage, since the branch on which it's perched would be weighed down considerably more if the creature were that size. Luke is wasting time in trying to identify it when Eunice cries "Go away."

It's almost a scream, and it crosses the park even though the window is shut. Luke snatches the mobile away from his face and holds it not too close to his uninjured ear. "You haven't told me where they are," he persists. "What do you want me to do?"

"Go away."

This time it's a plea in little more than a whisper. Luke isn't sure whom she's addressing, and he has no chance to ask, because the mobile is instantly dead. He could phone her again, but he knows she won't answer, and he can't bring himself to go over to the house. He feels hollow with frustration and guilty for having troubled her so much. He thrusts the mobile intro his pocket and is turning back to the path when he hears a sound behind him.

Something is running down a tree—down several. He can hear claws scrabbling at the bark. The trees are more than stout enough to hide the creatures, but he glimpses a hint of an outline on the tree trunk closest to Eunice's window. It must be a squirrel—it's racing down head first—though its tail is helping it appear to be as elongated as Luke is tall. Presumably the moonlight is making its outline look so pale. In a moment he can't see it, but he hears it and both its fellows reach the ground simultaneously, and then they're gone.

He waits for them to cross the grass, but there's no sign of them. They can only be hiding behind the trees. He does his best to make no sound as he paces towards them, but they aren't where he thought they had to be. When he darts around the middle tree, feeling as if he's performing some moonlit ritual, he's unable to find any of them. The impression of a tall shape seeping into a tree trunk must have been his shadow, however thin it seemed. He's acutely aware of how he may look to anybody in the houses; he wouldn't blame them for calling the police. He already feels ridiculous enough—a comedian forced to perform for no visible audience. He could think this sums up too much of his life, and he tramps back to his car.

16

GAZER'S HEAD

AFTER THE GIG IN GAZER'S HEAD Luke walks down to the harbour. In the steep narrow crooked streets the tipsy buildings have propped up their antiquity with souvenir shops and seafood restaurants and boutiques. Fishing boats nod and creak at the quayside while yachts wave their masts at the crescent moon. Its light has laid a pallid trail to the horizon, where the ocean leads into a darkness so immense the stars are lost in it. Luke feels as if his thoughts could suffer that fate too.

Tonight's show was in the function room at the town hall. The large solemn darkly panelled room was full, and yet he felt out of place. Some of the audience looked eager to be entertained but initially uncertain of his humour. At least they've heard of Brittan even this far south, not far from the lowest tip of Cornwall, and Luke could imagine that they want him to turn into the man or at any rate a caricature of him. He felt uninvolved with his own performance, more like a spectator, not least because Eunice is still on his mind. Sophie has done her best to persuade him not to worry about little Maurice, and he doesn't think she's trying to convince herself. If they needn't be anxious about their child, there's even less reason for Luke to play a victim's role. Whatever may have happened a lifetime ago at the hospital, it's surely too remote to affect him, and he has no excuse for fretting on his own behalf.

Staring out to sea doesn't help him to understand his encounter with Eunice, and he wanders back to the Atlantic View, three inns combined into a single hotel on the cobbled seafront. His room is centuries younger than the plump stone corridor. Beyond the window the pale thread that extends across the black water looks as though it's reaching out of the void to draw him into the ancient dark. When he returns from the bathroom, which is tiled as white as the moon, he feels unnecessarily like a child taking refuge in bed.

Despite having drawn the thick curtains, he's aware of the moonlight on the ocean. He keeps imagining that a pallid filament has found a gap between the curtains and is creeping across the room in search of him. Whenever he can't resist opening his eyes, the room is still dark. Surely this should help him sleep, but eventually he stumbles to the window and tugs the curtains wide.

No wonder he was so conscious of the moon. Its glow has intensified, so that the outlines of the clouds that hide it at the rim of the world are as sharp and bright as lightning. How is this possible when the moon wasn't even half full? The glow seems fierce enough to part the clouds; a colossal one is lumbering away, and Luke is put in mind of a stone being rolled aside from the vast black mouth of a cave. The image isn't too appealing, and he wishes he could look away from the slow inexorable progress of the cloud. It's revealing more than the segment of the moon, which is dwarfed to the size of a seed floating above an oddly regular bank of cloud that has been exposed at the horizon—a rounded mass the width of the skyline, above which it is continuing to rise. He's able to believe that the hairless whitish cranium is just a cloud until the upper section of the face heaves into view. The eyes are round and white as full moons, but he can't judge their expression, since they're empty of pupils. Perhaps he'll understand, however little he wants to, once the rest of the face becomes visible. Luke isn't the only watcher; several figures are lined up at the edge of the harbour, each of them stretching out a hand towards the apparition. They must sense Luke at the window, because they turn and extend their contorted hands to him. He can't distinguish their faces for the glare of the moon, but he's unnerved by how they turned at exactly the same time with an identical movement. That's among the reasons he lets out a laborious cry that jerks him awake.

He doesn't sleep much after that. At dawn he sees himself in the bathroom mirror, rushing through his morning preparations like a silent comic speeded up in the belief it makes him funnier. He's anxious to be on his way home to Sophie, that's all. In the breakfast room a slim middle-aged waiter with moderately long hair and a dancer's gracefulness ushers him to a table with a view of the harbour. He brings Luke a pot of coffee and watches him grimace, having taken a black gulp. "Oh dear," he says. "Not to your taste?"

"It's fine. Just trying to bring myself back to life before I hit the road."

"Oh dear again," the waiter says and gives his hand a twirl as though he's conducting his response. "Was our bed unkind to you?"

"The bed was fine too." Before Luke can stop himself he adds "My dream wasn't."

"Oh double dear." In case this seems insufficient the waiter flattens the hand against his cheek. "So long as it's behind you now," he says and peers at Luke. "Dear me, was it that horrid?"

"I don't know what the word would be." Luke points at the ocean. "Something was sticking its head up over there," he says. "A giant head."

"Well, I never expected to hear that from a guest. You should have sent me packing," the waiter says as he retreats towards the kitchen. "We don't want you starving as well as exhausted."

He reappears to escort several of breakfasters to a table on the far side of the room. Once he has taken their order he departs without glancing at Luke, who is drawn to gaze out at the ocean. The horizon looks thin, capable of supporting the sky only because that's so insubstantial. Beyond it lies the void from which he saw the gigantic pallid face arise. The waiter's remark has brought back the dream and its sense of awful imminence. When the man returns with a rack of toast Luke demands "What did you mean?"

"I wasn't doing my job as guests are entitled to expect, sir."

"You were, and I'm not talking about that. Were you saying someone else has seen what I told you about?"

At first all this brings him is a prolonged look, and he's about to put a sharper version of the question when the waiter says "I expect you came from around here originally, would that be so?"

"Not that I know of."

"Then may I ask where?"

"I wish I knew." Rather than admit this Luke says "What made you think I'm local?"

"You seem to know about Old Stary, that's all."

"I don't," Luke says, but uneasiness makes his voice harsh.

"Perhaps you heard the tale somewhere and guessed it was about Gazer's Head."

"I don't know that either." Another breakfast party has arrived, and he's afraid the waiter will use them as an excuse to move away, but a waitress greets them. "What tale?" Luke takes the chance to ask.

"Just the kind of thing you dreamed of. People used to tell it to their children to put them off daydreaming. They'd say if you looked out there too long Old Stary would look back at you."

Luke glances through the window at a bank of cloud that has started to protrude over the horizon. "What would happen then?" he's less than thoroughly eager to learn.

"What did was bad enough according to my grandmother. So many children started having dreams about him that the parents gave up telling them about him. She used to say it was like a plague that came in the night. She was one of the children, you see."

"Where would a story like that come from?"

"People stay here for the view. They do say you can see further from the headland than anywhere else in Britain."

"I don't see how that explains it."

The waiter fingers his lips as if he's searching for an expression. "My grandmother did say once—"

More guests have entered the breakfast room. Luke is about to urge him to continue when the waitress proceeds to deal with them, having sent the waiter quite a look. "Yes," Luke insists, "she said—"

"Her grandmother told her there were folk hereabouts who looked out for the old things. They were supposed to be trying to keep them alive or bring them back to life. I expect she might have said you've done it."

Luke finds the suggestion unwelcome if not worse. It makes the nightmare feel like a seed in his brain—the threat of a revelation. "Why would she say that?" he objects. "I had a dream, that's all."

"She believed if you could see the old things you gave them life. That's what the folk she was talking about lived for." The waiter wafts away the notion with his hand and says "It was just a tale, obviously."

Luke can't help thinking of Terence. "What old things?" he says.

"Old Stary for one." The waiter traces the hint of a frown with a fingertip and says "I've never forgotten how she put it."

In case the waiter hasn't made that clear Luke says "How did she?"

"I think she was quoting her grandmother. She said they were so old they showed you how the world was made. Now your breakfast will be ready. I hope I've left you with an appetite."

Luke isn't sure while he feels closer to the dream than to his body. No wonder when a girl on a yacht in the harbour is lifting her head and a telescope to watch something on the horizon—but the object in her hand is a bottle of lemonade she's draining. Nevertheless Luke continues to stare across the ocean until the waiter returns. "Careful, sir," he murmurs.

"Of what?" Luke blurts.

"Of your plate," the waiter says and plants it in front of Luke, using a napkin. "And your fingers."

Luke feels as if he has played a joke on himself, not even for an audience. He sees off the breakfast, because the waiter seems almost maternally concerned that he should; perhaps he's regretting some or all of what he said. "Is it home to the family now?" he says as Luke leaves the breakfast room.

Luke thinks of Sophie and the child inside her, and is able to say "That's the plan."

As he drives away from the hotel the masts of the yachts begin to nod at him and then at the horizon. He could almost fancy they're betraying that the ocean has grown nervous. The route leads past the headland, and as the road climbs he sees more of the sky rise over the brim of the world—just the sky and an enormous pale brow of cloud. Along the seaward side of the road bushes shaped by many years of winds stoop to point at the car. In a few hundred yards Luke comes to a layby from which a path leads to a bench overlooking the ocean.

He isn't there for the view. The bushes creak a greeting when he takes Terence's journal to the bench, and a wind leafs through the pages as soon as he opens the ledger. He glimpses a name and has to pin a wad of pages down while he searches for the entry. He would have been seven years old when it was written, and it does indeed say **GAZER'S HEAD**. Terence mentions how kind the people were—presumably his unnamed informants, whatever they told him—but otherwise the entry says only **LOOKED OUT, NEARLY SAW**. Who or what looked out from where, and did they nearly see him? Luke isn't sure he wants to know, and he's also troubled by an impression that he glimpsed something else while the pages fluttered. He's leafing through them when he realises he isn't alone on the headland.

Presumably the newcomers have climbed up from the beach. They're to his left, beyond a clump of shrubs that may well hide a path. He can just discern three figures through the tangled foliage—no, four. He can't see if they're facing him or the ocean. The thorny branches trap the glare of the sun on the water, so that the silhouetted heads look featureless, hardly even present, above bodies thin as twigs. Are they in fact unhealthily emaciated? He would have to venture closer to determine what they're wearing; he might even imagine they're naked. Perhaps they're senile, given their behaviour; they're imitating the cry of a seagull in chorus, and then they mimic the creaks of branches as the wind lets the bushes subside. If the performance is for Luke's benefit, he doesn't appreciate it at all.

He shuts the journal with a thud, and then he peers towards the group of figures. One after another they're reproducing the sound, so accurately that he can't believe they're doing so with their mouths; perhaps they're thumping their scrawny chests. He's tempted to confront them, but what would he say? Gazer's Head has troubled him more than enough, and he marches to the car without looking back.

He does glance in the mirror as he sends the car onto the road, and his eyes are drawn back to the reflection as he speeds away. Surely it's because the road is sloping uphill that the figures appear to have risen up to watch him, if they're even facing him. It's just an effect of perspective that produced the unnaturally simultaneous movement, and of course they haven't stretched themselves thinner still by growing taller; the glare from the ocean is confusing his vision. Just the same, he's glad when a bend in the road takes away the spectacle, and he tries to fix his mind on Sophie and their child. They're the safest things in his life.

17

THE OLD DAY

As soon as Freda heads for the kitchen Maurice murmurs "Any developments?"

"Only what we said," Sophie tells him. "Getting bigger and better."

"Not your little one," Maurice says and lowers his voice further. "I'm saying is Luke any nearer knowing where he came from."

"Nowhere I've been yet," Luke says. "I thought I had a lead but it wasn't one."

"Which was that?"

It's Maurice who asks, though Sophie could. Luke is about to mention Eunice when Maurice says "It's all right, son. No need to talk about our failures."

"He certainly takes after you there, Maurice."

"You can say Freddy and Terry as well if you like."

Luke feels as if they're trying to shape him between them, and he could think the same of Freda as she comes out of the house. She's singing happy birthday and carrying a cake, but how can they be sure this is his birthday? She brings the cake to the round wrought-iron table, pacing slowly enough for a more solemn ritual. The flames of thirty candles flicker in the July twilight, surrounding a 3 that resembles a crescent moon perched on top of its twin beside a full one. As Maurice and Sophie join in the song, birds begin to chatter in the hedge, and then at least a dozen of them soar up like ash into the darkening sky. Luke takes a breath as elongated as the prelude to a sneeze, a routine with which he has amused the Arnolds ever since he was very young, and expels it at the flames. As they bow and die virtually in unison Maurice says "Here's to every one you've had here, Luke."

"And to being a family," Freda says.

"To being even more of one," Luke offers.

He isn't meaning to prompt Sophie, but she lifts her glass of lemonade again and says "To the midsummer boy."

Freda looks puzzled. "Luke, do you mean? I suppose he is in a way."

"In the oldest one, Freda. It's Midsummer Day."

"I think you'll find that was last month, dear."

"Only since they changed the calendar. Before that it was the fifth of July."

"So that's what today is as well," Maurice says. "Can't mean as much as being our Luke's birthday, though."

Luke isn't sure why he feels uneasy. "What does it mean?"

"Quite a lot to some people," Sophie says. "They still have the old Celtic ceremonies. The Isle of Man has an official one. And there are songs about the day. I'll see if I can find them if you like."

As Luke wonders if he does Maurice says "Maybe that's what Terry had in his head."

"Here's to him as well," Freda says and lifts her glass of glimmering wine. "What did he have in it?"

"The song he sang on Luke's birthday about June."

"I thought that was yours," Luke protests. "You've sung it often enough."

"I remember," Freda says. "He kept on till the nurses told him to stop. We thought he must have been a bit drunk or something like that."

"So how did you end up with the song, Maurice?" Sophie says.

"I was reminding Terry on Luke's first birthday, that was what. He joined in, didn't he, Freddy? And it got to be a family tradition. I forget when Terry started leaving it to me. Maybe he was peeved I could have a laugh when he thought it was only him."

Luke can't grasp why he thinks Maurice has missed the point. He's left feeling that his birthday celebration is a pretence, a ritual substituted for another. How ungrateful is that to the Arnolds? He does his utmost not to let them sense his doubts, but he's glad when Freda's discreet yawn brings the evening to an end.

He doesn't want to trouble Sophie while she's driving. He stays as quiet as the lopsided moon above the river. Over the airport vapour trails hang down like threads, as if the otherwise black sky is fraying, its fabric unpicked by the needles of planes. Soon Sophie begins to murmur a lullaby to him or to their child or both. ". . . while the moon her watch is keeping, all through the night . . . " She interrupts herself to say "I don't mind if it's just the moon."

"What else would it be?"

She gives him an apologetic sidelong smile. "Just me being silly when you're not there."

The road swings inland, and the moon sails above the blanched roofs of houses as though it's tethered to the car. "Why," Luke says, "what happened?"

"Just a couple of odd folk at the club in Chester. They were at the back while I was on."

"How odd?"

"I couldn't really make them out. The lights were down." Sophie hardly seems to find it worth adding "I started thinking they were deaf, but they wouldn't have come to see me then, would they?"

"I'd pay just to look at you," Luke says but feels as if he's manufacturing the compliment to delay asking "Why did you think they were that?"

"I thought they were making signs to each other."

Luke clears his dry throat. "What kind of signs?"

"I only said I thought they were. I told you it was dark."

"But can't you give me an idea?"

"Not while I'm driving, and anyway I couldn't make my hands go like that." Sophie grips the wheel more firmly and says "It was just that they stayed in my mind. They'd gone when I finished, but afterwards I thought they'd followed me home."

Luke swallows, but his voice still comes out harsh and sharp. "Why?"

"Don't panic, Luke." She takes time to laugh and to coax a car out of a side road with a flash of the headlights. "I didn't see anything really," she says. "It was a bit like the dreams you used to have, and I expect that's where it came from. I thought they'd got into the bedroom."

Luke does his best to laugh as well, but his gift for imitation lets him down. "When?"

"I must have been dreaming about them and then the moon woke me up. Just for a moment I thought I saw one of them at the end of the bed, and then it went in."

"The moon did," Luke urges her to mean.

"That must have been it." Sophie ponders and says "That's what it was like."

Luke finds he has to conquer some reluctance to ask "What was?"

"I was dreaming, remember. It made me think of the moon going into a cloud, that's right. The gentleman who wasn't really there, he went into the wall."

She turns the car towards the road that leads home beside the river. As the moon recedes ahead of them it appears to be leading them towards the black void above the water. "At least nobody should blame Terence for my dreams," she says. "Am I ever going to get a look at his diary?"

"If you think it's worth your time. I don't even know if it's worth mine."

"I'll make some as soon as I can, then. I've got media interviews coming up and gigs as well. Stop me sounding like a prima donna, Luke."

"You're the first lady as far as I'm concerned, no, the only one. Don't go expecting too much from his diary, that's all. A lot of it doesn't seem to mean much of anything. He keeps saying how kind the folk he met were."

Sophie smiles as the moon begins to pace the car alongside the river. "So long as he wasn't away with the fairies."

"Fanciful, you mean?" When she shakes her head Luke admits "I don't understand."

"That was what people used to call the fairies to try and stop them getting up to anything too wicked, the Kind Folk. There are songs about them."

"He just meant people were helpful," Luke says and attempts to believe. The moon clings to the edge of his vision as he stares along the dark deserted road, but he's seeing the phrase he has encountered far too often in Terence's journal. **KIND FOLK HERE. KIND FOLK HERE.**

18

THE SECOND VISIT

"LUKE! WE WEREN'T EXPECTING to hear from you again so soon. Is everything all right?"

"No different from yesterday, and thank you for my birthday."

"It wouldn't be summer without it," Freda says, "and now Sophie's made it mean even more."

"I don't think that means much," Luke says and hopes as well.

"That's not like you. You're supposed to be the imaginative member of the family. Well, you definitely are." Having paused to let this gather weight, Freda says "It means people who know about the old ways are celebrating your birthday every year. Do you think Terry knew?"

"I don't know what he did."

"I think he may have and that song of his was his funny way of saying it was midsummer. I wonder why he gave it up." As Luke refrains from answering she says "What can we do for you today?"

"I've been thinking about last night," Luke says while his eyes remind him how long he lay awake. "When you were talking about me being born—"

"I'm sorry, Luke."

He feels dismayingly unsure that he'll want to learn "Why?"

"It wasn't actually you Terry was singing to that day, was it? But you know we'd never swap you for anyone."

Luke realises she means so well that she can't be aware of her turn of phrase. "I was just wondering—"

He's interrupted by the sound of a key in the lock. "What, Luke?" Freda says. "You can tell me. You always can."

"Sophie's just come in," he says and calls "It's Freda."

"Do you want to talk another time?" Freda suggests.

"Not at all." He feels as if he has been caught trying to conceal a secret from Sophie rather than having called Freda as soon as it occurred to him. "She's listening too," he says and turns on the loudspeaker. "What was he like when he was born?"

"Noisy and wriggled like a little worm. Sophie, we're talking about the baby I had." As Sophie gives him a searching look Freda adds "He was smaller than we might have liked and a bit frail. They nearly had to put him in an incubator."

"So when do you think—" Luke struggles to find words it should be safe to use. "When do you think it started to be me?"

"I've talked to Maurice about that, and we honestly don't know. It must have been early on, mustn't it? Only obviously we didn't notice any change. You didn't really start to put on weight till after we took you home, and that must have been you. If your baby turns out delicate you'll know you started out like that too."

"Delicate isn't the word, Freda," Sophie says. "He's just given me a kick to remind me, little Maurice."

"Maybe he knows we're talking about him." Less whimsically Freda adds "Well, I hope I've helped."

As Sophie gazes at him Luke says "Thanks, Freda. We'll see you soon."

He can see this won't do for Sophie. He ends the call and stows the phone in his pocket before saying "I think I know what happened. Nothing else seems to make sense. Terence swapped us at the hospital."

Sophie's eyes glisten. "Why do you say that?"

"He knew Freda and Maurice were desperate and he must have thought their baby wasn't healthy enough. We don't know how strange a state his head was in with the drugs."

Luke suspects the journal makes that plain. It doesn't matter what Terence came to believe, and Luke might well rather not know; his misgivings feel too close to the dreams he had as a child—too much like a threat of reverting to the condition he was in. He would rather ask "How were the press?"

"They're going to print the interview as well as broadcast it, and it'll be on national radio too." Her enthusiasm fades as she says "But Luke, what's bothering you?"

"I just feel I don't know enough about myself."

"I know plenty, and it's all good."

"I thought you'd say that. I'm not saying you shouldn't, but I wish—" All at once he realises the Arnolds aren't the only people who might help. He retrieves the mobile and brings up the list of dialled numbers and pokes the key to recall one. He knows what to ask now, but it seems to be too late. The mobile responds with a harsh drone and displays a red spot like a childhood disease. "That's not possible," he protests, only to grasp how it could be. "She's changed her number."

"Who has, Luke?"

"The nurse who phoned. I'm sure she knows what really happened at the hospital."

"Would you like me to try for you?"

"Try what? We can't call her. I don't even know her last name."

"No, but you know where she lives. Maybe if she sees me she'll talk," Sophie says, indicating her midriff. "How about right now? Let's use my car."

The Clio bleeps to greet her, and the echoes scurry into the corners of the basement. The downtown streets are swarming with pedestrians, though it's too late for lunch and too early for dinner. The way to Greenbank Park leads past Amberley Street, and as the jagged Christ teeters out from the wall of the church Luke remembers his impression of the multitude of windows swarming with a single face. He could imagine that the vision is reaching for his mind and reluctant to let go. "Straight on," he blurts, though Sophie doesn't need to be told.

In five minutes they're at the park. The trees seem to be empty of life, and the leaves are as still as the stout trunks. A repeated squeal like the noise of a rusty hinge accompanies a figure that keeps sailing into the air beside the lake. She's on a swing, and the playground is crowded with children. When Luke indicates the house where Eunice lives Sophie parks in front of it. "Stay in the car," she says. "Let me have a look."

She examines the names beside the doorbells before pressing the topmost button. She steps back at once, gesturing behind her back for Luke to remain where he is. Having gazed up at the house for a while, she gives the doorbell twice the push, but when this earns no response she eases herself in beside Luke. "At least we know her name," she says. "It's Eunice Norden."

"Let's see if she has a land line." The mobile shows him that she has, and almost as soon as a bell starts to trill at his ear a phone imitates it above him in the house. The sounds add a counterpoint to the squeals of the swing until Luke eventually breaks the connection. He's planting the mobile on top of the dashboard when someone strides out of the house.

The man's grey lightweight suit is hardly large enough for him. His midriff isn't much less prominent than Sophie's. His broad face is clenched with determination, and the corners of his thick lips look dragged down by the weight of all his chins. He stares at Luke before marching in front of the car to scowl at the registration number, which he mouths while he scribbles it on a notepad. He flourishes the pad at Luke as he tramps to the passenger window. "It's you again, is it?" he says in a voice that seems squeezed falsetto by his girth. "What do you want now?"

"Where do you think you know me from?"

"You needn't think I didn't see you and your friends the other night in the park."

"They weren't my friends. I've no idea who they were or what they were after."

"Ah, so it was you." The man takes a moment to enjoy his triumph, planting his hands between his hips and stomach. "Are you going to answer my question?"

"We're looking for Eunice Norden."

"And why might that be, may I enquire?"

"It's a private matter," Luke says very much in the fellow's manner.

"I'm in no doubt of that." With an effort the man stoops to peer at Sophie and notices her condition. "Good God," he mutters, "is the woman up to that as well?"

"I've no idea what you——" Sophie breathes hard as she understands. "We'll be keeping our baby," she says, "if that's what you mean."

"Then perchance you'd care to tell me what you're doing here."

"We're waiting for a word with Eunice."

The man straightens up with a grunt. "You'll have a considerable wait. I suggest you take yourselves elsewhere," he says and turns towards the house.

"Why?" Luke says loud enough to halt him. "What's happened?"

"See if you can think what might have."

"I really couldn't say." Luke feels close to imitating the man's language. "I've never met her."

"She worked at the hospital where Luke was born," Sophie says. "That's why we want to talk to her."

"I doubt you would have got much sense from her," the man says. "Until very recently we weren't even aware she'd been a nurse."

"But you are now," Sophie points out.

"Only because she was under the influence. I'm not saying which, but I know what I think."

Luke is more concerned to learn "What did she say about being a nurse?"

"Very little of significance. We thought she was trying to regain our respect after we'd been forced to raise her behaviour with her."

"What kind of behaviour, do you mind my asking?"

"Making a commotion in the middle of the night. Crying out and shouting heaven only knows what nonsense at people who weren't there. All about how she could have stopped something if she hadn't been afraid to. And," the man says louder to forestall any interruption, "there was the matter of the kind of person she attracted to the house."

Sophie twists towards him on her seat. "Weren't you saying Luke was one?"

"I'm prepared to accept I was in the wrong to that extent, since you assure me that's the case." Having pursed his lips while he gazes at her, the man says "But I'll hear no argument about the undesirables who were in the park when your partner was. We'd already seen them loitering after dark, and that night was the last straw."

"You didn't tell me about them, Luke."

"I didn't think there was anything worth telling." Luke senses the man is offended by this, and so he says "Did they do something else?"

"Far too much." With a frown that may be aimed only at the memory Eunice's neighbour says "They managed to find their way into the house."

"You saw them."

"The lady on the ground floor did. She saw one crawling up the stairs, the creature was in such a state. I would have dealt with them in no uncertain terms, I promise you. She was afraid to draw their attention, and so she didn't call the police or even tell me at the time."

With some reluctance Luke says "What state?"

"You must have seen them in the park. Too busy taking whatever they take to bother putting flesh on themselves. And let me add," the man says as if he's tired of the interrogation, "I may not have seen them in the house, but I heard them well enough."

Luke hopes he'll welcome learning "Was there much to hear?"

"Scrabbling about on the stairs to begin with. I thought someone had brought an animal in, quite against the rules. I was in bed or I would have investigated." With a look that warns his listeners not to think him inadequate the man says "Miss Norden must have let them in. She was being surreptitious enough about it, but I heard them talking in her room."

"Did you hear anything they said?"

"They kept insisting she could. I don't think that needs much interpretation." After a pause that challenges anyone to disagree the man says "They said it so often it sent me to sleep. If I'd gathered who they were I would have gone up to have the situation out with her."

Luke is searching for any response when Sophie says "But why do you think she's gone away?"

"I fancy she must have realised we knew what was afoot. If she hadn't left she would have been asked to do so."

"You wouldn't happen to know where she's gone," Luke says.

"None of us here would or would want to." The man's lips wince downwards at the squeals not just of metal in the playground, not just of metal. "Now you really must spare me," he says. "I was having a rest until you started ringing all the bells. There's more than enough unnecessary noise in the neighbourhood."

As he plods into the house Sophie says "Maybe I should leave the searching to you, Luke."

Luke swallows in order to ask "Why's that?"

"It sounds as if I brought us here for nothing," she says and starts the car. "Eunice wouldn't have been any use if she's how he said."

"You've enough of your own to do without trying to help me," Luke says and is glad she's watching the road rather than his face. At least he has been given the excuse to continue investigating by himself. Whatever is to be learned, he has a sense that he's best doing so on his own. He doesn't want to risk disturbing her in her condition, that's why—it must be. He won't even let her read Terence's journal.

19

NOT HIM

WHILE THE WORD that caught Luke's eye was **MAGIC**, it's unclear how it relates to the apparently haphazard list of names and references. **RICHARD DADD + ARTHUR RACKAM. RAPHEAL PAINTING, POPES HAND. MICHAEL PACHER PAINTING, SAINT SHOWS DEVIL HAND. DURER HID IN CHURCH ART. HANDS IN BAYUEX TAPPESTRY BACKGROUND. PAGANINNI + LISZT HANDS. BOSCH + BRUEGEL. IRELAND MUSIC. TOP OF CHURCH, CARVINGS YOU DONT NOTICE. BOOK OF KELLS. ILUMINATED MANUSCRIPTS. BLAKE SUPRESSED ART.** After all this Terence has written **END OF MAGIC PAGE.**

Luke can't see how it's supposed to be magical. Rackham and Dadd were Victorian artists who depicted fairies. Ireland could be the name of the place or of a composer like Paganini and Liszt, but what did Terence mean about their hands? The entry seems to leave too much unsaid. When the misspellings start to resemble a reversion to an older usage, Luke abandons the journal on the hotel bed and goes to the window.

He's in Edinburgh. In the afternoon light the mediaeval buildings of the old town look preserved in luminous amber. The city bristles with chimneys and turrets, some of which appear to be trained on the castle or the hill of Arthur's Seat, above which a bird of prey is circling against the featureless blue sky. On the slopes of the city the layers of roofs are robbed of perspective, as if the houses are less substantial than they're pretending to be. Luke can't help wishing he hadn't researched Edinburgh to find local references to make tonight; the place is rather too hospitable to the kind of thing Terence seems to have liked if not believed. Every May Eve the city is taken over by an all-night Beltane festival, and afterwards young women bathe their faces in the dew on Arthur's Seat. Up there seventeen small coffins were found in a cave—coffins rumoured to belong to stolen children, however mercifully empty they proved to be. Luke's thoughts are no more reassuring than the journal, and he throws it open once again at random. He has turned a few pages when his eye is caught by the name of a town.

The entry says **DESMOND LASSITER MIDDLESBROUGH COMPASS ME**. Luke doesn't understand the last phrase, but Middlesbrough isn't far off the route to tomorrow's booking. Just one D. Lassiter is listed in Middlesbrough, and Luke calls the number before any doubts can deter him. It rings long enough that he begins to wonder what he can say to an answering machine, and then there's a protracted plastic clatter. At last a voice croaks "Who is it?"

"Desmond Lassiter? My name's Luke Arnold. I—"

"It's not."

"That's what they've called me since I was born, Mr Lassiter. I—"

"I'm telling you it's not."

Luke has to take quite a breath so as to ask "What would you call me, then?"

"I'd call you nothing. I don't know the first thing about you."

For a moment Luke feels as if he knows even less than that, and then he sees where he may have gone wrong. "Am I speaking to Desmond Lassiter?"

"I've told you no twice."

"I'm sorry, Mr Lassiter. I was looking—"

"Not that either." As Luke begins to feel he has lost his grasp of language the voice croaks "Not Mr anything."

Has Luke's gift for observation deserted him? "I'm sorry," he says while struggling to contain a laugh.

"Don't be. I'm not. It's the fags that do it. They can do their worst just as long as they keep me calmed down."

"Well, I'm sorry I called the wrong number."

"You've not."

Luke rises to his feet, and the hill that hid the miniature coffins appears to imitate his movement. "You mean you're . . . "

"I'm Doris Lassiter. Desmond's my da."

"Well, that's something, or rather it's a lot more. Could I speak to your father?"

"What do you need him for?"

"I believe he knew my uncle. My uncle was in touch with him."

For the first time Doris Lassiter pauses before speaking. "What did you say the name was?"

"Arnold. Luke Arnold." When this prompts another silence Luke says "My uncle's name was Terence Arnold."

"Gone, has he? They all do." As though she's determined to keep any regret to herself Doris Lassiter says "I remember my da talking about him."

Luke sees the hill shiver, but it's his vision that does. "What did he say?"

"About how he sent your uncle off. He used to wonder what he found."

"Found where?"

"One of the places my da said I mustn't go when I was little. You'd have to ask him, only he's not here any more."

"I'm sorry." Luke is, and not just for her loss. "So which places—"

"Like I said, ask him."

"I'm sorry." By now Luke feels he's repeating the phrase simply because he has heard it used. "I thought you meant he—"

"He's being looked after with some of his friends. I coped as long as I could." Just as brusquely she says "Do you want the number?"

"I'd appreciate it."

"Wait there, then." She drops the receiver, and a series of coughs dies away into the distance. Luke is gazing at the hill and straining to hear her when she retrieves the phone with an unhandy clatter. "Here's the number," she says, and Luke writes it on a sheet of hotel notepaper, though the sprained tip of the ballpoint that resides in the room makes the digits sprawl so large that they might be imitating someone else's script. "It's the Longview Home," Doris Lassiter says. "Be sure and call now you've got it."

"I'll do it now if you like."

"I'd tell anyone the same that can bring back his memories. Aye," she says as if she needs some reassurance, "even those," and with a curt goodbye she's gone.

20

WHERE THEY DANCED

THE LONGVIEW RETIREMENT HOME is a small converted hotel with its back to the river. As Luke turns the car along the gravel drive a gondola glides towards him from the opposite bank. The vessel, which is big enough to carry several cars, floats above the wide river. By the time he parks in front of the sallow amber building he has identified the steel cables that suspend the vessel from the gantry of a bridge. Before Luke was born there used to be a transporter bridge near Terence's house, and he remembers Terence adding an older tale, telling him how you could walk across water if you knew the words to ask the spirits to bear you up. Luke is gazing at the bridge when a young woman opens the glass door of the home. "It's soothing, isn't it?" she says. "Most of our service users think so."

Luke wishes he felt soothed. She has a large face that looks rouged with scrubbing, and her auburn hair is tied back out of any sort of trouble. She wears trousers and a short-sleeved white blouse with the name Jaine pinned to the pocket. "Who are you here for?" she says.

"Desmond Lassiter. Whoever I spoke to yesterday said I could visit him."

"Our Desmond nearly always likes his visits. They bring him back to himself." All the same, Jaine says "Are you family?"

"I'm somebody's." Luke immediately regrets having said that. "My uncle," he tries saying, "he knew Mr Lassiter."

"I hope Desmond remembers. Come in while I see where he is."

She leaves Luke in the spacious hall at the foot of an enclosed staircase. As he sits on a straight chair next to a low table strewn with dog-eared glossy pamphlets about caring for old age, a woman peers at him out of a side room and screws up her already wizened face. Upstairs a man is practicing variations on a sneeze, which put Luke in mind of last night's gig. The audience laughed hardest at his sternutative routine, where he mimics and enlarges on a bout of sneezing that overcame Maurice many years ago. "Aaa-cha," he recalls Maurice declaring along with aaa-chash and aaa-chow and much else, growing red-faced with the effort to produce a sound that apparently never came out as it should. There was woogh as well, not to mention wrogh and weragh. Did Luke manage to imitate the apoplectic colour too? That's how his face feels whenever he performs the improvisation. His act has started to put him in mind of a rite he executes to amuse people without understanding how it does. He can do without feeling even more unsure of himself, and he's glad when Jaine reappears. "He's in the grounds," she says.

As Luke follows Jaine the old woman limps fast out of the side room and plucks at his arm. "Have you brought the little ones?"

"He isn't yours, Hettie. Your family's coming tomorrow," Jaine assures her and leads Luke through a large room where several oldsters are watching *Brittan's Resolutions* on a television. Some of them gaze hard at him, but at least nobody seems to associate him with the show. French windows open onto an extensive lawn that slopes towards the river. As she makes for a man in a wheelchair who is watching fellow inmates stroll haphazardly about, Jaine murmurs "What was the name?"

"I'm Luke Arnold," Luke says as if it's no more than the truth.

"Your uncle's, Mr Arnold."

"Terence." Luke feels as though his own name—the one he has always used, at any rate—is receding from him. "Terence Arnold," he says.

"Here's somebody to see you, Desmond. The nephew of a friend of yours."

The man swings the chair to face them, describing a trail like a twisted symbol on the grass. His hands on the wheels are gnarled as old roots, and his eyebrows resemble a transplanted greying moustache. His watery eyes and peeling nose and thin almost colourless lips look close to being overwhelmed by pasty mottled flesh. His blurred gaze is slow to find Luke, as if he's waking from a daydream. "Which friend's that?" he mumbles.

"Terence Arnold, Desmond. Do you remember him? This is his nephew Luke."

"Ah nold. Arn old." The old man's lips work as though savouring the name. "Did he want my advice about money?" he asks anybody who might know. "I liked all my clients to be friends."

"I'll leave you two to get acquainted," Jaine says. "Just you tell Mr Arnold if you start to feel too tired."

The old man's eyes sag almost shut as she bustles over to a resident who appears to have forgotten where he is. Luke thinks Lassiter may be dozing off until he sees a glint in the narrowed eyes. "Give us a push as long as you're here, laddie," the old man mutters. "No need to be letting the world know our secrets."

"Where would you like to go?"

"Down by the river. The ones there won't be telling."

Presumably he means a pair of residents who are gazing over the hedge at the gondola. As Luke grasps the handles—their rubber sheaths are sticky with the heat—he says "So were you a financial advisor?"

"Nothing to be ashamed of, is it?" Lassiter retorts and squirms around to squint at him. "It's what I did. It isn't what I was."

Luke is silent while they pass the residents who are wandering about the lawn. As he makers to ask a question Lassiter protests "Did you not hear what I said? Stay clear of them."

Apparently he has changed his mind about the couple by the hedge—there's nobody else in sight he could have meant—and Luke can only hope this doesn't indicate how unreliable he is. He wheels Lassiter to a deserted corner of the lawn, and the old man pokes a shaky hand in the direction of the gondola. "Not much machines can't do these days, is there? They're taking all the spirit out of life."

"I suppose I grew up with it."

Lassiter peers hard at him. "You want to be true to yourself, laddie."

"I might if I knew who that was."

The old man's lips wrinkle inwards as if they're searching for an expression or trying to conceal one. When it's clear that he isn't preparing to speak Luke says "Do you remember my uncle, then?"

"That I do. He was another one like me. His job was only what he did and the old places brought him alive." With another searching look he says "You'll be the same."

Rather than respond to this Luke says "Why did he come to see you?"

"Not because he was any client of mine, but I'll wager you knew that." Lassiter narrows his eyes again and says "Won't he be the man to ask?"

"I wish I could. He's gone."

"Doesn't mean you couldn't." Before Luke can determine whether the old man has misunderstood, Lassiter says "He was looking for places the old tales came from."

"That sounds like him. Any in particular?"

"What are all of them about when you look into them?" For a moment Lassiter seems to be expecting Luke to answer, and then he says "The Kind Folk."

Luke's attempt at a laugh sounds like none he has ever heard. "You mean the fairies."

"If that's what you want to call them. It won't change what they are."

Luke finds he's grateful nobody can overhear the conversation. "What are you saying that is?"

"I'm saying nothing about it." Lassiter scowls as if Luke has tried to trick him. "They may be dying out," he mutters, "but they'll be a good wee while about it yet. They aren't the sort to take kindly to it either, so I'll not be aggravating them."

This time Luke doesn't even try to laugh. "You mean you believe in them."

"No more than your uncle did, laddie, and I promise you we're not alone."

His choice of words seems to catch up with him. He stares about the grounds and then leans forwards with an effort to peer under the hedge. While Luke doesn't want to disturb him further, he still needs to learn a good deal. "What made him think you could help him?"

"He read about me," Lassiter says as if the question isn't far from insulting. "I used to do a column in a wee magazine round here. I told some of the tales I'd got from my nan about the Folk."

Luke assumes the old man is lowering his eyelids as an aid to memory until he sees the narrowed gaze is fixed on him. "I ought to be asking," Lassiter says, "what made you get in touch."

"I found your name in his journal."

"He wrote things down, did he?" Lassiter keeps his eyelids nearly shut as he enquires "What did he write about me?"

"Just your name and where you lived. Can you tell me what you told him?"

"I sent him off somewhere the Folk used to dance. They call it Compass Meadow."

"Any particular reason?"

"It's not far. Seeing as how you're so interested I think you should find out for yourself."

Luke wants to know why Lassiter sent Terence there, not the basis of the name. He's about to make this clear when the old man's eyes close, squeezing out a droplet each. "I'll go in now," Lassiter mumbles. "I've said enough."

Luke takes the clammy handles to steer him away from the hedge and murmurs "Did you ever go there?"

Lassiter grabs the wheels to propel the chair faster. "Just the once."

"And you found . . . "

The old man's eyelids tremble as if they're harbouring a bad dream, and he swings his head from side to side. "I almost saw them," he mutters and stares about like a sleeper attempting to wake up. "They were talking in the trees."

Luke lets go of the handles. "What did you think you heard?"

"They didn't ask my name, thank God."

"Why," Luke is compelled to enquire, "what would happen if they did?"

"If you told them true they'd pay you and your kin a few visits, and if you didn't you'd be feared they'd find you. You wouldn't want to know about it if they came to you after you'd lied to them." Lassiter turns away from Luke and thrusts his head decisively forwards. "Now I've said my piece," he declares, "and I want my rest."

Beyond the French windows Jaine crosses the room to meet him. "Has Mr Arnold brought things back to you?"

"He can take them with him," Lassiter says without looking at him.

As Jaine does her best not to look disappointed or bemused, the old woman who accosted Luke earlier calls across the room "Is that the little ones?"

"We said, Hettie, remember," Jaine says. "Your family's day is tomorrow."

"Some little ones were here," the woman insists and nods unsteadily at Luke. "I thought they came with him."

Luke feels no less confused than she has to be. He's making for the hall when Lassiter says "Mr Arnold?"

He's gripping the wheels of the chair as though to ensure that it stays where it is. "Yes?" Luke says.

Once the old man has responded Luke shakes his head like someone indulging a relative and hurries out to the car. He sets the disc of Sophie's album playing and drives away without a backward glance. He might feel more relieved to be done with the residents of the home if it weren't for where he's going. "Don't look back," Lassiter said, and Luke feels like the victim of a trick he doesn't even understand.

21

THE EDGE

THE PATH IS OFF A WINDING LANE half a mile from the nearest main road. A sign has fallen from a post and lies in rotten chunks beside the path, where the few surviving letters spell **PASS ME**. Luke almost couldn't find the place online; it's named on just one old map. It's where Lassiter sent Terence, but that hardly seems a reason for Luke to visit it, especially given his undefined nervousness. All the same, he leaves the car parked on the verge and starts along the path.

It's barely wide enough for anyone to pass him, not that anyone is to be seen. Thorny hedges fence it in, although if the fields on either side were ever cultivated, they aren't now. The sky teems with clouds, and Luke could imagine that their shadows keep weighing down the long grass. That's the play of the wind, which sets the hedges scraping their twigs together. Otherwise there's silence, not a murmur from the motorway over the horizon and no sound of traffic along the lane. When he glances back he can't even see the car. He's beginning to wonder how far he has to tramp, and whether it's worth the effort, when he catches sight of a line of trees ahead.

Lassiter said there were trees in Compass Meadow. As Luke advances they nod in unison to him. It's the wind again, but he feels as if part of the deserted landscape has become aware of him. The hedges twitch, and shadows flee across the path into the grass. When the wind relinquishes the trees their tops rear up as though unseen denizens have leapt from them. Several hundred yards short of them the main path turns away along the edge of a weedy field, but an uneven trail leads to them, not so much between hedges as through the middle of one. The track is so narrow that even when Luke sidles between the thorns they keep clawing at his sleeves. He struggles to the end and takes a breath that seems louder than the wind.

The hedge extends on both sides to encompass a field perhaps a quarter of a mile across from corner to corner. He has an odd sense that it isn't quite square, though he's unable to determine what shape is pretending it is. Otherwise it looks as nondescript as the surrounding fields—just one more stretch of unkempt grass scattered with wild flowers and piebald with lively shadows. There ought to be no reason for his mouth to have grown dry while his pulse sounds in his ears like a muffled drum.

He gazes at the meadow and then up at the trees, but they're just as empty of life. The path has brought him to a gap in the hedge, an opening not even as wide as the track. He has to assume that nobody has been in the field for a long time—at least, nobody of much bulk. He's tempted to decide that the gap is too narrow to fight his way through, but how can he justify that? It would reduce the detour to a joke he has played on himself. He can't retreat without learning whether there is anything to discover. He only needs a little courage, a ridiculous amount under the circumstances. He just needs to hear someone's voice—Sophie's voice. He fumbles the mobile out of his pocket and cradles it in his hand while he calls her number.

"Hi," she says, and he's about to respond when she goes on. "This is Sophie Drew and I wish we were speaking. I must be switched off or somewhere you can't reach me just now. Be sure to say who you are and where I can call you, and leave me a message if you like."

Surely she can't still be on the road. She has a gig in Manchester tonight, but that shouldn't be for hours. Her answering message leaves Luke feeling unrecognised and anxious for her. "It's only me," he says and almost adds his name. "Just calling to see how you are, both of you. I'm, I've come off the road for a while. No trouble, just a side trip while I have the chance. I oughtn't to be driving for I don't know, maybe half an hour, so call me if you pick this up before then. In fact, call me whenever you do."

By now he's talking for the sake of it, or rather to convince himself he can be heard. He could imagine that his words are being absorbed by the restless meadow. He has been trying not to raise his voice, although this makes him feels wary of being overheard. "I'll say goodbye for now, then," he says but keeps the phone in his hand. He might almost be holding it as a protective charm as he edges through the spiky gap in the hedge.

Darkness wells up from the grass to embrace him with its outstretched limbs. They're the shadows of the trees, released by a glare of sunlight through the clouds, and they're immediately engulfed by an enormous silhouette that spreads across the meadow. It's cast by a cloud that is racing onwards to leave the sky clear. Luke thinks he would rather be in the sunlight, and he strides through the clinging clammy grass, beyond the reach of the trees. He's well in the open by the time the sunlight catches up with him. As it does so he feels as if the meadow has abandoned some kind of pretence, because he's seized by a wintry chill that seems to rise out of the ankle-length grass.

It's an atmospheric condition, he tells himself. Perhaps there's water under the meadow. Certainly the ground feels as if it could grow unstable beneath his feet, and he moves forward before it can begin to yield. The atmosphere may have affected his phone as well; there's no longer a signal. He slips it into his pocket—it wasn't much of a talisman after all—and marches across the field as though he's challenging it to reveal its secret, if it has any. The wind has fallen, and the only sound is the brushing of grass against his wet ankles. He's about to glance back to see how far he has progressed when a thought halts him, and the chill that the sunlight can't defeat seems to close around him. When Lassiter called out that he shouldn't look back Luke assumed the old man meant at him, but suppose he was warning Luke how to behave in Compass Meadow?

Luke has no reason to believe it was more than a senile fancy or indeed to look back now. Doing so will only delay him when he's eager to be finished with the place. He'll cross the meadow to prove that he can—to show that it contains nothing to be nervous of. He won't achieve a thing by standing here, and he forges ahead, kicking at the sweaty grass. Perspective makes the far hedge seem more distant than it looked from the end of the path, and he appears to be no closer when he hears a wind behind him.

It must be caught in the trees, since the grass around him doesn't stir. Their foliage lends it a voice, a sibilant murmur that grows louder as he tramps away from it. Perhaps the pulse in his ears is giving it a rhythm, since it seems increasingly repetitive. He could even fancy that it contains syllables, as though a chorus is taking shape. If he were to think he's hearing words, what would they be? He might imagine they're "See us," except that the blurred chant is repeating more than two syllables; perhaps the insidious sounds are more like "You see us." Luke does nothing of the kind, but he can't outdistance the hypnotic whisper by taking longer strides. The wind must be easing, because the sounds are slowing down, although shouldn't they also have begun to fade rather than increasing in volume? The syllables gain more definition as they throb in Luke's ears along with his pulse, and all at once they're clear. They form the name Terence wanted him to have—Lucius.

It feels like the threat of a breath on the back of his neck—a concerted breath—and he's overtaken by a thought that has followed him from his encounter with Lassiter: they aren't supposed to know anyone's name. They don't, it's the wind, he thinks fiercely as he twists around, and then he gasps as though the ground has collapsed beneath him. He can't have been hearing a wind in the trees, because the trees are nowhere to be seen.

He has walked further than he realised, that's all. How far has he gone to have lost sight of the trees? He oughtn't to be surprised, given the pace he has kept up—but his attempts to understand can't distract him from an impression that's closing in on him. Something is wrong at both edges of his vision. There isn't much to see, and that's the trouble. He swings around, and before he can suck in a breath he's so dizzy that he almost sprawls on the treacherous ground. The inside of his skull is continuing to spin because he has no idea how far he's turned. The hedge has vanished. On every side the expanse of sunlit grass and weeds stretches to the horizon.

It feels as though his childhood problem has returned—as though that mental state is about to define itself at last. His mind seems close to swelling uncontrollably, drawn out by the boundless field. Which is worse—that his mind has revealed its true nature or that the meadow has? He can't even distinguish between them. All he can do is stare about in the desperate hope of finding a landmark, but there's none.

He shuts his eyes so hard that they throb with light and then opens them, willing the vision of the meadow to have left him. He still can't see any boundary, and he has the dismaying idea that if he looks closer he'll find that the apparently haphazard distribution of grass and wild flowers is far more regular than it ought to be—that the field repeats some kind of pattern over and over. He doesn't want to see that, but where can he look for any kind of reassurance? Not at the ground, not at the horizon, and he's beginning to suspect that if he heads in the wrong direction he'll never find his way out of the meadow. Perhaps he can call for help; perhaps he could, except that the phone still has no signal. The whispering has fallen silent as though it has achieved its purpose, and the meadow has grown so torpid that it might be feigning lifelessness. Luke is shoving the useless mobile into his pocket when he catches sight of an imitation of the movement. It's his shadow on the grass.

The sun is behind him. The shadow has to indicate the direction he was following. Might this be why the place is called Compass Meadow? Surely if he keeps on the way he was heading he'll eventually reach the far side, and this seems to be the only thought he can risk having. He strives to hold it in his mind and let nothing else in as he starts after his shadow. He hasn't dared to look away from it, to determine whether any kind of border is visible ahead, when the shadow dims and grows blurred and then is wiped out. The sky has clouded over.

He doesn't need the shadow to guide him. He has enough sense of where he was going—except that when he yields to the temptation to raise his eyes, nothing but the endless meadow is visible ahead. He falters to a standstill, battling to prevent the sight from taking hold of his mind. It has to be some kind of illusion, and he mustn't let it delay him—and then he wonders if his haste is outdistancing his ability to think. Surely his shadow wasn't his only means of orienting himself. He lowers his eyes and turns around, willing the indication not to have disappeared. It's still there: the track he has made through the grass.

It's only just evident. The trampled vegetation is already rising up to obscure where he has been. He's afraid the traces may not remain much longer, and sprints along the fading path. He keeps his gaze on the ground not merely to avoid seeing the extent of the meadow but to urge the trail to stay distinguishable. It is—it still is—it barely is—it's gone, and he's confronted by an expanse of grass and weeds identical to the sections of meadow around him. He can only dash across it while he clings to the notion that he hasn't lost his way. He's staring so hard at the ground that he can scarcely make it out; his eyes feel as though he's straining to waken from a nightmare. He has no idea how far he's run by the time he seems to glimpse a shape at the upper limit of his vision, and he doesn't trust the impression enough to risk glancing at it. There's more than one shape, and they're growing more definite. Once they start to tower above him he has to look. They're trees, and between the pair directly ahead of them is the gap in the hedge.

Or is this the illusion? Suppose it begins to recede as he struggles through the increasingly obstructive grass? He's afraid to let himself believe he is making his escape until thorns on either side of the gap pluck at him. He sidles along the constricted track as fast as he's able without snagging himself on any of the multitude of thorns, and then he hears movements behind him.

They're running down the trees. They could be squirrels; Luke can hear claws scrabbling at the bark. Whatever kind of creature they are, he doesn't have to look back; he needs to see where he's going. They aren't coming after him, however many of them there may be; they're scurrying into the meadow. The moist rustle of grass fades into the distance, though not before another noise makes him start nervously. His mobile has emitted the tone that means he missed a call.

He has just seen Sophie's name displayed when the phone begins insisting that it's June. Luke almost catches his arm on the thorns as he lifts the mobile. "Are you there now?" Sophie says. "I did try to call you back. Where did you get to?"

The question feels capable of sending his mind back to the meadow. "Just somewhere there wasn't a signal," he blurts. "Where were you?"

"Sorry, little Maurice must be making me forgetful. I switched off the phone while I was tuning up and I forgot to turn it back on."

"I'm glad that's all." Luke can hardly think for trying to determine whether the way back to the main path is longer than he recalls or just harder to negotiate in this direction. He's anxious to keep talking to Sophie, and hears himself ask "Are you on soon?"

"I've a few minutes yet. What are you up to right now?"

Luke avoids a bunch of thorns and then another, an effort that appears to bring him no closer to the main path. "Just walking," he says and hopes his desperation can't be heard.

"So long as you walk back to me. Have you found anything else on your travels?"

"No." His mind feels too close to the meadow again—too eager to betray him. "Nothing," he insists.

"Never mind, Luke. Maybe you will soon. I have."

He's dismayed to be nervous of asking "What?"

"The song I was looking for, the one about the Kind Folk. Shall I sing you some of it?"

"Not right now." He mustn't let her think he wants to end the call. "Save it till I'm back," he says harshly. "Sing me something else if you like. Sing me one you sing to little Maurice."

"I've been singing that one."

Luke can't say why the notion unnerves him. "Don't any more, all right?"

"Why?" Sophie says and laughs. "Do you think it might bring them?"

"We wouldn't want that, would we?" Luke blunders along the track, snapping twigs that scratch his forearms. He's too concerned to leave the meadow far behind to take care any more. "No point in playing with things like that," he says, "when there's no need."

"All right, if it bothers you." She sounds puzzled even before adding "Are you sure nothing's happened, Luke? You don't seem like you."

"I'm the same as I've always been." He's panicky enough to demand "What's going to change me?"

"Nothing if it's up to me." Just as gently she says "Tell me what to sing, then."

He can't think, not least because he has almost reached the end of the track. Shoving his way through the last thorny gap, he staggers onto the main path. When he glances back he can hardly believe he succeeded in making his way between the hedges; it doesn't even look like a route. Beyond it the trees and the meadow are as still as a painting of a landscape. "Never mind," he says. "You save your voice for the audience. I'm back at the car and I'd better be on my way." The last words are true, at any rate, and not too far from panic. He promises to see her soon and says goodbye, and heads for the road so fast that he could imagine he's leaving his breath in Compass Meadow.

— 22 —

THE GIFT

COULDN'T IT HAVE BEEN SOME KIND of optical problem caused by stress? Luke tries to convince himself as he lies in bed, nagged by an intermittent wakeful clanking that rises from the railway the hotel overlooks. At first he was afraid to drive in case he grew unable to distinguish boundaries again, but he was just as nervous of staying anywhere near Compass Meadow. Once he set off he felt as if he was leaving his condition behind along with the place that had caused it somehow, and shouldn't this be all that matters? Perhaps he ought to stay away from the sites Terence visited if they simply trigger some version of the state he had to overcome in his childhood, but in that case he may as well give up his search and never learn where he came from. He might be more than content to do so if he were searching only on his own behalf.

He isn't helped by an impression that he has overlooked or misunderstood some detail during the search. When at last he manages to doze it offers very little relief. There are dancers in the meadow, figures so thin he can't even be sure of their shape. They seem hungry for a kind of sustenance he would rather not define, and yet as they prance in a ring he could think they're celebrating some event. As the margins of the field recede out of sight while the moon swells in the starless dark, the circle of dancers expands. Their arms are growing longer and thinner, but their faces have taken on more substance. Their utterly black eyes glitter and their beaky lips part as all the heads swivel on scrawny necks

113

towards Luke, and stay turned to him despite the frenzied round of the dance. They're whispering the name he never used and reaching out their arms to him. They're inviting him with the ancient sign, and however far he retreats he won't escape them, because their arms can stretch as far as the meadow is wide. A cry struggles out of his mouth, and he's awake.

Where did all that come from? If it was based on one of Terence's stories, where did Terence find them? Luke is increasingly convinced he didn't make them up. If they're to be found in books, perhaps that would help lay them to rest—and then Luke thinks he knows what he misinterpreted in the journal. He gropes for the switch of the bedside lamp, and the boxy nondescript flat-featured room lights up around him. He grabs his mobile from the shelf that's level with the undernourished pillow and fumbles to go online, where he types end of magic page in the search box. As he sits up against the rubbery substitute for a headboard—a rectangular lump on the wall—he sees there is indeed a book called *The End of Magic*, and the author's name is Alvin Page. It was published more than forty years ago in California.

A Toronto bookseller, Once Upon A Tome, is offering a copy at fifteen dollars. The listing describes the book as "a study of the decline of the belief in magic and its significance in everyday life". The front cover reproduces a mediaeval image that may well be a detail from the Bayeux Tapestry: an image of three peasants kneeling to be blessed by a cowled figure. The penitent faces are flattened into a bunch, and they look identical. That's an artistic convention of the period, but aren't the outer fingers of the hand that gives the blessing stretched too wide? The cowl might as well be a mirror, the face within it is so similar to those of the faithful; Luke could imagine some mimicry is involved. The blurb beneath the author's name says *When magic came into our lives*. Luke needs to know what the book meant to Terence, but he won't have to buy it; somebody has stored it on a site called the Arcane Archive. He has just brought up the site when a pulsing inflamed icon warns him that the battery is almost dead.

He shouldn't risk leaving Sophie unable to contact him, and so he doesn't try to read the book while the phone is charging though he uses it to look up the hours of the public library here in Lancaster. He won't be able to go online there for almost six hours, and he drags the quilt over himself in the hope of capturing a little sleep.

He couldn't drive last night. After whatever happened to him in Compass Meadow, he couldn't face so many hours out there in the dark. He booked into the Frugotel and called Sophie to say he was too tired to drive. He couldn't judge what kind of performance he would give at the small packed theatre until he went onstage, and then his routine felt uncomfortably close to letting his mind loose, not too far from entirely losing control. Along with imitations he produced without having to think, he found himself replicating various styles of laughter he heard in his head: timid giggles verging on apologetic, belated guffaws that felt like waiting for a fuse to reach an explosive, mirth that sounded as if its perpetrator was announcing it to the rest of the audience, either to stake a claim on the humour or to prompt everybody else to appreciate the joke . . . Luke's audience had continued to laugh even when he started imitating them; in fact, those he'd mimicked had laughed harder. He'd ended by pretending to be seized by an uncontrollable fit of hilarity, until he couldn't even tell whether he was faking his struggles to restrain it. If someone hadn't started to applaud, Luke doesn't know how he would have finished the performance. He remembers digging his fingers into his sides, as people do, while his body shook so hard it seemed close to growing unfamiliar.

He has no sense of having slept by the time the dawn seeps through the thin brownish curtains. The phone is still charging, and will be for hours. Eventually Luke stumbles to the corner of the room that manages to cram in the essentials of a bathroom. The intermittently hot shower leaves him feeling sleepless rather than awake, and so do several cups of coffee from an urn in the breakfast room that resembles a canteen. He abandons some of a plateful of overheated items from the buffet, not least because he's anxious to be upstairs in case Sophie calls. But there's no sign of a missed call or a message, and as soon as the phone is charged he checks out of the hotel.

He moves the Lexus to the station car park and walks into the town. Beyond a crossroads where the traffic ends a market has risen on both sides of a street of small shops. Some of the traders sell books. Is *Make Your Life Magic* an occult volume or just a lifestyle manual? Annuals and other tattered books for children slouch in cartons on a folding table, where the foremost item in one box is *The Little Mermaid*. The cover shows that it's based on the Disney film, not the version Terence told Luke, which made a good deal of the mermaid's fears that she couldn't pass for human even after she was transformed. Luke doesn't need to think about it now, and he tramps faster downhill.

The library, a pillared building in a square, is full of bookshelves low enough to see over. Elegant graffiti about reading decorate the white walls, and a further room packed with computers at rudimentary desks is embellished with repetitions of just two words, *clickety* and *click.* Swarms of them hover at the edge of Luke's vision as he finds an unoccupied desk next to a teenager in conversation with his friend, who is opposite Luke. He checks his email and finds an invitation to perform in Goodmanswood, a town in Gloucestershire. He'll answer that when he's home, and he brings up the Arcane Archive site.

It looks arcane enough. Below the name in spiky Gothic script is a symbol that consists of an L to the right of a reversed one, together with an inversion of them that overlaps the upper pair. Luke feels he has seen something like it before, and he's gazing at it when the student next to him leans close, exuding a herbal smell. "Just give it a click," he advises, by no means under his voice.

"Clickety click," his friend confirms.

"I'll do that," Luke says but doesn't. The symbol is too symmetrical to represent a cross, at least the familiar religious kind; perhaps it's an older reference. When it begins to remind him of the hands in his dream he clicks on a button that says *Books.* The only P in a list of initials belongs to Alvin Page. In a breath—a conscious one that lasts some moments—Luke is staring at the first line of *The End of Magic.* Once upon a time there were fairies because people believed in them.

It's unclear whether this is a quotation, although much of the book is composed of them. Alvin Page sets about worrying the sentence, examining the language and counselling the reader to ponder how much of a difference a comma makes. Did the belief prove that fairies existed, or did they exist because they were believed in, or both? Page doesn't quite reach a conclusion. What did people mean by fairies? Plenty, to judge by the examples he cites. Some regarded them as agents for the chaos that existed before the world took shape, when all things were possible, a state they yearn to bring back; so said Thackeray Lane, an English academic. He was writing in Victorian times, and it was fashionable to believe in fairies, but Luke assumes he must have been analysing other people's beliefs. Peter Grace, a contemporary of Lane's, suggested that the Bible disguised the fairy folk as fallen angels, but he was a clergyman who turned to the occult and left the church. Page also quotes Roland Franklyn, an occultist writing in the 1960s. "Magic is the last trace of the shaping of creation . . . The ancient creatures often called the Fair Folk may be composed of the stuff of the stars . . . They took on life when the world still dreamed of itself and what it might become . . . As the world grows fixed, so magic withers and the Folk are robbed of sustenance . . . "

Luke thinks this reads like a product of its era and very probably of drug use. Perhaps that helps explain why Page's book appealed to Terence. The following chapter describes tricks, most of them malicious if not worse, that the fairies were supposed to play. Substituting pebbles and dead flowers for jewels was one, and the fairies were said to take even more delight in seeing people blamed for their mischief. Sometimes they contaminated food with herbs—if the victims were lucky, no worse than emetics. In mediaeval times and even later quite a few cooks were tortured and executed, having been charged with the pranks of the fairies—so the old tales say. The grimmest legend is German, and dates from the seventeenth century. A mother walking through an Alpine forest with her baby on her back found when she reached the family cottage that a lump of fungus had been substituted for the baby's severed head.

Some of Page's sources found reasons for the wickedness. Nathaniel Selcouth, a sixteenth-century alchemist or magician, maintained that the Good Folk felt an entirely understandable contempt for the human race, for its constricted beliefs and its lack of fluidity, both mental and physical. Thackeray Lane suggested that the Kind Folk resented human domination of the world that should have been theirs to continue shaping, and invaded it wherever they could. He noted a common belief that seeing fairies could drive you mad, and pointed out how some visions of sufferers diagnosed as insane resembled those of occultists. The idea doesn't appeal to Luke, nor does the suggestion that the visions caused the madness. Lane cited the case of Richard Dadd, a Victorian artist who painted fairies while he was incarcerated in Bedlam. Dadd composed a poem as a commentary on one picture, referring several times to "folk" and claiming that the fairies were unjustly regarded as evil. A fellow inmate insisted that the images, which have a hallucinatory vividness, were based on sights Dadd showed to him.

Surely Lane didn't accept this or the idea that the notion of benevolent fairies had been planted somehow by the Kind Folk, coinciding with the Victorian occult revival—that the spread of the belief had been a last concerted attempt to retain some power over the human race. In any case that was over a century ago, and what can it have to do with Luke's search? Why is he continuing to read if all it tells him is that Terence had too much time for fairy tales? He glances at his neighbour, but the student isn't looking at Luke's screen; he's busy patching passages from a web site into an essay. When he sees that Luke has caught him in the act he peers at the display of Page's chapter and gives his friend an incredulous grin, which provokes Luke to read on.

Dadd and his contemporaries weren't alone in painting the Folk. William Blake was rumoured to have destroyed a group of poems and watercolours that dealt too openly with them. Visual references can be found in cave paintings and various illustrated manuscripts as well as the Bayeux Tapestry, which is where the cover of *The End of Magic* came from. A painting by Raphael even shows the Pope's hand transformed into a fluidly inhuman secret shape, suggesting that the influence of the Folk extended to religion, though how can this be related to Dadd's urge to assassinate the Pope? Many of the occult puns in Dürer's work refer to the Folk, and the fifteenth-century Austrian painter Michael Pacher shows a saint's hand being transformed by one, an image generally misinterpreted as showing the saint warding off a demon. Similar depictions of hands are hidden in paintings over the centuries, but the distortions are usually rationalised as tricks of perspective or mistakes on the part of the artist if not his apprentices. What could any of this have meant to Terence that he listed the names in his journal?

The next chapter brings the saga of the fairies almost up to date. Roland Franklyn listed glimpses of the Folk some decades ago, surely only tales he'd heard if not visions caused by drugs. "They dance beneath the moon, and as it waxes so they put on flesh. In some languages they are named the Children of the Moon, since they took their original shapes as it did . . . Dark and secluded places are their thoroughfares, but they have not entirely lost the power to pass through matter . . . Where ancient magic slumbers they batten upon it and so regain traces of their old nature . . . " According to Franklyn they used to feast on the energy released by the dead in the process of dissolution, but now they're reduced to communicating with the tenants of the grave, drawing forth whatever memories may linger in the brain as it decays. Luke prefers not to linger over the notion, and scrolls down to the thoughts of Peter Grace, who blamed science for the decline of magic. In his view science sought to unpick the world and reconstruct it without its soul, a perception he claimed either to share with or to have learned from the Folk. Franklyn seems to have agreed but believed science hadn't quite triumphed at his time of writing. "While the charms continue to be spoken by the ignorant, the Fair Folk retain some purchase on the world. They will not die while their slyest charm is remembered, however mistakenly: the charm that summons the Gift of the Folk."

Which gift? For the moment the book isn't telling. The next chapter deals with places where the Folk are said to have been encountered during Page's lifetime, along with locations they might be expected to frequent. There's a tradition that they can or could be seen at a megalithic circle on a Scottish island, weaving their way in and out of the monument in a ritual dance. Walkers in the wild Welsh countryside between the Severn and the Usk should never look behind them if they hear a voice calling for help. Villagers in County Down will never take a valley road when the moon is growing full and a light as pale as mist seems to rise from the valley to greet it, although the road is the shortest route to the next village. Arizona has a hill that nobody local ventures near, where birds wheel constantly around the summit but are never seen to land or fly away. Prudent travellers avoid the path beside a Hungarian river, in which reflections hint at the invisible shapes that rush to meet the unwary at a bridge that must be crossed. In an Austrian forest you may notice that the shadows of the trees are stirring even though the trees are still—that the shadows are forming symbols you would be wise not to attempt to interpret. Compass Meadow in County Durham is best left unvisited, since they say that if you try to compass it—to grasp its nature or its boundaries—you may be lost for ever. Luke could do without this allusion, even though it explains how Terence heard of Desmond Lassiter; he's the source cited at the end of the chapter. Page carries on listing locations, too many of which sound familiar, presumably from Terence's journal. Luke scrolls fast through the text in search of some point, and then his hand falters. "In our time the Folk of the Moon may most often be encountered where they seek to draw upon the magic that remains." It isn't the quotation that has taken him unawares; it's the attribution of it to John Strong.

For an instant he glimpses the face he left on the floor in Terence's room—the face that's still lying there in fragments. He makes himself search for the name in Page's text, where the source is acknowledged at the end of the chapter: John Strong, unpublished papers archived in

Liverpool Record Office. That's a department of the central library, and at least some of the entries in Terence's journal are finally clear; he didn't leave papers in a library after all. Should Luke consult Strong's? He hopes he won't need to, and he scrolls down to the next chapter, **The Last Gift.** He has hardly started reading when he utters a sound that makes the students stare at him.

Page begins skeptically enough. The legend of the changeling—an inhuman or demonic baby substituted for a human one soon after birth—has been rationalised as a means of rejecting children who were born unhealthy or deformed. The supposed changeling tended to be stunted or unusually frail, and most of them died before their eighth birthday. "Perhaps these were indeed no more than sickly children," Roland Franklyn observed, "or did the Fair Ones leave them as distractions from the Gifts that flourished? Those quickly learned to pass for human by imitating traits they observed, a camouflage as innate as the chameleon's. Many displayed their talent for mimicry, while quite a few gained fame with it. Some parents came to suspect that their grown children had never been human but dared not acknowledge the possibility, which might well have seen the family ostracised if not persecuted. They kept the secret so close that it scarcely even passed into legend. Only a few may have confessed it on their deathbeds, where they would refer to it as the Gift for fear of offending the Fair . . . "

It's just drugs talking, Luke tells himself. To think otherwise feels too close to reverting to his childhood state. Franklyn names no sources, and if he did that would only mean they're folk tales, not the truth. There's no need for Luke's mind to grow unstable just because Franklyn's obviously was. What else did Page imagine was worth quoting? "As science robs religion of its dominance, so the faithful may swarm to embrace other beliefs," Peter Grace predicted. "What charms whose true purpose has been forgotten or disguised may the ignorant employ? Some unwary supplicants have been known to use the old spell to impregnate the barren. Few might have recourse to it if they understood that beneath its disguise it was designed to invite the Gift of the Kind Folk . . . "

Luke starts to shake his head, a spasm that feels capable of over-whelming the rest of him. He isn't mindful where his gaze has strayed until the student facing him demands "What's your problem?"

"What's it got to do with you?" his friend mutters at Luke.

He means stealing someone else's thoughts. Presumably the other student is up to that too, since he adds "Why don't you stick to your own stuff and never mind about us."

"That's it, stay with the fairies."

The student opposite Luke smirks. "What's he been doing?"

"Looking at a lot of fairy stuff when somebody could be using the terminal to work."

This, along with a good deal else, is too much for Luke. "Using it to steal other people's work, you mean, like you both are."

"Who are you calling a thief?"

"You want to watch who you are," his friend opposite says, no longer smirking.

"Tell me your names and I'll tell everyone who I am."

Luke hardly knows what he's saying, let alone what his words may mean. Isn't he a thief as well? At the very least he steals people's traits and puts them on show, but he feels responsible for worse than that. He takes the computer offline, blotting out the Arcane Archive but none of the thoughts it has lodged in his head, and is shoving back his chair when the young woman seated opposite his neighbour says "You aren't going to complain about him, are you? He isn't really homophobic."

Luke is so confused he feels as though he's spreading chaos, and then he understands. "I haven't got time to complain," he says and stumbles away from the desk.

His neighbour stares at Luke's hands. "What's that supposed to mean?"

Luke has no idea what kind of gesture he made, though he intended it for conciliation. He clenches his fists without glancing at them and leaves the computer room at not much less than a run. Perhaps just his look makes more than one librarian stare at him, but he feels as if they've found him out in some way he's desperate not to learn. As he dodges through the crowd outside he could imagine he has emerged into a foreign land, where the people are quite unlike him. He's almost out of the street market when he catches sight of the bookstall. *Make Your Life Magic* is still there, and *The Little Mermaid*. They seem to resemble phrases in the punch line of a joke, and he's its victim—the victim of a joke that is the world around him.

IT RETURNS

As SOON AS LUKE REACHES THE CAR he retrieves the journal from the boot and dumps it on the bonnet. Beyond the car park an express train rushes like a gale through the station, but around him the air is as still as the deserted sky appears to be. A woman who has just parked her car gives him a long look, surely only because she wonders what the ledger may contain, and then she hurries onto the enclosed bridge across the tracks. "Come and see," Luke is almost maddened enough to shout after her. "See if you can see what's here." He might be worse than distressed if anybody did, and he crouches over the journal. He only wishes he didn't have to read it himself.

Were Terence's summaries of fairy tales meant to convey secrets or to keep them? Here's an entry Luke overlooked—**HANDS GET MORE POWERFUL WHEN MOON DOES**—and he hopes it was simply inspired by the piece of ironwork Terence took home. He leafs through the journal so fast that he dislodges a pressed flower. He could fancy that it was an insect he disturbed; the desiccated twigs on either side of the withered stem appear to twitch as the souvenir drops to the concrete. Before he can examine it, not that he has much desire to, it vanishes under the car. If it was meant to mark an entry, that was **LIKE DREAMS** or **NOT MY DREAMS**. Terence didn't mention dreams until he brought the sculpted face home from John Strong's house, after which he learned about the papers in the library and, Luke deduces, copied something from them. The next entry is **SAYS IT BRINGS BLESSING**. Luke would be happy to leave this uninterpreted, along with **JUST LIKE PRAYING**. He turns the pages faster but can't avoid reading. **FREDA RADIENT. LIT FROM INSIDE. BIGGER AND BRIGHTER. LUCIUS + LUCIA COME FROM LIGHT. LUCAS HERE**.

He feels watched, found out, although he's alone in the car park. No face has dodged out of sight into the enclosed bridge; the impression didn't even resemble much that he would call a face. Down on the tracks a stationary train ticks like a clock if not a bomb. He yearns to be with Sophie, but he's afraid she will sense a change in him before he can grasp it himself. Whatever nearly surfaced in his childhood feels much closer now: some sort of explosion of his mind. He slams the ledger so hard that he might be trying to crush all its significance out of existence. He's tempted to consign it to the nearest bin, except that the notion that someone might read it fills him with undefined shame. He drops it in the boot, and as he slams the lid his mobile begins to sing the song that was Terence's secret joke.

Luke snatches out the phone and sees Sophie's number. His finger hovers over the keypad as he realises he has no idea what to say to her. Suppose she has something urgent to tell him? Even if she hasn't, how can he leave her wondering why he won't answer? He jabs the key but can't speak until she says "Are you there, Luke? Don't try and talk if you shouldn't."

He could use this as an excuse if it weren't obscurely ominous. "Why shouldn't I?"

"If you're on the road."

"I'm just about to be."

"Oh good. Don't let me hold you up if you'd like to get going."

"I don't mind talking for a few minutes." Even this seems capable of betraying his unease, and so Luke blurts "How was your gig yesterday?"

"They all seemed to enjoy it, little Maurice too. Maybe he'll grow up to be a dancer." Having waited in case Luke wants to respond, she says "And how was yours last night?"

"Just what you'd expect, me pretending to be what I pretend to be." He heads off any response by asking "Is everything all right at your end?"

"My end is fine. Sorry, I should leave the jokes to you." After a pause that might be inviting one she says "Dr Meldrum's secretary did call."

Luke draws a breath so fierce it seems to attract all the sounds around him: the ticking of a dormant train, the gasp of a lorry that has halted on the road, a footstep or something like one on the bridge. "Why," he has to ask, "what's wrong?"

"Oh, Luke, don't worry. Nothing at all that I'm aware of. She said he was just wondering if you'd found out any more about your parents."

"Any more," Luke says and swallows, "than what?"

"Than that they weren't Freda and Maurice, I suppose."

"That's all I've got to tell him."

"I said you'd have been in touch if there was anything new. I mean you'd tell me if there was."

"What do you think?" Luke says and is acutely conscious of pretending that's an answer.

"You haven't had a chance to look any further, or you didn't turn anything up?"

"Nothing that means anything to us," Luke says, though it's more like a prayer.

"That's what I meant." All the same, Sophie pauses before saying "Anyway, guess where we are."

"You and, and our forthcoming event, you mean." Luke is afraid she'll wonder why he stumbled over referring to their baby, and hastens to ask "Where?"

"At Terence's house."

He hasn't time to take a breath. "What are you doing there?" he demands not quite before his voice gives out.

"Just some of what needs to be done, Luke."

"Yes," he says more urgently, "but what?"

"Getting it ready for whatever we decide to do."

Her vagueness brings him close to panic. "You don't have to do any of that by yourself."

"I thought I was giving you less to do."

How can he warn her when he can't define his fear? "Suppose you hurt yourself on something," he says, almost relieved to have thought of it. "You could be infected, the state of that place."

"I don't think I'm that clumsy even just now. Are you worried because it isn't only me?"

For a panicky moment Luke wonders who is with her in the house, and then he realises. "That's it," he says not much less than eagerly. "You can't be too careful with little Maurice."

"Don't you think that's what I'm being? He can't help getting in the way a bit, but he's really no hindrance."

"He needs you more than the house does," Luke says in desperation. "You don't want to be tiring yourself."

"Honestly, Luke, he isn't taking much out of me. I don't think I've felt much better in my life."

This isn't reassuring; it's just another of her arguments Luke can't think how to surmount. As he searches for a reason that she won't be able to dismiss for her to leave the house, she says "Anyway, we're done here for today."

"Lock up and head for home, then, and I'll be on my way as well." He only wishes he were as close to home as Sophie is. "Be careful on your way out," he can't help adding.

"I'm already out, Luke."

He feels as though he has played a bad joke on himself. He's about to acknowledge it with a laugh, even if he can't predict what kind, when Sophie says "I suppose you were right about one thing."

Luke isn't sure how much he wants to learn "What was that?"

"I was a bit clumsier than usual, I'm afraid. I broke something. I'm awfully sorry, Luke."

"All I care about is that you're in one piece." Presumably she thinks she broke the plaque of John Strong's face. He doesn't like to imagine her alone with it, but at least she isn't now. "None of that stuff can be worth much," he says. "I don't think it would even mean much to anyone but Terence."

"This might have."

"Well, I can live without knowing, can't you?" When she doesn't answer he says "Which piece of junk was it?"

"It was in the room where he kept his souvenirs. I only meant to tidy it away for safety. I was going to put it on the desk and it just fell apart in my hands. It must have been awfully delicate."

"Never mind," Luke says with some urgency. "You aren't telling me which it was."

"I'm not sure what you'd call it. I thought it looked Oriental." Sophie hesitates and says "Some kind of carving of a skull, only the top looked more like coral."

Luke feels as if reality is about to collapse around him. He remembers how the object that he took to be a sculpture crumbled in his grasp.

Through the phone he hears an approaching rumble that suggests Sophie's words have summoned a presence, and he has to remind himself of the railway above Terence's house. He has found nothing he can say by the time Sophie adds "That's one thing that happened."

"Why," Luke says as his mouth grows drier still, "what else did?"

"Just an encounter I had." She laughs as a preamble to saying "Not in the house. Someone you didn't tell me you met."

This applies to quite a few of Luke's informants, which is one reason he's nervous of asking "Who?"

"The lady from the church."

Perhaps Luke is beyond being reassured just now, and by no means only now. "I didn't think she was worth mentioning."

"You must be the opposite of her, then."

He feels as if he's speaking only because it's expected of him. "In what, in what way?"

"Didn't she want to know your whole life history? She pretty well did mine."

Luke doesn't want to be reminded of his own, but he can't forget by saying "She'd have wanted to know what you were doing at the house."

"She certainly did, and what we are to each other, and even whether we're religious. Because of the baby, that would have been. That's right, little one, we're talking about you." Having drifted away from the phone, Sophie's voice returns. "Did she say anything to you about Terence?"

"Just that he'd started coming home drunk at night."

"About his religion, I mean."

"He didn't have one."

"That's what I thought. It was just something she says he said."

Sophie's pause makes him strain his ears, but the only sound this brings him is another footstep on the bridge. Or is that what he hears? It puts him in mind of a restless insect scrabbling in a crevice, and he lurches towards the bridge. "What?" he has to prompt.

"Let me see if I can get it right. She thought at first he was talking about praying. That's how religion came into it."

Luke has an unobstructed view along the enclosed bridge, and it's deserted. This doesn't reassure him; he has a sense that nothing can any more. "Why does she think he wasn't?" he would very much rather not ask.

"Because he told her it was like a prayer, except it wasn't even that. I'm not being very clear, am I?"

Luke has an unhappy notion that he understands all too well. Remembering where Sophie is brings him closer to panic. He's about to tell her to head for home when she says "He said he thought it was a charm but it turned out to be a trick. Do you know what I think he meant?"

Luke can only hope she's wrong. "What?"

"I think he got it into his head that he had to help Freda and Maurice. He found some kind of spell somewhere and must have thought it worked when you were born. He might have until we all went on the Brittan show, but once he heard the test results he'd have felt tricked, wouldn't he? The sad thing is he's the only one of us who ended up thinking they mattered."

Luke wants to believe all this. He feels as if he's clenching his mind so as to keep hold of Sophie's explanation, but his mind won't shrink to that size any longer; it already contains far too much. He has found nothing that he dares to say by the time Sophie prompts "Do you think?"

"I can't argue," Luke says, feeling false to the core.

"Anyway, shall we make a start? I shouldn't be keeping you when you've so far to come."

That's yet another thing Luke wishes she hadn't brought to his mind. He says goodbye and gazes along the bridge. The boxy enclosure gapes at him while a train at a platform ticks off the empty seconds. He feels as if he's issuing a challenge—an idiotic useless one. Nothing is visible, and nothing responds. He turns away, pocketing the mobile, and tramps to his car. He's desperate to be with Sophie, and yet he falters as he fumbles for his keys. He's wondering how much longer he'll be able to maintain the pretence that appears to be his life.

— 24 —

THE VOICES

"ARE YOU GOING TO TRY and turn my show into a joke again, Mr Arnold?"

"I don't think you need my help to do that, Mr Brittan."

"You're out on your own there, but let's check. Anybody agree with him?"

"Noooo."

"Maybe you like to think you're one of a kind, do you? I wouldn't have a loyal audience like them if I didn't show people the truth."

"And what do you think I show them?"

"I don't know. What do you think you show them, Mr Arnold?"

"Now you're really sounding like a joke, and you're proving my point as well."

"All you're showing us is that you're nothing like the rest of us. Or am I wrong? Anybody else get his jokes?"

"Noooo."

"He shows us ourselves, don't you, Luke? You're a human mirror."

"Don't say that, Sophie. I'd never use you in my act."

"Now that is a laugh, but do we think he meant to make a joke?"

"Noooo."

"Less of working everybody up, Mr Brittan. This isn't what we came for."

"You want to run things, do you, Maurice? Go on then, tell us why we're here."

"To sort Luke out for good this time, isn't it, Maurice? To make him content with himself."

"That's a fine ambition you've got for your son, Freda. Only that isn't him, remember. We don't know where he is or what happened to him."

"No call to bring him up just now. We're happy with Luke."

"Maybe your son isn't if he watches my show, Maurice. Aren't you at all bothered how he ended up?"

"We'll find out if Luke tracks down his birth parents, Mr Brittan."

"I wouldn't hold your breath for him to do that, Freda. And do call me Jack. We're all the same here, well, nearly all of us."

"Spit it out then, Jack. What are you trying to say about Luke?"

"He's not as eager for the truth as he'd like everyone to think, Maurice. This show's about honesty, and he isn't even being honest with himself."

"You can't say that. You don't know him."

"I can say exactly what I like on my show, Sophie, and my gut feelings never let me down. I'm telling you there's a lot the people he's pretending are his family don't know about him."

"Then how do you, Mr Brittan, Jack?"

"That's what researchers are for, Freda. He shouldn't be here if he doesn't want us finding out the truth."

"So let's be hearing what you think you know if you're not just shooting off your gob."

"I never do that, Maurice. I know him so well I might as well be living inside his head. He saw your brother off for a start. You might want to wonder if he thought Terence knew too much about him."

"This isn't even funny any more. He didn't kill Terry, he tried to save him."

"Did I say anything about killing?"

"Noooo."

"I can't believe anyone would think I'd make an allegation like that on the air. All I said was that he was with your brother at the end."

"You want to be careful how clever you're trying to be. What else are you going to make out about our Luke?"

"You won't like this either, Maurice. He's been disturbing a lot of old people. One was in a home and your boy still kept on at him, and another ended up in hospital because of him."

"I won't believe that. How did Luke put him in hospital?"

"It's just the kind of person you are, isn't it, Luke? And another one was dead but Luke still managed to disturb him."

"I think you're having a joke now, Mr, Jack."

"Look at his face and tell me if he thinks I am. Doesn't want to meet your eyes, does he? And as if harassing old people wasn't bad enough, he's been stalking a nurse."

"Why would you do that, Luke?"

"I can tell you, Freda. I was with him. She said she saw what happened after he was born but then she wouldn't say what it was. I'm sure it wasn't Luke's fault she left where she was living. It was some folk she was supposed to have brought into the house."

"You can understand that, Mr, Jack. He just wants to know where he came from, the same as the rest of us. He's only human."

"No I'm not."

"Don't say things like that to your—Don't say them, that's all. You can see you're upsetting her."

"I thought we were meant to be here for the truth, Maurice."

"That can't be it, Luke. You oughtn't to say such things about yourself. You're just like us."

"That's what I had to be, Freda. That's how I'm made."

"It isn't all there is to you, Luke."

"You're right, Sophie, there's Terence as well. I don't think he was too happy when he realised what I was, though. Maybe he was fascinated to begin with, but then he got scared and tried to tone me down."

"You're telling everyone you've only just found all this out? You've gone through life thinking you were just like the rest of us? Do we think that's the honest truth?"

"Noooo."

"Can't everyone make a bit less noise? You've woken me up."

"Why, it's little Maurice inside me. Do you want to contribute anything, Maurice?"

"Nobody's asked me what I think."

"Well, we're asking you now. You tell your father if there's something you'd like him to know."

"I think he's got to be out of his head, talking to himself like this."

The accusation jerks at Luke's consciousness. He's on some unidentifiable stretch of motorway, speeding along the outer lane at almost

130

ninety miles an hour, with no idea how long he has been unaware of driving. It does indeed feel like having lost his mind. A van twice the height of the Lexus is racing closer behind him, and he tramps on the accelerator. He has travelled several hundred yards without being able to take a breath before he's able to retreat into the middle lane. His heartbeats feel considerably larger than his heart, and his mouth is as dry as the sunlight that has burned the sky clear above the flat green fields flanking the horizonless road. He swings into the inner lane as soon as he can, peering ahead for a signboard that may remind him where he is. When the monotonous landscape eventually produces one, it seems to offer at least a hint of relief. It's a sign for a service area, and he indicates so prematurely that the arrow flashing on the dashboard appears to be urging him to leave the motorway at once.

A lorry brakes ahead of him on the slip road, trailing fumes. They drift into the hedge that separates the route for lorries from the way into the car park, and Luke does his best to ignore the vague stealthy movement among the twigs. He needs a break from driving and from the clamour of his thoughts, which felt as if they were rehearsing his life. He's distracted while manoeuvring the car into a space, by a dog or a child that rears up at the window of the van next to him. He must need a respite even more than he thought, because once he's out of the car he can't see anyone through the grimy window above him. Unless they've dropped to the floor, nobody is in the van.

Low clumps of privet help define the grid of spaces outlined on the concrete. As Luke heads for the block of shops and restaurants he could think he's glimpsing activity in the hedges. At first it puts him in mind of birds, since it appears to be dodging from clump to clump, but it can't be, since it isn't visible in the open, although some of the hedges are at least fifty yards apart. He's seeing twigs behind twigs, that's all, and nobody around him thinks the sight is even worth noticing; quite a few seem more troubled by the look of him. If he's noticeably uneasy, he has yet another reason. He has just realised that the name of the motorway services is somewhere in Terence's journal.

A security guard decorated with a waistcoat the colour of a buttercup is watching the car park from beside the entrance to the block. He scowls at the automatic doors as they glide apart although nobody has approached them. His ruddy weathered face grows neutral as he turns to Luke. "Can I help you, sir?"

131

"Would you happen to know why this place is called Stonebridge Valley?"

"The valley's there." He nods in the direction of the car park. "They knocked the bridge down," he says. "No loss."

He must be indicating somewhere beyond the perimeter, although all that Luke can see out there are fields and a scrap of moon like the remains or the beginnings of a skull lying low on the horizon. He could fancy that the landscape is an illusion betrayed by its name. He mustn't let that kind of idea into his mind; its bounds already feel unstable, too close to giving way. He stares at the hundreds of parked vehicles and tries to believe there's no more to the place than he sees, but he can't avoid asking "Why do you say that?"

"Too many people went off it."

Luke wonders how deep the unseen valley can be. "Killed themselves, do you mean?"

"Maybe some meant to." The guard frowns at the doors, which have parted again for no visible reason. "Some were supposed to have went across too fast," he says, "and not looked where they were going."

There's no need to assume they were looking behind them. The guard won't know, and Luke doesn't want to. "Thanks," he says and feels as though he's mimicking politeness. As he makes for the doors, which open so readily that he could imagine somebody's ahead of him, he hears the guard tell a mobile phone "The doors are playing up again."

The floor and ceiling of the lobby are tiled white, reminding Luke of a hospital. Beside a Frugonews shop a Frugostop food court is crowded with diners. A girl in a generic overall is clearing tables in the territory of the Frugoburger counter. Someone has spilled sugar across most of the top of a table and drawn in it too, but the girl sweeps the spillage into a bucket before Luke can be sure he recognised the scribbled symbol. Would he prefer to hope it was a misperception, another sign that his mind isn't to be trusted? How much of a danger does that make him on the road? Surely he needs to be more awake, and he hurries around the food court—Frugasia, Frugoveg, Frugofish, Frugitalia—to the Frugo-quench counter.

He buys a black coffee and a slice of carrot cake on a Don't Just Drink deal and finds a table by a window overlooking the car park. The vigorously bitter drink reminds him how raw his senses feel, so that he seems to be aware of every crumb of a mouthful of cake. The fluorescent tubes muffled by overhead tiles are the colour of the moon and the chatter of diners all around him feels like a version of his unstoppable thoughts blurred into incomprehensibility, as if they've swarmed out of his head. Gazing through the window doesn't help; he thinks he keeps glimpsing figures in the parked cars, and whenever he glances at them they aren't where he imagines they were—they've shifted to another vehicle at the edge of his vision, as if overgrown yet scrawny children are forcing him to play a kind of hide and seek. He gulps the coffee and leaves most of the cake, and pushes back his chair with such a screech that diners provide a variety of winces for him to observe. The idea of incorporating their behaviour into his stage act almost makes him let out some kind of a laugh.

He dodges through the crowded lobby to the doorless entrance marked MEN. The long white-tiled room is divided by a double row of cubicles back to back. As he joins the line of intent men at the urinals he could imagine he's enacting one more imitation. It takes him some time to get going—long enough for him to wonder if his neighbours are growing suspicious of him. Can they tell he's an intruder? He's close to uncontrollable laughter, though of a kind that wouldn't amuse even him.

He clamps his teeth together as he succeeds in his task at last. When he heads for the sinks he's confronted by a mirror the length of the wall and as high as the top of his head. Besides the reflection of men washing their hands—some with theatrically masculine robustness, some with careless brevity, several not bothering with soap—the mirror shows the doors of all the cubicles facing this side of the room. Thin red rectangles indicate which doors are bolted. The door directly behind Luke displays a sliver of green, but as he squirts jade soap onto his hand from the bottle with its back against its double under glass, he sees the cubicle is occupied.

Someone is standing just behind the door. He could be retrieving a jacket from a hook, but he needs to do more than that about dressing, since his feet and ankles are bare. They're as pallid as the tiles, and so thin that Luke would rather not envisage what kind of body goes with them. The toes are considerably longer than anyone's ought to be, and the grubby elongated nails are almost indistinguishable from them, as if the claws are composed of exactly the same substance. Luke cups his soapy hands and dashes water into his face, but that doesn't charm the sight away—indeed, the feet shift with a faint desiccated scraping on the tiles as though their owner has begun to grow impatient. Luke rubs his eyes so

133

hard they sting and glares at the mirror, and speaks before he knows he means to. "I can see you."

Both of his neighbours glance at him. Perhaps they think he's talking to a child, and he has a sense that whatever is hiding behind the door is far too like one. It must have heard him, because it's giving him a sign, stretching the toes on either side of the left foot away from each other until they point in opposite directions. In another moment the right foot imitates the gesture. Luke clenches his fists but can't keep quiet. "Is that the best you can do?"

His neighbours stare at him. They could have decided he's mentally ill, and who's to contradict them? He's very close to urging them to look at the cubicle and say what they see, if anything—and then a newcomer makes for it. As the man shoves the door with the flat of his hand Luke sees the clawed feet draw up behind it. The occupant of the cubicle is riding the hook on the back of the door.

Luke holds his breath until his head starts to throb like his fists. The man vanishes into the cubicle, and the door has hardly shut when the bolt slides into place. Luke stares into the mirror as his neighbours watch him sidelong, and all at once he's sure that he has been tricked into making a show of himself. He hurries to a hand dryer, which emits a miniature gale so fierce that he wonders if it's blotting out sounds he ought to hear, but when it falls silent there's no further sign of anything wrong in the cubicle. He stalks across the lobby and sees the exit doors sidling together, although nobody appears to have just left the block. As he emerges into the sunlight, a car alarm starts to yap ahead of him.

It has uttered just a couple of notes when an alarm several hundred yards away joins in. Almost immediately an alarm on the far side of the car park adds to the clamour. If this is a demonstration of power it seems even more banal than it's vindictive, or could it be meant to greet Luke? In either case he feels guilty and isolated, singled out for what he is. The security guard has taken out his phone, but before he can use it there's a metallic thump and a smash of glass. Two cars have collided near the entrance to the car park.

Luke thinks the drivers were distracted by the babble of alarms until he glimpses a thin sketchy figure scuttling away from the accident. It dodges into a hedge and hides among the twigs, which it instantly resembles. Luke is afraid he has provoked this latest childishly senile trick, and he's nervous that his guilt will be apparent to the guard beside him. When the man strides towards the crash, where the drivers have stormed out of their vehicles to bellow at each other, Luke thinks of following, but how could he help? If he tried to explain they would all think he was mad, which he still isn't sure is so far from the truth. If he's responsible he ought to leave before he causes worse, and he sprints to his car. As he speeds onto the motorway he does his utmost not to think he glimpsed spidery limbs groping out of a hedge as though to draw him back.

— 25 —

THE FOLLOWERS

"LUKE, WHERE HAVE YOU BEEN?"

"I went to the library."

"You didn't say you were going there. Didn't you say were out in the open?"

"I was there all right. Out where you can't come back from."

"Except you have. You've come back to me and little Maurice."

"Maybe I haven't, not who we wanted to think I was."

"I won't believe you. You'll always be who I want."

"I'll still put on a good show, you mean. That's the story of my life. You know what kind, don't you? A fairy tale."

"I'm not following you, Luke."

"Let's just hope nothing else has. Look, can we start again? I want to tell you everything but I don't know how."

"You only have to say it to me. It can't be that hard when you're so good with words."

"Maybe they don't belong to me. They're something else I've stolen from everyone I've known."

"You're going off the point again. Just say what you know. If you can't tell me you can't tell anyone."

"That has to be true, but maybe not how you'd like."

"Now you're just putting off telling me. Is it something you found out at the library?"

"It's far too much."

"Go on. You've come that far."

"I've got to do this in my own way or I can't do it at all. You remember what happened when you went to Terence's house."

"I broke that ornament, you mean."

"It wasn't an ornament. I'm not sure what it was, but you didn't break it. I already had."

"That can't be right, Luke. I know you're trying to make me feel better about it, but—"

"I'm not trying that at all. I'm saying that's the kind of thing it was and maybe still is."

"Well, let's go to the house and see what's there."

"Let's leave that for now. The point is the things Terence ended up believing were all true."

"Which were they?"

"His neighbour you met, she told you about one. You remember."

"Some kind of charm he'd believed in, you mean."

"You said it was a spell. And you said he eventually realised it was a trick. You were right, Sophie. You just didn't know how much."

"Are you going to let me into your secret, then?"

"He thought it was a way of making someone fertile when they hadn't been able to have a child, but that's just how it was meant to seem. Or maybe it helped Freda get pregnant, but that was only so her baby could be stolen. That's what happens when anyone does what Terence did."

"I can't believe what you're saying, Luke."

"You have to, Sophie. You wouldn't want to see the proof. Remember you said singing about, about what we were discussing might bring them. Promise you won't do that any more."

"Luke, do you honestly believe what I think you mean?"

"I've got to. If it isn't true it has to mean I'm mad, and you wouldn't want to make me worse by arguing, would you? So humour me if you care about us and little Maurice."

"That's really unfair. You know how much I do. All right, enough not to sing about them to him if it bothers you that much."

"I hope that keeps them away, then."

"Why, what else is going to bring them?"

"I might, and you know why, don't you?"

"You have to tell me, Luke. You have to say it."

"Because they brought me in the first place."

"Don't say that," Sophie cries. At least, Luke does—he can't even judge how much he sounds like her—and stares at himself in the windscreen mirror. His face looks indefinably unfamiliar, as though he's seeing it with new eyes. He could fancy it's a mask he dons when he's performing, which is all the time. Yet another rehearsal has gone wrong. Perhaps his attempts at preparation have had no use except to let him feel less alone while he drove home, in which case he could have wished for better company than himself. He's as far from knowing what to say as ever, but he can't practice any more without putting off the moment Sophie sees him. He's home.

He drives down the ramp and parks beside her car. As he crosses the basement, thin footsteps imitate him while vague shapes dodge into corners to sink into the bricks. He's hearing his own echoes and seeing the shadows the lights make him cast, but he could think they're just as real as he is, or exactly as unreal—imitations of an imitation. All at once he's afraid he may not be able to choose the voice Sophie hears when he opens his mouth, since he was possessed by so many voices on the road. He doesn't have to choose, he just needs to be natural, an ambition that brings him close to sniggering aloud. "This is me," he hears himself repeating as he climbs the steps to the lobby. "This is me."

Somebody is singing upstairs. If it's Sophie he's anxious to distinguish the words. The clatter of his footsteps on the wooden stairs doesn't help, so that he's nearly at the first floor by the time he's certain that the singer isn't her. The song is accompanied not by her guitar but by several musicians. It ends as he reaches the second floor, and then it recommences. While he doesn't catch the first line, the second one is clear: ". . . all day contrive our magic spells . . . "

It halts him for a moment, and then he climbs faster, desperate to learn where the song may be. His footsteps blot out some of it, but he keeps hearing words. ". . . shakes as if for fear . . . " ". . . we to some flowery meadow stray . . . " Which of these is more ominous? ". . . by mortal eyes unseen . . . " At least this ends the song, which is still above him, but it's revived as he climbs the last flight of stairs. "We fairy elves in secret dells . . . " He gropes for his keys so clumsily his fingers feel contorted, and sprints to his apartment. That's where the song is coming from.

He scrapes the key into the lock and slams the door behind him. "What are you doing?" he demands as he strides along the hall.

Sophie is at the computer. She pauses the playback, and as she swivels the chair to face him he has the disconcerting fancy that their unborn child is steering her. "Where have you been, Luke?" she says. "I almost started thinking you weren't coming home."

It could be a cue for one of the attempts at explanation he's rehearsed, but the sight of the lyrics on the screen is too immediate. "I've been on my way," he only just takes time to tell her. "Why are you doing that? You promised you'd leave it alone."

"I think I said I wouldn't sing that kind of song to him within."

"You might as well be. It's still near him."

"I honestly don't think this can do him any harm. It's Beethoven." When Luke gazes at her as he struggles to find words she says "I was only doing some research while we were waiting for you. You might as well say reading the words is too close to him."

"Maybe, maybe you shouldn't take the risk."

"Oh, Luke." For a moment Sophie seems reduced to leaving it at that, and then she swings around to the computer. "Look," she says and points at the first line of the song, which is called *The Elfin Fairies*. "Did you know that was what they used to call the moon?"

We fairy elves in secret dells
All day contrive our magic spells,
Till sable night o'ercast the sky,
And through the airy regions fly,
By Cynthia's light so clear . . .

Luke gathers this is what she wants him to see, and it has no appeal for him. He thinks it reads as though the writer was striving to disguise a reality he was afraid to acknowledge, unless it showed how accepted the innocuous version of the fairies had become. It occurs to him that Shakespeare has a good deal to answer for. "Have you finished with it now?" he blurts.

"If you have."

Sophie sounds a little disappointed. She's shutting the computer down when Luke says "You aren't planning to use that, are you?"

"I don't break my promises, Luke."

"In your act, I meant."

"I wasn't thinking of it. Shall I check with you in future that everything I do is acceptable?" Sophie wheels around as if she's ready for a confrontation but relents when she looks into his face. "Luke, I'm sorry," she says. "Has it brought something back?"

Though her sympathy is plain, her words feel ominously closer. "Such as what?" Luke hears himself ask.

"Maybe something about your childhood."

"Why do you think it would do that?"

"We decided Terence believed in magic, didn't we? A lot of his generation did. It was like the Victorians but with different drugs." She gazes into Luke's eyes while she says "Did that song make you think of him?"

"A lot of things have lately."

"It isn't just him that's on your mind, is it?" Luke sees her trying to gaze deeper as she says "Have you been feeling how he used to make you feel?"

He can't quite take the cue. "Meaning how?"

"However you did when the doctor sent you to the specialist. Are you afraid you'll end up like that again?"

What can he accomplish by trying to convince her of ideas that he has no reason to expect her to believe? It's a great deal easier to agree with her, particularly since he isn't wholly sure that she's mistaken, and he blurts "Don't you think I ought to be?"

"I think you shouldn't let it bother you too much. You overcame it by yourself when you were just a little boy, didn't you? And now you've got me if you need me."

"You know I do." That's a formula people use in this kind of situation, and he doesn't want to feel he's nothing but a mimic—and then he thinks he sees how to deal with his fears without being forced to define them. "You made me a promise before," he says, "and now I'll make you one. If I ever think I'm any kind of a threat to you or the baby I'll see whoever I have to see. And if that doesn't work I'll do whatever else needs doing. If I have to I'll go far away."

"You won't, Luke." Sophie takes his hand and rests it on her midriff. "Maybe I know you better than you know yourself," she says. "You'd never do us any harm."

Luke believes the last few words. If he ever could have been a danger to them, surely he's sufficiently aware of himself not to be. "Going away so much hasn't helped you, has it?" Sophie murmurs.

"Why," Luke says and hesitates, "what do you think it's done to me?"

"I think it's giving you too much time on your own with everything that's happened lately." She strokes her midriff with Luke's hand as she says "Remember you've still got nearly all of us."

"I can do without my real parents."

Once she has searched his eyes for the meaning behind this Sophie says "Won't you be trying to find them any more?"

"Would you mind if I gave up?"

"I wouldn't mind anything that meant you weren't away from me so much." She lets go of his hand at last and says "Let's make sure people realise we can travel as a package."

"I suppose we won't be able to after Maurice is born."

"Not for a while, but maybe he'll be as precocious as you were." Sophie smiles down at herself and says "Do you know, I think he heard that."

Luke feels as if he's putting on a show that's himself as he says "What would you like me to make for dinner?"

"I've already made it. Just salad and spaghetti and a lot of bolognese. I fancied that, or the little one did."

"That's three of us."

"Lead the way then, little Maurice," Sophie says and heads for the kitchen at a stately pace. The round black glass top of the table is already set for two. As the tureen full of pasta rotates in the microwave Luke finds all the tasks he can—bringing the salad bowl from the six-foot refrigerator and the wooden utensils from the drawer beneath the hobs, dislodging cubes from the frosty tray to ice a jugful of water, refilling the compartments to the brim before returning the tray to the freezer—until Sophie says "You sit down, Luke. You've been on the road since I don't know when."

"I've only been driving. You're being a vehicle."

"Not too cheap for fuel but runs well otherwise." Sophie watches him pour out two glasses of water and says "Just because I can't drink at the moment doesn't mean you have to be like me."

It seems a petty way to prove he's not an imitation, but he finds a bottle of Chianti in the built-in wine rack and serves himself a glassful while Sophie tosses the salad. "Here's to us," she says and clinks her glass against his. "To our family."

"Thanks for being one for me."

Perhaps he should have come up with a more orthodox response. Sophie is quiet until he enthuses about the meal they're eating, and then she says "I didn't tell you yet, the label wants the new album as soon as I'm ready."

"That's great news. I couldn't be happier for you." This sounds like a routine he has learned from someone else, however genuine it is, and so Luke tries saying "When do you think that will be?"

"I'll be trying out some of the songs onstage tomorrow and then I'll know better. Before this little one's born is the plan. That way it'll earn us money while I'm resting, except that's the last thing I'm likely to be."

"You'll be doing some of that and that's a promise." Even this feels too much like a standard rejoinder, though he means it. When her smile suggests she'll wait to be convinced Luke says "Have you got a title for the album?"

"I've used a lot of traditional material, so I was thinking *The Past is Alive.*"

"I don't know if I'd buy that."

"You won't have to, will you?" Somewhat more gently Sophie says "Tell me if you think of a better name."

He has downed a second glass of wine by the time she lays her fork to rest. "That's what I call a wethl-fithled bethly," she declares and turns a wince into a wry grin. "I wouldn't be much good at your act, would I?"

"You shouldn't want to be like me." Luke wishes he'd been more careful with his words. "As far as I'm concerned," he says, "you ought to stay exactly as you are."

After dinner he listens while Sophie rehearses. *Kisses Sweeter than Wine* sounds to him like her next hit, especially when she improvises a fugue on the tune. It's growing dark by the time she unstraps her guitar. "Do you mind if I go to bed now?"

"Do you mind if I do?"

"I'd mind more if you didn't," she says and heads for the bathroom.

Luke goes into the bedroom to draw the curtains. The crop of high buildings that Terence deplored has cut off much of the view from this window, but a section of the bay is visible between two of them. A moon waiting for its features to be filled in lends a pale glint to the watery horizon, which sprouts a single spindly windmill isolated from its identical companions. Its vanes stir as if they're fingering infinity or making a secretive sign to the moon. Luke reaches for the curtain cord, and then he leans so close to the window that his breath swells up like a gust of fog to meet him.

Along the front of the apartment building the Strand is almost deserted. A knee-high concrete strip divides three lanes from three more on the road. A car has just swung around the bend that takes the road inland. For a moment the headlights illuminate a group of objects on the far edge of the strip. They could almost be abandoned plastic bags, variously misshapen by their meagre contents; the four of them are nearly featureless except for the glint of eyes deep in their pallid substance. Their chins are resting on the edge of the meridian, and each of them is flanked by a pair of hands, not so much gripping the concrete as displaying how wide their elongated fingers stretch. The headlight beams sweep onwards, but the heads appear to be growing more definite. Sketchy mouths have begun to split open, each one a hint of an identical grin.

Luke feels as if he can't move until they do—as if the sight has trapped him into imitation. It seems to have stolen his senses too, because he's aware of Sophie only when she joins him at the window. "What are you looking at, Luke?" she says, and by no means immediately "Good moon."

If there's any reassurance to be had, it's surely that she can't see what he's seeing. He glances at her to make sure, and when he looks out of the window again the watchers have gone. As Sophie slips into bed he tugs the curtain cord like a lifeline. He mustn't let her overhear, but he mouths so fiercely he feels his lips stretch. "Go back where you came from. Leave us alone. There's nothing for you here."

26

A PARENTAL INTERVENTION

"YOU'RE LOOKING UNCOMMONLY PLEASED with yourself, Luke."

"Don't you think he has plenty of reason, Ambrose?"

"Most emphatically. I wasn't intending to suggest otherwise, Delia. You were very splendid tonight, Luke."

"And you equally were, Sophie."

"I was on the cusp of saying so, dear. If I may be allowed to sum up, I've rarely seen more skill and confidence in a performer, and that applies to you both."

"It's because Sophie's new songs went down so well," says Luke.

He has another reason, but nobody else need know. It came to him in the night, when he crept out of bed to peer down at the road. All six lanes were deserted, and so was the concrete meridian. He'd silently vowed to protect Sophie and their child however he had to—and then, as he slipped under the quilt beside them, he'd wondered if he was too fearful on their behalf. Whatever happened when he was young had never really threatened him, even while he was most vulnerable; why should it be more of a threat to his family? No matter how disturbing his uncanny glimpses have been, there's no reason to regard them as a menace to Sophie and the baby—no reason to believe that the others won't keep their distance so long as he does nothing to entice them closer. The notion let him sleep, and now it's allowing him to appear normal, even sure of himself. Everyone is silent for a moment, and then Ambrose Drew is less so until his wife says "Scarlatti."

They're all in the bar of the Unity Theatre, where a poster for the show Luke and Sophie have just finished occupies a prominent place on the wall. Maurice and Freda are perched on a small couch while Luke and Sophie face her parents from another. The elder Drews are tall and slim with hair so discreetly silver it suggests that owning up to more of their age would be inelegant. When either of them speaks the other commonly responds with the sort of patient look they might give their music students. Whenever there's a lull Ambrose has a tendency to hum a sample of a melody, which Delia identifies with a tolerance Luke suspects is many years old. It amuses Freda, who says "Maurice only knows a few songs, but you can always hear when he's in the bath."

"I know plenty," Maurice protests. "You just wouldn't thank me for singing them."

"When's your new record out for us to buy, Sophie?"

"It's racing little Maurice. I need to find out when the studio is free, and I still have to think of a title. I thought *The Past is Alive*, but Luke didn't care for that one."

Her father's eyebrows hoist some of the expression out of his eyes as he turns to Luke. "So long as you've vetoed it, might you have a substitute?"

As Luke opens his mouth Maurice says "It hasn't got to be up to him."

"That's right," Freda says, "we can all have a think."

Luke is touched by the notion that they're playing the roles of his parents, protecting him as if he's still their child. Freda suggests *A Girl and Her Guitar*, which Ambrose counters with *Folk Baroque*. It takes his deprecating smile and his admission that he had folk rock in mind to prompt Maurice to contribute *Folk for Folk*, and Delia is diffident about offering *Attuned to Folk*. There are too many repetitions of the word that haunts Luke, but at last he has a chance to say "I was wrong about your title, Sophie. I wasn't thinking of you enough."

"Well, that's decent of you." As Ambrose lifts his glass of wine he says "Here's to bringing the past alive."

"The past." Delia sips her wine and says "If you were thinking of yourself, Luke, I expect it was out of concern for Sophie."

"And our baby," Sophie says.

Ambrose shuts his eyes for the duration of a nod. "Obviously you're saying Luke has been."

"I certainly would."

"In the appropriate departments." When she looks puzzled Ambrose says "He'll have had a satisfactory report."

"What your father's taking such a time to ask," Delia says, "is whether Luke has had a medical check."

"Nobody's suggested he should."

"He had a few when he was little," Freda says.

"He had the lot," Maurice says. "All the ones they said he should have."

"We'd expect no less of you," Delia assures them. "Only now we're talking about parenthood."

Freda gives her an understanding smile. "It'd help to put your mind at rest too, wouldn't it, Luke?"

Luke can't see how to avoid asking "What would?"

"Any tests they need to do before the little one is born. We're like you," she tells Sophie's parents. "We were thinking he'd have had them."

"I don't suppose they can do any harm," Sophie says.

"I'm certain they would make everyone happier." With scarcely a pause Ambrose says "If that's possible."

"Here's to them, then," Delia says and clinks her wineglass against Sophie's glass of lemonade.

Luke can only imitate the gesture as everyone else joins in. They drain their glasses and Ambrose stands up. He's consulting Maurice about a loft conversion before they reach the street, while Delia tells Freda almost apologetically how uncomplicated Sophie's birth was. Outside the theatre they say their various goodbyes, and the couples head in three directions. Ambrose has hummed just a pair of notes when his wife says "Bach."

It reminds Luke of Terence, as far too much does. Sophie takes his hand as they start downhill towards the city centre, past pubs and wine bars outside which smokers stand like pickets. A moon that puts Luke in mind of an infected face peers over the skyline alongside the river. Before Luke can think of anything he dares to say he hears Sophie in the distance, as though she has found out about him and fled. No, her voice is closer but minute. It's in the headphones worn by a girl who's waiting next to him at traffic lights, and it's singing *A Song We All Can Sing*. Sophie squeezes his hand, so that for a moment he shares what she must be feeling, and then all that he's keeping from her catches up with him again. The lights halt the traffic and the girl hurries downhill. Being alone with Sophie seems to release him to speak, and he has already come to the only decision he can think of. "I want you to read Terence's journal."

27

THE SECRET ROUTE

"I THINK I UNDERSTAND NOW, LUKE."

"Do you? Well then, well, go on."

"I don't think there's very much to understand."

"Then maybe you haven't. Tell me what you think you know."

"Don't be upset, but I'd say Freda and Maurice were right about him."

"Just tell me why I'll be upset."

"Because I feel as if you were looking for more than there is. I'm not trying to put him down. He'll always be the person who did most for your imagination."

"You do, Sophie, but we aren't talking about that. How were they right?"

"He was very sixties, wasn't he? He used a few drugs and maybe even dabbled in a bit of magic like some musicians did. It was just a fashion. I'm glad it's over, though."

"Why should you be glad?"

"I wouldn't want little Maurice to grow up with it, would you?"

They're at the kitchen table, which is laden with Terence's journal. Sunlight is working its way around the block, and although the room is bright Luke feels as if he's urging more illumination to reach them. The clinic has given him an appointment tomorrow, and he wants to convey the truth to her before the tests betray it, but he's desperate for the journal to relieve him of at least a little of the burden of explanation. "Why should that matter," he tries saying, "if you don't believe in it?"

"I believe in drugs all right. Believe they have effects, I mean. But shall I tell you what I think his diary really shows?"

"That's what I want to hear."

"I think he wanted to be a writer but his imagination got the better of him when he couldn't find a proper use for it. A lot of this looks like a kind of story he was telling himself." When Luke opens his mouth she says "I know that isn't all that's there. You can see how much he cared about you and the Arnolds. I'm afraid my parents might think he went too far, so perhaps we shouldn't mention it to them."

"I won't be discussing it with anyone but you. How are you saying he went too far?"

"We'll never know exactly, will we? I did wonder if there's anything at his house that might show us."

"Like the skull you found. You remember what I told you about that."

"I don't think I do, Luke."

"You have to. You can't have—" Just in time, if even that, he realises that he never had the conversation with her; it was only part of one of his rehearsals as he drove home from Lancaster. He feels as if his mind is close to giving way, as it may almost have done during his childhood. "It wasn't what you thought," he blurts. "It was some sort of magical thing."

"I'm sure you haven't told me that before, but let's not argue. I can see how Terence may have thought it was."

They're straggling further from the point than ever, and Luke tries to lurch beyond caution. "One thing you'll remember," he says and has to take a breath. "What you said about the Kind Folk, that he was involved with them."

"Did I say involved? I don't think—"

"It doesn't matter what you said, that's what he was. You must have seen he was looking for them."

"Because he keeps using the phrase, you mean? I don't understand why you're being so fierce."

"You have to see what's here." Luke lifts a hand but points it at the journal rather than himself. "He was trying to find them," he says, "so he could find out what to do about me."

"About——" Sophie is quiet for a moment. "Oh, Luke," she murmurs. "You're saying he was worried because you'd been sent to the psychiatrist."

"No, that's not it, not all of it anyway. I'm not angry with you, Sophie, just myself." Luke still can't step over the edge of revelation; he feels as if his nature has clamped on his mind, crushing the words too deep to reach. "One thing you won't have understood," he manages to say. "What do you think he meant by the end of magic?"

Sophie seems to welcome the respite as she leafs through the journal, and doesn't speak until she has read the entry at least once again. "Did he think some kind of magic ended with these people? I'm not sure why he keeps mentioning hands here unless he had some kind of secret sign in mind."

"It's the one the Kind Folk use to show what they are." For an instant that feels like losing all control Luke is aware that his fingers have begun to stretch wide, and then pain makes him clench his fists. "But the end, that's the title of a book," he says. "The author's name is Page, Alvin Page."

"Have you read it, Luke?"

He nods and feels as if the burden of knowledge weighs too much for his head to hold up. "In the library while I was away."

"You look as if you think it says something important."

"It says . . . " He has to open his fists, since they make him feel he's clenching the whole of himself to keep the revelation in. "It says if you ask them to help you to have a child you'll end up with one of their own."

Sophie looks away from him. He thinks he can't bear what she has realised she's seeing, but she's regarding the journal. In a moment she raises her eyes to him. "That's even sadder," she murmurs. "If that's what Terence thought it's a pity he won't be here for your test results."

Luke feels his mouth open and close again. He might almost have forgotten how to speak. He hasn't begun to think of a response by the time Sophie says "And if you're a changeling you'll do for me."

Too late he realises that she's already familiar with the idea from songs she knows. That's all it means to her—a folk tradition, a fairy tale. If he tries to convince her that it's so much more, will she think he needs to see another sort of doctor? Just the same, he's about to try when she says "Don't inherit his obsession, will you?"

"Don't you think I already have?" It feels like a last opportunity to persuade her of the truth. "If he were here," Luke says, "he'd be telling us we ought to remember some of the things that have happened."

Sophie looks as patient as her mother often does. "Such as what, Luke?"

"The kind of folk who got into the house where the nurse lived, for a start."

"Her neighbour said they were after drugs, if you recall."

"You didn't see them." This is no use, since Luke didn't either—not that night, at any rate. "But I'll tell you what you did see. The ones you said were making signs when you were performing in Chester."

"I thought you might have that in mind. I know what it must have been now."

"What?" Luke has to discover.

"I said I couldn't do that with my hands because nobody could. They must have been taking off their gloves and I thought those were hands in the dark."

"Who'd wear gloves," Luke says desperately, "when it's midsummer?"

"I can't say when I didn't see the people properly. Maybe it's the new fashion or it's going to be."

Luke takes a breath and forces himself to remind her "You said they followed you home."

"That was a dream, Luke."

"Have you had anything like it since?"

"Once was enough."

Surely all that matters is that she's left alone. Suppose talking about the unwelcome visitors summons them? He can sense that she's troubled by his insistence; does he really mean to distress her further while she's pregnant? He doesn't even know what continuing to pursue the subject could achieve. He has done as much as he reasonably can, but as he starts to experience a feeling not entirely unrelated to relief Sophie says "That wasn't what I meant by his obsession."

Luke finds he's reluctant to learn "What was?"

"I was thinking of the way you've arranged your tour."

"I don't understand," Luke says without necessarily inviting it.

"Now that we know what he was looking for you don't need to go where he did." Sophie gives the journal a light slap that seems close to parental and says "I noticed that all the bookings you've accepted recently, they're in places he visited too."

151

28

THE EYES

"ARE YOU CERTAIN WATER'S all you want to take onstage, Mr Arnold?"

"I need to drive home to my partner after the show."

"Can't you bear to be apart? How long have you been together?"

"Eight years, and we're having a child."

"That's the best reason to go back. Still or sparkling?" Trixie Hammond deals her quick grin a light slap with her fingertips as though admonishing the inadvertent joke. "Not your forthcoming event," she says. "The water."

She's a small woman with boyishly short hair that's counteracted by enough makeup for someone twice her size, and she's the manager of the Old Well Theatre in Snugsby New Town. They're in her boxy office, which is decorated with posters for shows at most a few years old, and the name of the theatre next to the almost identical concrete block of the library is the most venerable element Luke has encountered in the little town south of Leicester. "Make it still," he says, which sounds less like a joke.

"I'll fetch it now, and is there anything else we can do for you?"

"You could tell me something. Don't take this the wrong way, but what made you get in touch?"

"One of our regulars said we ought to book you while we could afford you. I hope that doesn't make us sound cheap."

"I've no complaints, don't worry. It was just one person, you're saying. Somebody you know."

"Valentine's the name. He rang me when you were on the television. He knew who you were," the manager says and touches her lips again as though groping for a smile she can't locate. "Are you over that now, what you found out about yourself?"

"I've had to be. Will he be here now?"

"I expect he's in the bar. Would you like to say hello?"

"I would," Luke says, though it's hardly what he has in mind.

Snugsby is mentioned in the journal—just the name, which must mean Terence visited it solely for the place itself—but Luke has seen nothing in the immature streets that he can imagine Terence would have found significant. He follows Trixie Hammond to the bar, a long concrete windowless room with tables and benches of the same pale pine as the counter. She orders a bottle of water for Luke and then makes for a man sitting alone in a corner with a tankard of murky beer. "Valentine," she says. "Here's someone who'd like to meet you."

The tall balding man rises from his crouch, but not entirely. His extravagantly broad shoulders seem to weigh him down, thrusting his wide flat reddish face at Luke. When he extends a large veinous hand Luke thinks for a grotesque moment that it's about to give him the secret sign. As Luke reciprocates its grip the man says "Good to know you."

His voice has almost expelled its regional accent and sounds as though it's braying about the achievement. "Likewise, Mr Valentine," Luke says.

"You can leave the mister out," Valentine says and lets go. "Not being rude, but who are you again?"

"Don't make me out a liar, Valentine. He's who you asked for."

"Not guilty, Trixie," Valentine says, remaining stooped while he peers at Luke. "Are you tonight's attraction? Looking forward to it, but I never put in for you."

"Think back," Trixie insists. "You rang me up."

"Is that a fact? Did I say it was me?"

"You didn't have to, Valentine. I'd never mistake your voice."

"Sorry, but you did."

"Wait a second, I was wrong." As he straightens up triumphantly Trixie says "I kept calling you your name and you didn't set me straight."

"Then it was somebody pretending." Valentine sits on the bench with a

153

decisive thump and keeps his gaze on Luke. "Maybe," he says, "it was someone like your comedian here."

"Why would anyone want to do that?" Trixie says before Luke can respond.

"No point asking me. You're the one saying they did. Maybe it was some kind of stunt for the show."

He's still watching Luke, who retorts "I hope you don't think it was me."

"You copy people, don't you? That's what you're known for. It could be extra publicity for you, convincing everyone you're somebody you're not."

Luke is struggling to appear as innocent as he wants to feel. They've all been victims of a trick, but he's sure it had more of a purpose. He's reduced to demanding "Tell me how I could have imitated you when I've never met you before."

"I'm not that clever." Red patches swell up on Valentine's face as he adds "But you're doing it now."

Luke feels as if he's losing all sense of himself. When he turns to his companion she says "You did sound rather like him then."

Luke strives to hear his own voice say "Would you have thought I was him on the phone?"

"The show will be commencing in five minutes." The announcement sounds as if identical members of a chorus are trying to imitate one another, since the loudspeakers throughout the building aren't quite synchronised. It silences Trixie, and Luke has to repeat "Would you?"

"Not as much as whoever rang up."

"There you are. It couldn't have been me." Presumably Luke no longer sounds like Valentine, since the man's face has reverted to its ordinary ruddiness. "I'm sorry if I seemed to be taking you off," Luke says. "I didn't realise I was."

Valentine makes him wait for the duration of a pair of gulps of beer and says "I suppose your whole life's a rehearsal."

"It feels like one," Luke says and trails the manager out of the bar. Beyond her office a bare corridor leads backstage past dressing-rooms. Luke hears a monotonous xylophone clatter of seats as people take their places, and then the lights dim. If he feels apprehensive, this isn't stage fright, though it might as well be. He leaves his mobile switched on, but only to ensure that Sophie can reach him. He takes a breath and strides onstage, where the boards exaggerate his footsteps. "I'm Luke Arnold in case anybody's wondering," he says. "I think."

While the pause isn't meant as timing, the afterthought gains a laugh. Even Valentine, who is sitting halfway up the wide concrete room in which the eighteen rows of seats are mostly full, throws back his head to emit a titter. Luke tries to ignore him in case he's tempted to imitate the man, and tries a routine about yawns, reminding everyone how infectious these can be; indeed, several people demonstrate it and reward him with rueful mirth. He performs a series of yawns, each setting off a more dramatic and elaborate imitation on his part, and then he wonders aloud if other tics could be catching too. He's portraying a variety of people losing a fierce battle with their compulsion to scratch, a spectacle the audience greets with increasing hilarity, when he notices someone at the very back of the auditorium.

It isn't just the dimness that makes it hard to distinguish the intruder's shape. The spindly figure, which is loitering behind the last row of seats, puts him in mind of a sketch that's waiting to be filled in. It looks bare, and not only of garments. Apart from the coaly glint of eyes and the glimmer of a grin, Luke suspects there isn't much of a face to see. He feels as if he has invited the intrusion by encouraging the audience to mimic him, because the figure has begun to copy his performance. The sight drives Luke to act more extravagantly still, stretching his arms in search of an inaccessible itch while he glares at the back of the theatre. The audience roars, but a few people glance behind them, though it's plain they see nothing significant. They must think Luke's glare is part of his routine, and surely he can ignore the unwelcome spectator, because he has realised how he can avoid being aped. "Suppose it's words as well?" he asks the audience.

Some people laugh. A few even sound as if they understand or want everybody else to think they do. For the moment the figure at the back has stopped moving, though that's just another imitation of Luke. He could think it's losing definition, unless he's seeing what he hopes to. It's still watching him, and he's sure that it brought him to Snugsby. He's close to demanding why, but he sets about representing a loquaciously inarticulate customer at a bank. "I'd like to pay in some, you know, some of that paper stuff and some of those little metal round things into what do you call it, that thing of mine where you keep the whatsits I bring in . . . "

There's a good deal more of this, which seems to bemuse some of the audience at least as much as it amuses them. He isn't helped by the distant spectator, which has begun to stretch its forefingers and little fingers wide, driving Luke to overstate his gestures in a bid to retain control of his hands while the customer is replaced at the bank clerk's window by a robber. "Give me all your, don't say you don't know what I'm talking about, the stuff you keep there in a drawer. I've got a how's your father and I'm not afraid to use it, one of the things that go bang and shoot bits of metal . . . "

The audience has seen the joke by now, but Luke wonders how many of them are mistaking his desperation for the character's, if there's any difference. He thought the acoustic had changed, and then he realised that the echo comes from the intruder, which is reproducing his voice despite scarcely having enough of a mouth. He can only keep the robber babbling until the clerk consults his superior. "Excuse me, Mr Whatsyour-name, this gentleman's got a thingummy there and he wants me to, you know when people take stuff out of the bank they haven't got in it . . . "

The audience laughs even harder at the policeman and the judge, though Luke hardly knows what he's saying any more. Even worse, the intruder seems close to anticipating his dialogue; they're speaking in unison now. Luke is so desperate that he releases the thief from jail to appear on *Brittan's Resolutions*, a move that's greeted with applause. He has no idea why everyone finds the routine hilarious; they would be less delighted if they knew that all his words and gestures are being mali-ciously replicated behind them. He feels like a puppet their enthusiasm is jerking about the stage until at last he finds a payoff. "Ladies and what's the other thing, this has been the Luke Whosit show . . . "

As the lights come up there are cheers and whistles and even a drum-ming of feet in the midst of all the handclaps, none of which means as much to him as the sight of a figure dropping to all fours behind the back row. He sees it scuttle into a shadowy corner, and then it's gone like a spider into a crevice, though the concrete is unbroken. Luke retreats into the wings, where Trixie Hammond meets him. "Very edgy," she says. "Good value. We'd have you again."

"Thanks," Luke says, mostly for the envelope she hands him.

He has an uneasy sense that he's yet to learn the purpose of his visit. Feeling enervated by his performance, he tramps out of the Old Well. Vehicles are leaving the car park, a concrete enclosure overseen by floodlights. Although he's anxious to be on his way home, he waits for the exodus to finish. At last he's alone with a few empty cars under a crescent moon pregnant with darkness. He stares about in case this brings any response, but everything is as still as the multiple shadows of the vehicles. Perhaps he's in the wrong place, and he stalks onto the road.

A few hundred yards beyond the Old Well it turns aside from the town centre, which is closed to traffic. An unpopulated pavement the width of the street leads between shops that put Luke in mind of glass cases at an exhibition. The pavement is served by the occasional rudimentary bench, and it's barren apart from a few saplings supported by splints in wire cages. The street feels cloned from shopping areas Luke has encountered throughout Britain, and he could think somebody has painted the cartoonish figure on the nondescript exterior of a Frugobank in an attempt to render it more individual. It's the only example of graffiti to be seen, and as Luke peers in its direction it appears to shift. Perhaps it isn't made of paint at all.

It doesn't stir as he strides along the road. He keeps his gaze on it until he arrives at the junction, where he can't help glancing aside to check there's no traffic. When he looks back at the figure he thinks for an instant that it has vanished. No, it's visible again, as though his attention has called it forth—a shape reminiscent of a spindly insect the height of a man, flattened against the pallid concrete wall. Instead of making it clearer, the white glare of the streetlamps that crane over the trees seems almost to be draining it of substance. As Luke crosses the junction he's afraid the loiterer may disappear before he can challenge it, and he shouts "What do you want? Why did you bring me here?"

There's no response of any kind, and he feels he's on the edge of giving in to laughter, though not mirth. Has his mind finally collapsed, leaving him to rant at a childish drawing on a wall? An unexpectedly chill wind blunders into the street, twitching the frail trees in their cages and rustling bunches of brownish leaves, but it has no apparent effect on the shape that's pressed against if not into the wall. Luke has passed several shops by the time it turns its head to him.

It has little enough of one—even less than it appeared to have while watching him at the Old Well. The object that nods out from the wall and twists towards him has just a single eye now, which seems to be swelling twice the size to compensate. A whitish scrap of lipless mouth bares a few teeth, the beginnings of a grin, but otherwise the concave bony mass would hardly be identifiable as a head if it weren't perched on a flimsy neck. In a moment the hands sprout from the concrete and describe the sign Luke knows all too well. As he digs his fingers into his palms to ensure they won't move, the figure darts out of the wall.

For a breath that he holds until his head begins to swim Luke can't see where it has gone, and then he glimpses movement inside the nearest wire cage. There's so little to the skulker that it's almost hidden by the gaunt tree, and at first he mistook its hands for diseased swellings of the trunk. He has barely identified them when they're snatched back, and a spidery figure bounds away on all fours. The impression vanishes before Luke can grasp it, and at once the next cage rattles thinly, a hundred yards from its neighbour. He's put in mind of an ape playing tricks in a zoo. "Where are you going?" he calls. "You haven't told me why I'm here."

Fingers like stripped twigs shift on the tree in the cage, but that's the only hint of life. Luke tramps fast along the street, which seems to be trying to live up to its name, Lily Avenue. Several displays in shop windows involve vegetation, presumably artificial; there are even water-lilies at the feet of mannequins in a boutique. Luke is well beyond the first tree by the time the cage ahead of him jangles as an ill-defined incomplete shape darts away. "Aren't you going to answer me?" Luke shouts. "You can talk if you want to. Don't pretend you haven't got a voice."

This appears to prompt a response—a mutter that might be echoing his last words. It's coming from the third caged tree. "I didn't catch that," Luke calls, "say it again," but there's silence until he's nearly at the cage. Then two knuckly swellings disappear from the tree, and he hears a faint scrabbling of claws on the flagstones of the pavement. It's gone before he can locate it. "Don't try to hide," he shouts. "I can see you if anyone can."

It isn't anything to boast about, he thinks. He could wish it weren't true. He runs to the junction with Bulrush Way, a street very much like the one he's following, but can't see a trespasser to either side or ahead on Lily Avenue. Suppose the prowler has sneaked behind him? As Luke turns he glimpses activity to his left; a shape with some of a face has ducked out from behind the nearest tree. It retreats into hiding at once even though the tree is too slim to conceal it, and Luke feels as if he's being mocked. "Is that your best trick?" he yells. "Try answering my question."

The whisper that replies seems as wordless as the hiss of a reptile. "Speak up for yourself," Luke shouts without provoking any further response. He's no more than a few strides from the tree when a lanky shape breaks cover and is instantly behind the next tree. Luke sprints after it, past shops that have indeed included bulrushes in their displays. Some of the shops must be draughty, because the heavy-headed stems beyond the windows stir as a cold breeze meets him, bearing a faint stagnant odour. The branches of the saplings scrape together, and an object that falls short of resembling any welcome notion of a face peers around the tree ahead of him. Before he can even take a breath it reappears from behind the tree beyond that one. "How long are you going to keep this up?" Luke demands, and anger makes him blurt "Don't you want to be seen?"

The answer appears to be no. He hasn't reached the further tree when an unpleasantly embryonic shape springs out of hiding and vanishes in the direction of the next cross street. There's no sign of it when he reaches the junction, but he hears a whisper to his left, as thin as a wind through wire. "Lucius," it seems to say, which is enough to take him into Marsh Passage.

The shops there are illustrating the name. Reeds sprout among mannequins and pools of water gleam, or at least sheets of plastic shaped to resemble miniature ponds. Some of the dummies in an unlit window appear to have weeds tied around their limbs, but Luke hasn't time to be distracted from the chase. A figure that looks too flimsy to support its unfinished outsize head dodges from behind a tree, though not the closest one. After that it stays unseen all the way to the next junction, where Luke hears another almost mouthless whisper to his left. "Lucius," it hisses.

Or is it "You see us" this time? It leads him into Steppingstone Lane, where the window displays are more distracting than ever. Several mannequins are virtually overgrown with vegetation, and the window-dressers have even gone to the trouble of beading the leaves with moisture. Quite a few of the dummies seem to be up to their ankles in water; could a recent downpour have flooded some of the shops? Certainly the saplings are rooted in mud. A wind brings a smell of stagnant water, and a soggy plastic bag that's pinned against a cage winces like a dying fish while the trees fumble at the wires. There's no sign of the fugitive Luke is pursuing, and when he hears a whisper it's so distant that he wouldn't understand it if he hadn't previously heard it. He dashes towards it, and then he falters. Has he grasped it at last? Perhaps it said "You see true" or "You see truth."

It seems he may have, too late. Perhaps the pursuit was intended to distract him from the kind of place he's in, which has begun to live up to the street names more fully than he likes. Moisture is outlining the flagstone beneath him, and he suspects it's seeping up from the marsh the streets are built upon. Either the swamp wasn't drained properly or something has summoned it back. The pools of water in the shops on both sides of him aren't fake after all—ripples are fading from them as the wind dies—but why do they make him feel watched? He peers at the window on his left, and the contents of the pool swivel to return his gaze. The oval object as black as the depths of a cave is an eye—and then he realises it's worse than that. Although it's bigger than his head, it's just the pupil.

Another one is spying on him from the window opposite. The pool that contains it covers half the floor, and yet the eye that's using it to observe him is larger. He has to take a long unsteady breath as a preamble to looking behind him. Steppingstone Lane is strewn with torpid pools, and whatever has been roused underneath it is employing them to watch with its myriad eyes. For a moment—no, much longer—Luke can't move, not least because he has no idea which way to flee. There's a cross street ahead, but how often has he turned left? One way will lead him deeper into the maze, to whatever lies at its heart. He can only flounder towards the crossroads as the flagstones tilt underfoot, releasing a stale miasma as water wells up around them. If he doesn't know which route to take by the time he reaches the junction he's sure that the place will have captured him—captured his mind. Surely going left will take him back the way he came. A flagstone rears up beneath him with a squelch of mud, tipping him backwards into Steppingstone Lane. He stumbles forward and trips over the edge of the slab, and then he's in the middle of the junction.

He has reached Lily Avenue. To his left are the shops he passed earlier, and their window displays look reassuringly artificial. He lurches towards them and makes himself look back at Steppingstone Lane. It's absolutely clear of water, and every flagstone is in its place. Perhaps he simply experienced a vision, although that's bad enough; why should it have been conjured up? He's retreating along Lily Avenue when he hears sounds in Steppingstone Lane—a sibilant chorus. It's some kind of chant, and although he doesn't recognise a word he can tell it's a celebration. He would rather not understand—it puts him in mind of reptiles or something even less human—but he feels unhappily responsible, and so he sprints back to the junction. He's almost there when the hissing chant falls silent, and by the time he comes in sight of Steppingstone Lane he's alone beneath the moon. He gazes at the caged trees until he's convinced that nothing is about to show itself. He has done all he can—perhaps more than he would have wanted to achieve—and he makes for his car.

— 29 —

THE NEXT SECRET

THE LIVERPOOL STREETS ARE DESERTED by the time Luke reaches home. He drives down the ramp and parks next to Sophie's car. His shadows and the shrivelled echoes of his footsteps imitate him as he makes for the lobby. However furtive the activities seem, they needn't remind him of anything. He's safe home now. Surely home is safe.

It's nearly two in the morning. The building is silent except for his hushed footsteps on the stairs. He pads up to the fourth floor and lets himself in. Darkness as quiet as soil fills the corridor when he eases the door shut, but he can just see that the bedroom door is ajar. He tiptoes to the bathroom opposite and is feeling for the light-cord when Sophie mumbles "Is that you, Luke?"

"Who else is it going to be?"

He's glad she doesn't answer. He suspects and indeed hopes that she may not be fully awake. Once he has finished in the bathroom he leaves the light on while he peeks into the bedroom. Sophie's eyes are closed, and she has one arm around his pillow. She's facing the corridor with a faint smile that looks anticipatory if not reminiscent, so that Luke wonders whether she's dreaming he has come home. He switches off the light and slips into bed, at which point Sophie turns over and gropes for his arm to draw it around her capacious waist. "Go sleep now," she murmurs.

She might be urging this on him or their child or addressing herself,

162

quite possibly all three. For Luke it's a task, and long after Sophie and the child inside her have united in stillness he's awake. The drive home gave him hours to imagine how many places like Snugsby there may be in the world—banal everyday locations that mask ancient dormant presences. Perhaps the only way to deal with these survivals is to ignore them; he's afraid that the chase through the streets built over the old marsh could have made its denizen restless. Surely if Luke reins his awareness in he won't be responsible for any more revivals of that sort. Whenever he begins to drift towards sleep he feels in danger of relaxing his vigilance; he has an unhappy sense of needing to remember what will happen then. He's overtaken by slumber before he can identify the problem, and is wakened by Sophie's puzzled voice. "What are you doing, Luke?"

"Just holding you," he says and then realises what he has allowed to happen by falling asleep. His hand on her midriff has taken advantage of his inattention and stretched its fingers inhumanly wide to form the ancient sign. "That's not me," he cries, though his words feel too clumsy to find their way out of his mouth. A less articulate cry does, and this time he's awake.

He's alone in bed. The curtains are keeping sunlight away from him. In a moment Sophie says something in the main room and approaches down the corridor. She's wearing her most voluminous new dress and carrying a phone. "He's woken up," she tells it and covers it with a hand. "Are you all right, Luke?"

"I am now," he says and does his best to be.

"You'd better speak to him, Freda," Sophie says and hands him the phone.

"I'm sorry if I woke you, son. Sophie says you weren't in till very late."

"Don't worry, I'd rather be awake. Why were you calling?"

"We were wondering if you'd decided what you're doing about Terry's house."

He's disturbed to realise that he hasn't thought of it for days. "The house," he says to Sophie. "We'll be selling it, won't we?"

"It's your house, Luke."

He assumes this means yes—it will have to. "We'll be selling," he says, mostly to Freda.

"Then Maurice and I thought we could give you a hand. You've both got more than enough to do as it is."

Luke is uneasily reminded of his dream by asking "What kind of hand?"

"Maurice and the boys can get the house cleared and then I'll tidy up before you put it up for sale. If it needs sprucing he'll see to that too."

Luke can't see how to turn the offer down; surely there's no reason why he should. "That's very kind," he says and wishes he'd thought of a different word.

"It's nothing of the kind, Luke. It's just what families do." Less reprovingly she says "Was there anything else you wanted to keep from the house?"

This revives his unease. "Besides what?"

"Sophie was saying you'd found Terry's diary. Was there anything in it to help?"

"It shows how obsessed he was with, with things Maurice didn't have much time for." Luke is speaking to Sophie too as he says "That's one way you wouldn't want me taking after him."

"You'll keep it though, will you?" Freda seems anxious to be assured. "It's still a souvenir of him."

"I wouldn't want anyone else to have it," Luke says and askes Sophie "There's nothing else we'd like from the house, is there?"

"I'm not sure there's even that, if you mean the journal."

"So if anything else takes our fancy," Freda says, "you won't mind if we have it."

At once he's nervous on their behalf. "There's a room full of junk and more of it scattered round the house," he says. "I shouldn't think there's anything that would look good in your home."

"We'll see tomorrow. I wouldn't mind something to remember Terry by. Now I'll leave you two together, well, it's more than two."

Luke says goodbye, not having thought of anything more useful, and swings his legs off the bed as he hands Sophie her mobile. As he stands up she says "You'd rather they dealt with the house, then."

"I was a long way away and worried, that's all, with you being twice as precious just now." Luke is hoping this may placate her—surely it's how people manage these situations, whichever this one is—but feels compelled to add "I'm sure they'd like to feel they're helping when we've so much else to handle."

Sophie gazes at him before she says "You're giving me a lot of reasons, Luke."

"Will they do?"

She pauses long enough for him to see they won't. "I've been reading while you were away. *The End of Magic*."

She's keeping too much of her expression to herself for Luke to be sure of her feelings. All he can risk saying is "And so . . . "

He could easily take her silence for an accusation, and her sigh as well. "I didn't get much sleep while I was waiting for you," she says. "I'm going to try and have a nap."

Luke doesn't think she is inviting him to join her. By the time he has finished in the bathroom she's asleep, and he hurries to the computer. While he doesn't know what Sophie has in mind, perhaps that's because the students at the library distracted him from finishing Alvin Page's book. He brings it onscreen and goes to The Last Gift, though even the title of the chapter makes him nervous. As he scrolls through the material he previously read he wishes he could leave all of it behind. He's doing his utmost to feel that it no longer matters when a paragraph he hasn't previously read crawls up the screen, and his fingers clench on the control.

It's another quotation from John Strong. "Whereas once upon a time the Gift was the means by which the Folk of the Moon infiltrated the upstart race, in this barren era it has the function of a charm. That which is least known may be most potent, and the Gift gains power from its ignorance of its own nature, which allows its essence to preserve its secret dream. Its occult strength lies in the depths of its mind where even its own vision, having grown mortal, cannot penetrate. Thus it is capable of reawakening such magic as is hidden in the world, and perhaps the Folk may revive themselves by battening upon the dormant forces it has roused . . . "

He's surprised not to find this more disturbing. He feels as though he has already dealt with it in the streets that were built over the marsh. Perhaps by acknowledging it he can extinguish its power. As his hand relaxes on the control he hears Sophie murmur in the bedroom. He shuts the computer down and keeps his footsteps quiet in case she's still asleep. A thought appears to have wakened her, and she looks unexpectedly apologetic. "Luke, did you mean what you told Freda?"

"I told her a few things. I should think I meant them all."

"You said you weren't going to inherit Terence's obsession."

Luke doesn't think he quite said that; perhaps Sophie dreamed he did.

Nevertheless he says "I shouldn't think you'd want me to any more than she would."

He can see the answer in her eyes, but there's a question too. She parts her lips for a breath and then says "Do you believe what it says in the Page book?"

"No more than you do."

"Then I don't at all."

"I won't either," Luke vows and takes her hands, which makes his grasp feel sure of itself. "I won't even think of it. Let's never mention it again."

— 30 —

ON THE BALCONY

"Just Water in a Bottle, thanks. I'll be driving home after the show."

"So long as you aren't sober in the wrong way, hey? Your act is what I'm saying."

"I'll be whatever they want me to be. That's how it works."

"Champion. Here's your tipple, so are you fixed up?"

"Do you mind if I ask you an odd question?"

"The odder the better. I'm more than a shade odd myself."

Luke thinks it's more that the man would like to be. He's Alasdair Hull, the manager of the Elysium. He's wearing a pale green three-piece suit with a leather trilby, beneath which his plump amiable face might look too youthful to have left school if it didn't bear wrinkles several decades old. As Hull resumes his puffy chair behind his office desk, having shut the miniature refrigerator that stands on top of a safe, Luke says "What made you get in touch with me?"

"No other way to book you that I could see. You independent types don't go in for agents any more. You're all the folk you need to be all by yourself."

"Yes, but why did you when you did?"

"Your reputation's spreading, that's all. I'll bet you there are folk here tonight who've never been to the Elysium."

"So what had you heard that prompted you?"

"You won't let me off with saying I got the idea out of my own little head."

"I will if it's true."

"Well, it's not." Hull tweaks the brim of his hat as if he's greeting somebody and says "We have one of our local critics to thank. She does it for the paper and the radio."

"She came to see you about me, you mean."

"As good as. Rang up and I don't know when I've ever heard her sound so enthusiastic."

If Luke were to say he's not surprised it would be mistaken for bragging, and so he says "Would you happen to remember what she said?"

"I do." Hull tips his hat back with a finger, though not far enough to expose his receding hairline. "Don't take this wrong," he says, "but she said we ought to book you while we can afford you."

They're reduced to imitating themselves, Luke thinks. "Will the lady be here tonight?"

"Sadly she won't. I haven't had a chance to tell her you'd be on since she rang, and she's still away on a course. She'll be sorry to have missed you."

Luke knows there's no reason to assume anything of the kind. It has occurred to him to cancel any bookings like this one, but he doesn't want to let anybody down, and what has he to fear? Just because the theatre is close to Crakemoor, which is mentioned in Terence's journal, he isn't about to be tempted to visit the site. As Hull ushers him backstage the manager says "Don't worry because we're empty upstairs. We're renovating but we haven't had to turn anyone away."

An unlit balcony looms over the stalls, which are indeed almost full. It's supported by caryatids Luke assumes are Victorian, however ancient they're feigning to be. Its front edge bears a brass rail divided by a pair of irrelevant decorations, two ridged knobs framed by of the elevated aisle. As the audience greets Luke with applause he could think the vibrations have made or are about to make the incongruous objects stir.

He earns more applause and a chorus of sighs by announcing that he's soon to be a father, though he only means to lead into a routine. Here's a father who appears not to know which way up to hold the newborn. Here's another who's afraid he may drop it or squash it or upset it or cause it to spray him. Here's a fellow who's determined not to shed a single joyful tear and grimaces so much that the audience claps as well as

168

laughing. This would encourage Luke more if the items on the balcony weren't responding as well, letting go of the rail so as to stretch their fingers wide and perform a parody of applause. In a moment they grip the rail again, and the body rises into view between them.

Too much of it seems to be elsewhere. It puts Luke in mind of a foetus that has withered in some inhuman womb. He could easily imagine that the bloated head, which is still working on some of its features, has floated up like a grinning balloon and drawn the pallid fleshless torso after it. It isn't unexpected, he tells himself, and it won't distract him. Here's one of those aunts who are convinced you have to address children in a special way, as if you're really talking to everyone else within quite a distance. Here's a relative who uses babies as an excuse to revert to speaking in no recognisable language. Here's one who doesn't care for children but feels bound not to show it, except that every wince and nervously valiant smile and earnest bid for friendship does . . .

The occupant of the balcony is displeased by all the laughter. Perhaps it feels that Luke should be paying it more attention. While the tiny eyes are unreadable—they're so deeply sunken that they appear to have shrivelled into the head—the corners of the lipless mouth have sagged on either side of the toadstool lump of a chin. Luke is inspired to portray someone determined to ignore a child, which produces several minutes of fun, and so does an impression of a father desperate to pretend he isn't wheeling a baby in a buggy, that unmanly task. The antics of the intruder in the balcony prompt Luke to demonstrate the lengths to which people will go in their attempts to disregard others while trying not to seem to do so. A whitish tongue, unless it's a discoloured worm, has writhed out of the mouth to dangle down the chin as the figure wags its head at him and lifts its hands on either side of the undeveloped face to give the ancient sign twice. Luke is reminded of a child who's eager to provoke a chase, except that the antics strike him as senile. They aren't going to put him off, although eventually he falls back on trusted material: the infectious tics, the verbal ones, the bank robber who ends up on the Brittan show. He feels as if he has been driven to imitate himself, even if the audience can't know. The waves of mirth appear to goad the intruder to desperation, and it prances back and forth on the balcony, grimacing so hideously that the contortions look capable of wrenching such features as it has into a different shape, not necessarily that of a face. Luke hears boards clatter beneath its tread, and some of the people seated under the balcony glance up. Suppose somebody on the staff goes to look? No doubt they wouldn't see the culprit, and Luke applies himself to doing likewise. At last his show is over, and he glimpses a shape crouching out of view as light floods the auditorium.

He suspects he's meant to know that his tormentor is hiding and to look out for it elsewhere. It isn't visible as the audience makes for the bar or the street, and Luke can't see it when he leaves the Elysium once Alasdair Hull has finished enthusing about him. Even if the presence helped intensify his nervous energy onstage, he can live without that kind of stimulus. The payment machine at the entrance to the multi-storey opposite the theatre sticks out the tongue of his parking ticket, and a shivering lift carries him up to the fifth level, past floors indistinguishable from one another except for the occasional parked car. Nothing moves on the expanses of concrete blanched by fluorescent lights, and he could imagine that the July heat has grown so stagnant it has sapped the night of life. But as he steers the Lexus out of its space he sees a figure waiting for him.

It's crouching on top of the wall at the far end of the fifth level, gripping the concrete edge with its toes, which are as long as his fingers. He has to drive towards it there's no other way out of the car park—and as he does so it lifts its hands to frame its face. The hands are describing the sign and perhaps also drawing attention to the absence of a mouth in the round whitish lump. In the middle of the floor Luke swings the car down a ramp and glimpses the figure dropping like a spider off the wall. As the car turns onto the fourth floor he sees that his follower has perched on the wall there to await him.

It plays the trick all the way down to the last floor but one. He wouldn't be surprised to find it loitering like a hitchhiker at the exit barrier, but the ground level is deserted. As he drives through Leeds towards the motorway he thinks he sees a figure scuttling past the far ends of terraced streets. When he arrives at the lonely junction the motorway overlooks, at first the only sign of life appears to be the operation of the traffic lights that guard the empty roads. He's driving up to the motorway when a scrawny malformed shape vaults onto the ramp and scurries ahead of him.

It's out of sight by the time he speeds onto the motorway, but he knows where he's likely to encounter it again. The lights of the city fall behind, and soon the lamps above the motorway come to an end. As the road

170

climbs towards the moors and the unfinished moon it grows almost as deserted as the sky between the stars appears to be. On both sides bleak slopes that seem too gloomy for the moon to begin to illuminate stretch to the horizon. A lorry lowers its headlamp beams as it races around a bend ahead, and Luke dips his. A mile further uphill he repeats the routine on behalf of a solitary oncoming car, and then he's alone on the road. His headlights find nothing to fasten on until a signboard comes into view— the sign for the Crakemoor road. The board sails by, and the raised beams light up a figure standing at the junction with the side road.

It's grotesquely reminiscent of a policeman directing traffic. Its right arm is extended towards Crakemoor, not pointing but forming the sign of the Folk. "I'm going home," Luke says loud enough to be heard on the moors, "and nowhere else." Before he has finished speaking he tramps hard on the accelerator.

He's nearly at the junction when the shape lurches in front of the car, flinging its arms wide and thrusting its mouthless head forward so violently that the eyes almost sink out of sight. He doesn't brake; he floors the accelerator, and the car runs the scrawny figure down, having struck it in the region where its genitals should be, a withered tangle more like bone than any species of flesh. Luke doesn't feel an impact, but the car shudders as though it has been seized by a wind across the moors. As he races past the Crakemoor road he sees a dim glimmering shape stagger to its feet in the mirror and stretch out its claws to the car. The arms are lengthening; they're yards long now—they're even longer. Then they appear to merge with the night, and eventually Luke lets the car lose speed on the ascent to the highest moor. "Don't bother trying to entice me any more," he says and doesn't care if anything can hear. "I've left you behind. I'm not your kind of folk."

A TOUCH IN THE DARK

"WHILE YOU CAN AFFORD ME. Of course I'm not offended, but was that your idea?"

"Now you mention it," Amy Greenaway begins and then gives Luke a blink of her glittery eyelids. "Well, that's an old song."

"Not as old as some," Luke says and reads the onscreen name as his mobile continues to sing about last month. "Excuse me while I take this. It's my partner and she's pregnant."

"I'll be fetching your water," the manager says and leaves Luke in the dressing-room.

Luke swivels his chair towards the mirror, which frames his face with lights and allows him to spy on the corridor. The visible section stays deserted as Sophie says "Can you talk?"

"I hope I'll always be able to do that. I won't be much use otherwise."

"You know what I mean," she says with a nominal laugh. "You aren't putting on a show."

"I'm not onstage for a few minutes, if that's what you mean." Having said just the first part of this aloud, Luke adds "How's everything at home?"

"I think somebody's anxious to see the world. I've been asking him to wait till next week."

"It isn't likely to be that soon, is it? I thought we had months."

"Won't you be happy if he's here sooner?"

"You know I will whenever it turns out to be. Why next week?"

"That's when they've booked me into the studio, and by the way, we were all wrong."

Luke finds he hasn't run out of apprehensiveness. "About what?"

"They've convinced me we should call the album *Drew Two*."

"If that's what sells." In case this seems insufficiently enthusiastic Luke says "It's more you, isn't it?"

"That's all my news." As Luke wonders if anything made her anxious to hear his voice she says "The Arnolds have been to the house."

He feels uneasy and can't quite grasp why. "How did it go?"

"Freda's taken a fancy to something. She wants to be sure you don't mind."

"I don't see how I could," Luke says, only to realise what he shouldn't have forgotten. Suppose Freda has told Sophie that she found the deformed skull? It reconstituted itself somehow after he destroyed it, and may it have reappeared again? Sophie will know something is very wrong, and not just at the house. "What thing?" he makes himself ask.

"The piece of ironwork with the moon in it. Maurice says he can make it into part of a gate for her."

"They're absolutely welcome to it. Was that all?"

"It's all they liked."

"No," Luke says as a shadow darts along the corridor. "Was that all whoever you spoke to said?"

"Just about." As the owner of the shadow, which was thin because Amy Greenaway is tall and slim, enters the dressing-room Sophie says "She thought they could take anything that's salvageable to one of the charity shops."

"They could," Luke says as he's handed a bottle of water. "Thanks, Amy."

"I didn't know you weren't alone," Sophie protests. "I'll let you go. Just don't drive all that way if you're too tired. I'd rather you stayed overnight if you need to."

"I'm not tired," Luke says and vows not to let it catch up with him.

"Why don't you decide when you've done your gig. If you aren't coming home just let me know and then I can bolt the door."

"I've decided now. At the latest I'll be home by two."

That would mean driving slowly, which he doesn't plan to do. "You're on in a couple of minutes," Amy Greenaway murmurs.

"I heard that, Luke. You do whatever's safest afterwards, and now go and be a star."

As Luke pockets the mobile the manager says "Ready for your audience?"

"Bring them on," Luke says and has to ensure she takes his vehemence for a joke.

He's thinking of intruders, and he doesn't have to wait long for one. As the lights go down in the auditorium that reminds him of a lecture theatre, the dimness appears to lend substance to a figure beyond the aisle that climbs between the rows of seats. It could be the spectator he encountered at the Elysium; there's little to distinguish it, and even less that bothers to seem human. As Luke portrays a variety of characters bent on ignoring children or beggars or some aspect of themselves, the figure grows frantic to attract his attention. It lurches at the aisle as though it's threatening to distract his audience, and all the laughter seems to madden it; perhaps it thinks it's the butt of the jokes. When Luke finds more improvisations to perform, it prances behind the back row, plucking at people's heads. Some people wave their hands as if they're fending off an insect, but that's all the reaction it provokes, and so it starts capering behind them while its elongated fingers drag so fiercely at its face that they might be trying to render it even less complete. Ignoring its antics energises Luke, and he feels as if he could go on all night. It isn't until the audience sounds exhausted by laughing that he ends the show.

When the light swells up it seems to shrivel the intruder, which collapses on all fours as if there's no longer enough of a body to support the head, and the scrawny remnant dodges behind the highest seats. Luke is sure he hasn't seen the last of it, but it doesn't appear to be eavesdropping while Amy Greenaway enthuses over his performance, and there's no sign of it on the way out. Once the car park empties he could imagine that he's on his own.

The Tarnside Theatre is close to one of the English lakes, although not on the shore. A pallid trail suggests that the ungainly lopsided moon has crawled across the water. This isn't Mountain Swallow Lake, which is some miles along the route to the motorway. While Luke has passed it once without incident, he suspects the drive back may be less uneventful. He's determined to deal with whatever confronts him, though the energy that sustained him onstage has dissipated. At least Sophie doesn't know how tired he has suddenly grown. He isn't about to search for lodgings this late in the small Lakeland town. He wants to be home to see Sophie and their child are safe.

The road winds as though it's trying to wriggle away from the moon. In a few minutes the headlights find the sign for Mountain Swallow Lake. No doubt most people would assume that it's named after a species of bird. It's mentioned in Terence's journal, and it reminds Luke of a tale of Terence's about a submerged mountain where the drowned enact an ancient ritual whenever the moon lends them a kind of life. Luke expects to see a figure attempting to beckon or otherwise entice him to the lake, but the only active presence is a shadow that the headlamps send to sprawl next to the hedge before the silhouette reverts to hiding behind the signboard.

Has he managed to persuade the Folk that he isn't worth the effort? His journey takes him close to quite a few locations Terence listed; he could think this part of the country is riddled with them. Nothing is waiting to divert him onto the road to Old Moon Fell, and he tries not to think of the tale it brings to mind. When he sees the sign for Broken Neck Ridge he can't help recalling the story Terence told him of the hill where the hanged came back at night to dance. It hardly seems an ideal tale to tell a child, but then Luke wasn't the ordinary kind. The road leading to the ridge is deserted, and so is the route to Deep Toll Bay, where according to Terence swimmers dived to worship at the sunken church—swimmers who came mostly from the ocean rather than the coast and grew to resemble the polypous occupant that had made its nest on the altar. The bay is well over the horizon, and the road Luke is following has straightened towards the motorway at last. In a few minutes he sees lights chasing lights as though they're searching for the dawn.

It isn't even midnight yet, and fatigue is starting to overtake him. When he reaches the first motorway services he pulls into the car park. He can nap for half an hour and still be home by two if not earlier. He sets the alarm on his mobile and closes his eyes. At first he thinks the glare of floodlights will keep him awake, and he feels himself nod in agreement. But it's sleep that is tugging his head down, and soon he has no more thoughts.

The rest of the drive home isn't worth remembering once Sophie is beside him, caressing his face. He hadn't realised pregnancy could affect her temperature so much; her slim fingers are unexpectedly chill. He could imagine that as well as being cold as fog, they're little more substantial, because they feel as if they're not merely on his skin but somehow on the flesh inside it. Even this sensation doesn't waken him; it's the word that is breathed into his ear. The voice is thin and shrill, and the breath feels like an exudation from a swamp. He jerks awake so violently that his fist punches the horn, which resounds through the car park. He's alone in the car, but the word lingers in his brain. "Page," the intruder whispered. "Page."

— 32 —

THE PURPOSE

PERHAPS THE INTRUDER is still in the car. All the way home Luke expects to see its unfinished silhouette rear up behind him in the mirror, and when it doesn't he keeps thinking it's about to poke its bloated temporary face over his shoulder. He has to switch off the air conditioning, since its chill feels too reminiscent of a cold hand fingering his face. "Stay away," he mutters whenever he fancies that he senses a presence, "I've got nothing for you," and much more of the same.

At least he reaches the outskirts of Liverpool. The miles of deserted lamplit streets don't let him feel as alone as he would prefer, and the sight of the occasional late pedestrian isn't reassuring even once he's close enough to be certain they're human. When he parks the car under the apartments and makes for the steps he has to persuade himself that only shadows and echoes are imitating him—on the stairs too. It's almost two o'clock, and he eases the apartment door shut in the hope that Sophie will have fallen asleep. As he finds his way along the dim hall, however, she says indistinctly "You, Luke?"

"Just me," he murmurs before mouthing "And nobody else. There better hadn't be."

He repeats the words while he's in the bathroom. If he indeed has any powers, he hopes they'll help the formula to work. He doesn't feel as though he's being followed across the hall, but then Sophie mumbles "Come to bed." Of course she's inviting nobody except him, and he slips under the thin quilt, where she takes his hand as if she's using it to measure her girth. Now his back feels exposed, and he could imagine that an uninvited visitor is about to press against it, mimicking his embrace of Sophie's waist by slithering a boneless arm around him. More than once he feels the wormlike limb not merely holding him but insinuating itself beneath his skin. It's a dream, and it keeps jerking him awake, so that daylight has started to brighten the room before he's able to sleep.

A touch on his face wakens him. While it's light enough for a kiss, it isn't one. Although it's with him in the bed, it isn't a hand either; it's too insubstantial. He manages not to cry out as he recoils to the edge of the mattress. By this time his eyes are open, and he laughs instead, although mostly because that's how someone would behave in the circumstances. On the pillow is a notepad page, which a breeze through the open window must have blown against his cheek. *Didn't want to wake you*, Sophie has written. *Gone to supermarket.* That's all except for a string of kisses like a censored version of his first name.

The supermarket he and Sophie use is several miles away. He sends her a text—Don't carry anything upstairs. Ring when you're back—and tugs the quilt over himself. He's wondering whether he has time to catch up on his sleep when a thought overtakes him. His fear that an intruder could have followed him home has distracted him from another possibility. He assumed that the whisper in his ear was meant to remind him of ideas he'd found in Alvin Page's book, but was he being directed to the section he still hasn't read? Might Sophie have been thinking of that too if she has read further than he did?

Luke flings off the quilt and hurries to the computer. Several emails are waiting for him. Some are from theatres—more invitations, he presumes, and wonders who's responsible—but one is from the clinic where they tested him. A spasm passes through his fingers as he opens the message. All the fluids he provided and the rest of the evidence of himself have passed the examination. He's as good as anyone could hope—as good as human.

Perhaps he'll be able to relax once he has finished reading Alvin Page, and he conjures up *The End of Magic* on the screen. The material has begun to seem familiar, like a collection of tales told long ago—tales of the Fair Folk, the Good Folk, the Kind Folk, the Children of the Moon, the Folk of the Moon, the Fair Ones and the malicious tricks that were part of their nature. The notion that their sign can be found in paintings as early as prehistory doesn't surprise him any more, and he can live with the idea that some luminaries may have been changelings, Spenser and Shakespeare among them. He skims the chapter about the last gift; he doesn't need to be reminded of that—it's already deep in him. Then a phrase snares his attention: "the purpose of the Gift". It has sailed upwards almost out of sight before he grasps it, and he takes a long breath as he drags it back.

It's the beginning of a quote from Roland Franklyn. "The purpose of the Gift was never simply to infiltrate the upstart race, but rather to draw upon those powers the human mind never suspects itself of containing: the shared and most secret unconscious. As the Folk wither and grow senile with the dwindling of magic, so they seek to add human strength and stability to their lineage. Having bestowed the Gift, they take not just the child whose place it has assumed . . . "

Perhaps only nervousness makes Luke's fingers feel unfamiliar, scarcely capable of wielding the control. He's suddenly certain that Sophie read as far as this, and the rest as well. As he scrolls down he has a sense of dredging the secret up from a depth where it ought to have remained hidden. ". . . they take not just the child whose place it has assumed but any hybrid that the union of Gift with human may produce. Some they seize from the cradle, but human years are less than a breath to the Folk. Many a vanished child or grown youth has been borne away to mate with them and dwell with them in their secret lairs, reverting to the ancient fluency of shape . . . "

In the midst of the clamour of Luke's thoughts one seems even more urgent: he told Sophie that he didn't believe this before he knew what it was. His mind feels close to losing its boundaries, and he struggles to bring it under some kind of control. He's staring at the screen when his mobile breaks into his birthday song. The sentiment is anything but welcome, and Sophie is on the phone. "I haven't woken you, have I?"

"I was awake." He feels as if the onscreen revelation is responsible. "Don't bring anything," he blurts. "Just lock the car and come up."

If this is a bid to deal with his fears by reducing them to banality, it's important in itself as well, and he dresses as fast as he can before dashing to meet Sophie on the stairs. For a dreadful moment he has the impression that she's carrying their unborn child in front of her like a sacrifice. She doesn't know that, and he vows she'll never have a reason. She's carrying a Frugo bag of groceries in each hand, which lets him pretend this is all that's wrong. "Why have you brought those?" he protests and grabs them. "You could have waited till I was awake to go with you."

"I'm not an invalid, Luke. I want to do as much as I can for as long as I can."

"You don't want to risk little Maurice," Luke says and feels atrociously dishonest; if anyone's responsible for endangering their child, he is. "I'm sorry," he makes haste to add. "I know you wouldn't really. I know you."

"You can say that about yourself as well."

"That's me, an echo."

"You know what I mean, Luke," she says fiercely enough for impatience. "And I'm sure your test results will bear me out when you get them."

"They're here."

Sophie looks away from inserting her key in the lock. "And I'm right, aren't I?"

"They say I'm all you'd want me to be."

"Then that's the end of your worries, Luke."

He feels as if she's repeating his name as a charm to conjure up her version of him. She's silent until he plants the supermarket bags on the kitchen table, and then she says "Am I going to see your results?"

He can't recall whether he took the Arcane Archive off the screen, which has grown as black as a plot of earth. He hurries ahead of Sophie and reactivates the monitor. It's showing only the Frugonet homepage, and he retrieves the email. "There," he says and waits for her to sit at the desk. "You stay here. I'll fetch whatever needs fetching."

He's barely out of the apartment when he grows nervous over leaving Sophie on her own. Surely their child isn't in danger until it's born. He hurries to the basement and hauls the three remaining bags out of the Clio. Suppose he has another reason to be apprehensive? Would she ever check the history of his online searches, perhaps because he has left her at the computer with not much else to do? He tramps upstairs while the supermarket bags surround him with an incessant rustling that suggests he has companions as thin and desiccated as they're unseen. Sophie is in the kitchen making coffee, and the computer is switched off. "You've time for breakfast, haven't you?" she says. "You must have."

He would like to think she's no more eager for him to be on his way than he is. "I ought to have more time for you," he says.

"You will when it really matters, Luke."

180

"I should at least let all the bookers know I may have to cancel at short notice."

"You've already kept a month free when he's due. You don't want to start anybody wondering if you won't show up."

At once Luke sees that she's right, although not in the way she imagines. He needs to go where he has been invited—where the Folk will be waiting for him. He needs to confront them, to do whatever's necessary to protect the child. "Well," Sophie says, "you look as if that's given you a new lease of life."

They breakfast late enough to call it lunch, and then Luke drives south. The Clifftop Theatre is near Bristol and, more important, close to Ten Steps Cliff. During the several hours the drive takes, he keeps recalling Terence's tale of the steps that lead to the lonely pebble beach—just ten steps to climb while you heard the sea grinding its teeth, and then the same steps while you realised you weren't hearing pebbles grind together, and the identical ascent towards the cliff top that seemed never to come any closer as the waves swept the vast black maw onto the beach, where it would gape in anticipation of your exhausted fall . . . Luke can imagine how the Folk would delight in this as well as feasting on the power of the location. He doesn't bother asking the manager why she has booked him; he's sure he knows. Afterwards she's extravagantly grateful that he put on such a show, half an hour longer than she expected, and he tells her that the audience was so enthusiastic he didn't want to bring it to an end, though they weren't the spectators he was anxious to engage. There was no sign of an intruder, in the auditorium, and there's none in the car park under the crumbling grin of the moon. It seems as though the Folk have lost interest in him—as though their attention is somewhere else.

— 33 —

THE VISITOR

"IF I'M HOME BEFORE YOU ARE, shall I come and find you at the studio?"

"Don't rush back, Luke. I'd rather know you're safe."

"I want to be sure you are."

"What's going to happen to me at a recording session? Unless little Maurice decides to join in with a dance."

"Is he more active, are you saying?"

"He's full of life all right. He keeps letting me know he's there."

"Are you saying he's about to put in an appearance? Because if that's what you think—"

"I'm sure he'll be a while yet. Don't let him put you off your performance tonight."

"How can you be so sure?"

"I don't know who else would have any idea what's going on inside me. even you, Luke."

"Somebody could. The hospital, I mean."

"I can't imagine I'll need them for weeks. If I should need anyone, which I'm certain I won't, I can always call my parents."

"Or maybe even stay with them while I'm away."

"Even that if I have to, except I know I won't. Honestly, I'll be fine on my own, well, I won't be that, of course."

"This is the last time I'll stay away overnight till, as long as it has to be."

"You shouldn't disappoint your public, though. Seems like there's nowhere they aren't after you, doesn't it? Still, maybe I'll be glad when you stop ending up where Terence did."

"There won't be too much more of that, I promise. You said yourself I shouldn't cancel any bookings till I absolutely have to."

"So long as that's all they mean to you. It is now, isn't it?"

"Do we even need to talk about it any more?"

"You're right, we ought to be on our way. I'm due at the studio in half an hour. I'll call you tonight and tell you how things are shaping up."

This is among the remarks that repeat themselves in Luke's head as he drives to Somerset. The journey leads him along a motorway that eventually leads onto another, which takes some hours to reach a third. Whenever the traffic grows sluggish it feels as if the August heat has weighed it down, though Luke could imagine that the Folk have caused the delay with one of their haphazard acts of malice. Cars with raised bonnets gape beside the road. Often the only hindrance proves to have been a matrix sign that said there was slow traffic, so that Luke wonders if the Folk can tamper with the electronic messages.

At last the motorway brings him to the road that winds west through Somerset. It's flanked by fields and hills, an English landscape of countless paintings and tourist posters, but the undulations make him feel as though the peaceful countryside is growing restless, incapable of holding down whatever may slumber beneath it. Distant spires are dwarfed by ponderous white clouds, and the churches look too small to have much weight—just tokens of human beliefs far younger than the world. Can Luke see all this because his mind is reverting to its true nature? If that has to happen so that he can intercede on behalf of Sophie and their child, surely he shouldn't resist it. He might even try to summon the Folk while he's driving if this didn't seem too dangerous; having one of them in the car while it was parked was distracting enough. "I'm coming to you," he says in a voice that sounds less than entirely familiar. "Wait for me."

He's hours along the road but well short of the coast when he arrives at Cranstone, a town surrounded by a coronet of low hills. Most of the houses are as white as the clouds the hills are holding back. All the windows are crisscrossed with lattices, and even the Frugotel on the outskirts appears to be trying to fit in. The courtyard beyond the stone wall is cobbled like the streets, and the windows of the concrete mansion are so thoroughly latticed that the architect might have been trying to cross out its youthfulness. The interior keeps up a pretence of the palatial—thick carpets, heavy furniture, wall lamps that imitate in miniature the lamps on brackets in the streets—until Luke reaches his room, which proves to have no windows, just a painting of the vista outside that confronts him when he draws the curtains back. He mistakes the bathroom for a wardrobe, and the furniture sounds hollow when he knocks on it. He booked one of the inexpensive rooms but didn't expect it to be quite so cheap. He isn't about to complain; it will do for his purposes. The lack of a window won't exclude any visitors he needs to invite.

He showers and changes and drives along one of the few unpedestrianised streets to the far side of town. The delays on the motorway haven't left him much time before his performance. The Woodland Theatre overlooks the fringes of a wood. Though the place isn't mentioned in Terence's journal, it wouldn't be the first time Luke has seen the Folk in trees. "Don't miss my show tonight," he mutters. "You'll be in it one way or another."

The manager is Archie Banton, an extravagantly red-bearded man in a white suit that suggests he's leaving room in case his tremendous body has a last surge of growth. "Just water?" he says in disbelief if not pique. "You're staying in Cranstone, aren't you?"

"I want to keep my head clear," Luke says, which is certainly the truth, and doesn't even ask why Banton booked him. Mentioning his imminent fatherhood earns him just a partial smile not unreminiscent of a shrug before he heads for the auditorium. While the seats aren't raked, they're staggered so that all of them except the front row have a view of the stage between the pair in front. Behind the back row is a wide aisle, on the far side of which a pair of exit doors gives onto the car park bordered by the forest. Luke thinks intruders should find it inviting, but even once the lights dim there's no sign.

He can only try another version of the trick he's been playing onstage for over a week. He talks about how kind folk are, the folk we're supposed to think are kind. His portrayals of relentlessly helpful relatives earn him a good few laughs of recognition, and so do the folk who address the disabled like children or become effusively friendly whenever they meet a member of a different race. None of this brings him the response he's desperate to provoke. He's reduced to reminding the audience how many

184

things seem to go wrong for no reason, as if the fairies are playing pranks—fairies or some other bunch of meddlers just as idiotic. Some of the spectators appear to be more puzzled than amused by his depiction of the folk responsible—the creature in charge of mislaying car keys, the one whose job it is to delete material from computers and cameras and mobile phones, the miscreant that spends its entire protracted life in hiding half a pair of socks and then another. . . The only word for the breed is losers, Luke suggests, but this doesn't prompt much laughter. He wins back the audience to some extent with his increasingly manic impressions of victims of the frolics, but how is that helping his real aim? He's inspired, if that's the word, to make Brittan interrogate the pranksters, bewildering as many members of the audience as it entertains without achieving what he hoped it would. The spectacle of Brittan overcome by tics and jabbering in an attempt to continue his presentation while searching his pockets for keys and his phone for lost elements does save Luke's act to some extent, so that he manages to end in the midst of mirth. He stares towards the exit in case the lights flush out a lurking spectator, but nothing of the kind betrays its presence, and he wonders how many people think he's glaring at their departure. "Well," Archie Banton says as Luke encounters him in the backstage corridor, "that was alternative and no mistake."

"Not to comedy, I hope," Luke says without knowing whether it's a joke.

He waits until the audience has finished emptying the car park, and then he gazes into the woods. The glow of a bloated moon a yellow as an old skull leaves most of the trees in shadow. Glimmering trunks resemble bony limbs with cracked flesh, and the forest looks as he fancies a lair of the Folk should look, as though it's being secretly transformed by their presence. "I know you're there," he says and tries again, louder. When not even a leaf stirs—he could imagine the Folk are holding the entire forest still—he drives back to the hotel.

As soon as he's in his room he phones Sophie. The ringtone that's pretending to be no more distant than his mobile falls silent, and a moment's pause is enough to make him blurt "Are you there?"

"Here I am, Luke. Who else would be? Is anything the matter?"

"I just wondered why you hadn't called."

"I didn't know if I'd spoil your performance. I know you like using calls onstage, but I don't think I'd have given you anything to build on."

Luke is glad he didn't have to try and incorporate her into tonight's travesty of a performance. "How was your day?"

"I've laid down nearly half the tracks. We ought to be finished tomorrow."

"Here's to celebrating. I'll say goodnight, then."

"To someone else as well," Sophie says, and is gone.

Her place is taken by a muffled development suggestive of a presence but falling short of any identifiable sound. In a moment Luke grasps that she has laid the phone against her midriff. "Goodnight," he murmurs and finds himself adding "Look after your mother."

Is the soft restless noise a response? Before Luke can define it Sophie says "Did you hear him?"

"I'm not sure what I heard."

"Well, I'm sure he heard you. It felt as if he knows his father."

Luke wishes he could find this more welcome. Surely he can once he has dealt with his kind. "Remember we love you," Sophie says, "and have a good night's sleep."

"You have a better one," Luke says and means it to be true. As he uses the bathroom he feels as though he's preparing for a ritual, and can only hope he doesn't need one. He could find nothing of the sort online, and the papers Terence apparently consulted seem to have been stolen or destroyed, though the library denies that they ever existed. Suppose there's no rite for summoning the Folk because people were too afraid to do so? If there's a way to call them up, surely it's instinctive to Luke and his kind. He gulps a glass of water as he returns to the bedroom, but his mouth stays as dry as the August night. When he clears his throat it sounds absurdly like a preamble to delivering a speech, but then he's desperate for an audience. "You know I'm here," he says and sits on the lanky upholstered chair next to the bed. "You know what I want. It's time we talked."

A face is beside him—a replica of his own. It's in the dressing-table mirror. Luke is distracted by the mimicry, and drags the chair around to turn its back. Now he feels more watched than ever, as if the room is concealing a vindictive gaze. "Show your faces, all of you. If you've got any," he adds with some kind of a laugh.

He hears a surreptitious flutter above him, and he's touched by a chill breath. The air conditioning has produced the illusion of a response. Otherwise the room seems as inert as the blank screen of the television squatting high up in a corner. The place is beginning to resemble a cell in which his obsession has trapped him. He's aware of the lack of a window; he's close to snatching the curtains apart in case unseen intruders are posing as images on the wall. "You don't need a window to let you in," he urges. "You're too thin for that. There's nothing much to you at all."

Could the light be holding them back? He pokes the switch beside the headboard and at once is buried in darkness, so that he has to grope his way back to the chair. A strip of light not much wider than the edge of a knife is visible under the door to the corridor. "Dark enough for you?" he calls. "You must look bad if you're so afraid to be seen. You can let me know you're here now. See, I'm holding out my hands."

In a moment he sees them—his outstretched hands. He can distinguish the angular outlines of the bedroom furniture as well. Is he seeing too much in the dark? Have his attempts to summon the Folk opened up his mind? He's suddenly afraid he may have fallen for another ruse of theirs, unless their refusal to appear is one more instance of their senile malice. "Stop pretending," he whispers in case lowering his voice may bring them closer, "I know you're listening," and twists around in the chair. The dim shape that lurches towards him, jerking out its hands, is himself in the mirror.

He tries sitting still and keeping quiet. He doesn't know how many hours he spends watching the luminous sketch of a room. Every so often the vent in the wall emits a tinny clatter and expels a frigid breath, but otherwise the room outdoes even him for stillness. When he begins to nod as if he's acknowledging the futility of his bid to entice the Folk, he crawls into bed. He wants to be alert when he goes where he's sure he can find them.

Something has waited for him to fall asleep. He's wakened by a sense of being watched. A face, or an attempt to assemble one, is peering in at him. No, not in; the curtains are still shut—it's peering down. For a moment Luke has the fancy that a window has appeared overhead, then that a mirror is above him, and then he's fully awake. A shape considerably taller and scrawnier than Luke is spread-eagled against the ceiling above him. Its limbs are stretched so wide that it's clinging to all four corners overhead. It's facing downwards, although this doesn't involve much of a face.

As Luke reaches for the light-switch he sees the figure tense all its spindly limbs. "Let's stay in the dark, then," he says in a voice he barely recognises, "and talk." He hasn't finished speaking when the shape scrabbles across the ceiling and disappears into the corner furthest from the door. It's scuttling backwards, and the lopsided head is the last of it to be dragged into the niche beneath the roof, where the pale lump shrinks like a punctured balloon. By the time the light comes on there's no trace of the intruder—no movement other than the icy breath from the vent in the wall. Luke should have known that his visitor wouldn't linger; perhaps it came just to mock his desperation, to remind him how malicious the Folk are. He ought to have recognised that there's only one way to entice them, and the knowledge actually lets him sleep.

34

THE WALLS

HE'S UP AT DAWN. He has no idea how much he may have to do before driving home. Apart from a brace of waitresses, he's alone in the banqueting hall decorated with prints very like the one that does duty as a view behind the curtains in his room. He makes do with cereal and coffee; he has an instinct that he shouldn't eat too heartily before his task. He doesn't bother looking around for intruders. He means to encounter the Folk soon enough.

He checks out of the hotel before eight o'clock. The receptionist is dabbing at her eyes with a tissue behind the counter that's pretending to be antique. Her face looks remodelled—identical eyebrows, sculpted cheekbones, lips painted with pink gloss, a nose as regular as her tan. "New contacts," she says, apparently to explain the tissue. "Are you off to see the sights?"

Luke hopes so, but hardly in the sense she has in mind. "Are there many round here?"

"We've all our old towns, and there are houses you can visit," she says and passes him a handful of brochures. "Or there are lots of walks."

Luke glances through the brochures but doesn't see his destination. "Isn't Round Hall Way one?"

"I don't know it." She risks wrinkling her smooth brow for an instant and says "I really don't know that one at all, and I've lived in Cranstone all my life."

He can tell that she's speaking the truth. He found just a single reference online to Round Hall Way, giving only an approximate location. It no longer appears to be on any map, if it ever was. "Forget it," Luke says and hopes she will. "It's my mistake."

As he steps out of the hotel a gout of blackness runs down the wall of the car park—the shadow of a crow that Luke has put to flight. The blue sky is empty apart from the sun, and looks close to growing as bright. Magpies chatter in hedges beside the road and fly off at the approach of the car. Beyond the hedges hills are keeping their rounded heads down, and he could imagine the parched land is dormant, waiting to be awakened. A blue flower flutters up from a verge, or rather a butterfly does. It jitters above the hedge as Luke notices the remains of a stone circle on the far side of a field. He doesn't need the ruin to remind him where he has to go.

Some miles along the road he comes to a lane that seems to lead towards his destination. It's even more circuitous than the main road, and in another mile or so he has to turn along a track that meanders more nearly in the direction he wants. The tarmac is as cracked as an old tree and scarcely wide enough for a car to pass his, if there were one. The route looks as if it may have been unfrequented for some time. Swifts dart across it with high thin cries, swooping to pick invisible life out of the air. Then they're gone, leaving the landscape as motionless as the sky, and Luke has to trust his instinct that he's close to his goal. He drives onto the yielding verge and parks the car.

He's surrounded by fields with no obvious path to follow. As far as he can judge, Round Hall Way lies to the west. There's no point in looking for the vanished mansion, let alone the prehistoric circle that was incorporated into its structure centuries ago. Apparently the alchemist who had the mansion built was hoping that the ancient stones would aid him in some occult task. Even his name has been forgotten; perhaps it was expunged wherever it was found. According to the single reference Luke managed to locate, Round Hall and its owner "collapsed of their own corruption" as a result of the alchemist's bid "to recreate the making of the world", which involved attempting "to transform his very substance into the stuff that was made out of the primordial dark". This sounds to Luke as if the alchemist was trying to become like the Folk, and shouldn't this make the place significant to them? All that Terence wrote about it in his journal was a single phrase, presumably addressed to himself: **FOLLOW PATH.**

There's the barest hint of one inside the nearest field. Beyond a gap in the hedge the faint track leads westwards. The gap might have been made by walkers, but perhaps that was long ago; spiky twigs have grown across it, so that there's scarcely room for Luke to squeeze through. Even though he can see nobody about he feels watched. The path leads along the border of the field to the far hedge, where Luke has to snap off several twigs before he can sidle through a gap. Beyond it he can see nothing he would call a path, but has anybody visited Round Hall Way since Terence did? When Luke makes his way along the edge of the second meadow, coloured fragments flutter ahead of him as though he's bringing the land to life. Despite the August sunshine that is withering every shadow, he has a sense of walking towards an unseen darkness.

He has crossed a field diagonally and struggled along the edge of a further one before he arrives at what he suspects is his goal. To the casual eye it's just another neglected meadow. On the far side, beyond a line of trees spiked with crows' nests, the landscape continues in the same fashion. Luke's route has brought him to a barely visible gap in the hedge. Although it doesn't give onto a path, he thinks he sees what Terence meant. In the middle of the field, almost hidden by ankle-high grass, he can distinguish the start of a stony track.

At least, that's what it looks like. It curves away in both directions under the grass, and he guesses it's all that remains of the outer wall of the mansion. He's sure that it's also the path Terence had in mind, not least because Luke feels much closer to the lurking darkness, practically on its brink. When he glances around, nothing is to be seen except the fields; his car is well out of sight. He grasps the branches on either side of the gap and forces the hedge apart until he's able to squirm through. The parched grass snaps underfoot like spindly bones as he tramps to the edge of the stone arc. "I've come this far," he declares at not much under the top of his voice. "Your turn."

The hedge beyond the remains of the mansion creaks in a breeze that visibly dissipates in the grass before it comes anywhere near him. Otherwise the landscape is as dormant as the stones, and he isn't even sure he's being watched. He has to believe that the Folk are waiting for him to rouse whatever the place conceals. There's a gap wider than a man between the exposed curves of grey stone to either side of him, and an intermittent stony line almost buried in the hard earth beneath the grass extends straight ahead from the left-hand section. It's framed by two swathes of dead grass, each about two feet wide, which is all that the ruin seems to offer in the way of paths. Luke takes a breath that only turns his mouth drier and sets foot on the track that follows the near side of the vanished wall.

At once he's sure this is what's required of him. He feels as if he's venturing into or more accurately under a mass of darkness, though none is to be seen. He does his best to reassure himself by thinking of Sophie, who ought to be at the studio by now. He's reluctant to call her, not just in case she's recording but for fear that contacting her while he's within the ruins might send some of the Folk to her. How irrational is that? Perhaps no more so than the rest of his behaviour. He's here to protect her and their child, and he mustn't let any doubts trouble him. He follows the line of the fragments of wall until it brings him to an angle that he deduces was the corner of an extensive vestibule. Some yards away along a transverse line of stones is a break wide enough for a doorway, to which the path beside the stones leads. "How far do you want me to go?" Luke demands as he heads for the gap. "Isn't it time you showed up?"

Raising his voice doesn't seem to help. It sounds oddly flattened, cut off before it can travel far. He could fancy that it's muffled by the unseen darkness, which feels closer. The ground encircled by the ruin has begun to smell dank, and he represses a shiver. Perhaps the circle has trapped the chill of all the stones somehow. Once he's through the doorway he locates the next one, on the opposite side of the almost invisible remains of an enormous room. The route to it stays close to the walls, and Luke concludes that he's meant to walk the outlines of the rooms, even if he can't guess why. "I'm doing my part," he calls. "How about showing me that's what you want?"

His voice seems more enclosed than ever. It does appear to startle a bird somewhere nearby, though the piping notes sound at least as much like a shrill drip of water. Otherwise the only noise is a muffled creaking—a restless branch, he supposes, however motionless the trees and hedges look. "Get on with it," he almost shouts, tramping into the next obliterated room.

Will he really have to wander through the entire ruin? He hears the shrill notes again, a series of them even more reminiscent of moisture dripping in a stony place. They're behind him, but he can't see any birds in the distant hedge. He hasn't time to let this matter, and he strides around the outline of a vast room. "Come on," he shouts—his voice has to be louder than it sounds—as he stalks across another threshold formed by dead vegetation. This time he sees movement, the trees on the far side of the field nodding towards him before they appear to expel a breath that whispers through the grass. The wind emphasises the dank smell and revives the creaking somewhere high in the air; he could even imagine the wind has dislodged moisture from one of the vanished ceilings, since the stream of shrill notes is renewed—and then, as he trudges along the edge of another hidden wall, he realises that none of these developments is caused by the wind. The grass within the circle of the outer wall is absolutely still. Some barrier is keeping the wind out of Round Hall.

He feels the mansion rear up around and over him—the dank walls, the saturated ceilings, the creaking floorboards overhead. He has a sudden awful notion that the house and its occupant may have merged somehow before they collapsed, having been transmuted into a single primal substance. Perhaps the medium that feels like darkness, all the more oppressive for its invisibility, is a lingering trace of that substance. Luke has halted somewhere in the middle of the building, which no longer feels ruined enough, when he hears a voice.

He doesn't need to start quite so violently; it's in his pocket—it's the phone. He seems to have to remind his fingers how to function so as to fumble it out. When he sees Sophie's name, for a moment he wants to cut the call off unanswered; suppose it alerts the Folk to her whereabouts? He suspects they know already, and he blurts "Hello?"

"Luke."

It isn't Sophie. It isn't even a woman, and Luke feels as if the breathless dark has closed around him. He's nowhere close to expressing all his rage and fear by demanding "You can talk now, can you?"

"Of course." The answer sounds puzzled as well as defensive. "Using mobiles is only prohibited inside the hospital."

Luke's rage fades, making more space for fear. "Sorry, who am I speaking to?"

"Forgive me. My fault entirely. This is Ambrose, Sophie's father."

Luke has to resist an urge to shout, because his voice sounds even more thoroughly trapped by the unseen walls everywhere around him. "Why, what's happened?"

"Only the event we were all awaiting. A little precipitately, that's all."

Luke swings around to find the quickest way back to the gap in the hedge. "She's had the baby, do you mean?" he says like some kind of plea.

"Not quite yet, but she's in labour. It came upon her just after she started recording today. One more example of the power of music, perhaps."

Luke promises himself he isn't going blind, even if his perceptions are somehow falling short of the landscape outside the stone circle. He's so distracted that he says "Why, what was she singing?"

"Pardon my witticism. I really couldn't tell you." Still more briskly Ambrose says "Have you an idea how soon you'll be able to join her?"

Luke steps back from the path of dead grass and has to shut his eyes at once. "I'm in Somerset," he says as if this may return him to the ordinary human world.

"Not driving at this moment, I hope." When Luke keeps his wish unspoken Ambrose says "You'll be a few hours, then. I'll advise everyone."

"Say I'll be as soon as I possibly can," Luke says and risks opening his eyes.

"I'd expect no less. I should reassure you everything's in order here. Let me not delay you any further. Take good care on the road."

Luke is about to speak in case conversation—any kind—may help him back to the world when he hears the phone go dead. It feels as though the unseen building has cut him off even more decisively. He isn't quite blind, at least not in the conventional sense; it's more as though his other senses have overwhelmed his vision, blotting it out with the presence of Round Hall—the taste of the dank stale air, the smell of mildewed walls, the sound of dripping moisture that has acquired an echo where none ought to be, the chill that gathers like fog on his skin, the sensation that the surface underfoot isn't earth. He feels surrounded by a structure that doesn't require visibility to imprison him, having demonstrated how it can shut out every breath of wind. If it's able to do that, there can't be so much as a chink in the walls—and then he remembers the last thing he read about Round Hall. In preparation for his final experiment, which had to be conducted in absolute darkness, the alchemist had every outer door and every window bricked up.

He believed that the powers he sought to acquire would mean he had no need for doors, but presumably this proved to be no truer of him than it is of Luke. Too late Luke grasps that Terence's reminder to follow the path may have been not just advice but a warning. This time he hasn't even been tricked by the Folk; he has trapped himself, leaving Sophie at their mercy. "Stay away from her," he shouts and hears his voice echo through the enormous empty rooms of Round Hall.

The echo is the final confirmation of the presence of the alchemist's domain, the element that closes the trap on Luke for good—and then rage overwhelms him. Is he really going to behave as if he can't reach Sophie and their child? He's afraid that any movement he makes will simply add more substance to the unseen building, but how can he assume that? He shoves the phone into his pocket and lurches at the path, thrusting out his hands. He doesn't know whether he means to fend the wall off or to challenge it to be tangible. He lets out a cry—it's hardly a word—as his hands cross the boundary of the exposed stones and find nothing but air. It doesn't matter that his cry sounds blocked, shut in. Stepping off the dead path, he plants both feet on the remnant of wall.

It's all he can do not to recoil and stagger backwards into the invisible room. The surface on which he's standing feels less like stone than flesh. It yields a little and shifts like a restless dreamer. He wasn't mistaken, then; the alchemist and the site of his experiment did indeed become one. "Stay still," Luke says with a grin not far away from crazed, "stay down," and sets off around the walls towards the way back to the car.

The remains squirm beneath his feet like segments of an enormous scaly worm. They're doing their utmost to dislodge him—to fling him into one vanished room or another—which convinces him that he has found the right course. He's preventing Round Hall from manifesting itself, and he feels it growing frantic. Spasms pass through the transformed stones as he treads on them; they feel capable of rearing up from the earth. Just as he reaches the wall closest to the gap in the hedge his foothold swells up beneath him, sloughing off clods of earth. He totters backwards into the stone circle, and then he lurches out of it, almost sprawling headlong on the grass. He stumbles away from Round Hall and looks back.

It might never have moved. Except for a scattering of earth among the weeds around the section of buried wall where he last stood, the ruin is just as he found it—a broken arc of exposed stone and a hint of more remains beyond. The field is placid with sunlight, and there's no sign of any watchers. He can't linger in the hope of seeing that he lured them to Round Hall. "Keep away now," he mutters as he dashes to the hedge. "Keep away from me and everyone to do with me."

35

THEY WAIT

THE POST AT THE ENTRANCE to the hospital car park sticks out a mocking tongue and then retracts it before extending it more fully to Luke. When he snatches the ticket the barrier hesitates over raising its metal bar to admit him, and the engine roars as his foot jerks nervously on the accelerator. He can't bear any more delays; he has already been held up on more than one motorway—outside Birmingham it took him almost an hour to drive a mile—without ever seeing a reason for the hindrance. Where's a parking space? Both sides of the car park are occupied by unbroken lines of vehicles. Why did the barrier let him in if there's no room? He's thinking of parking where no space is marked, even if cars have to struggle past, when headlamps light up behind him. As soon as the car pulls out and past him Luke reverses so hastily that the engine snarls again. He backs fast into the space and then has to line the Lexus up to give himself room to climb out. Though this takes just a few seconds, it's enough to turn his hands clammy and parch his mouth. He slams the door and almost doesn't lock it before dashing to the hospital.

The evening isn't far from dark. He can't tell how black the statue of a giantess outside the entrance is supposed to be. Her eyes are as inky as the rest of her, and they gaze down at a baby cradled in her left arm. She might be ignoring the women in pyjamas seated at opposite ends of a metal bench, chattering on mobile phones while they brandish cigarettes.

Each of them gives Luke a stare bordering on hostile as he sprints past them.

The automatic doors muse about admitting him. He's on the edge of clawing them apart by the time they separate, and he runs to the reception counter. A solitary girl is consulting a computer, and doesn't immediately look up. "Maternity," Luke gasps with all the breath left in him.

"Take the first lifts." She points with her right hand, displaying glossy manicured nails. "First floor," she adds and belatedly glances at him. "Only—"

He can't wait to hear. He dashes along the corridor, which is composed mostly of raw red brick. The pounding bass of a car radio distracts him; is anyone allowed to make so much noise so close to the hospital? In fact it's inside the building, and surely it can't be a radio; it must be some item of equipment that's gone wrong, given the din. He's wondering what this may suggest about the standards of the hospital when he identifies the sound at last—his own heart thumping in his ears. That can't delay him either, and he runs faster along the corridor.

Where are the lifts? They aren't around the corner. Perhaps he should ask the women he just passed, all of whom are pregnant—and then he sees a pair of lifts ahead. His heart redoubles its thudding as he pokes the button between them. The button starts to glow with an upturned arrow like a brand, but the number above the left-hand set of doors seems stuck on 2, while the symbol above the other lift is nothing like a number. Luke's heartbeat recedes from his ears, and he becomes aware of a muffled voice. "Can someone let me out?" it's calling. "Someone come."

Luke has the unappealing fancy that it's like an appeal from the womb—the cry of an unnatural child demanding to be born. "What's happened?" he calls.

"Just testing. Making sure."

The answer comes not from the lift but behind him. When he glances around, the corridor is empty all the way to the corner. Was it a passing member of staff? "They say they're testing," he's prompted to call.

"Testing what?" When Luke finds no reply the voice pleads "You'll help me out, won't you? Be there for me."

How can Luke do that when he needs to be with Sophie? He twists around, hoping to accost someone, but he's alone except for his heartbeat, which sounds capable of blotting out every other sense. Where are the stairs? While he uses them he can contact the hospital on his mobile, though surely they must know that someone is trapped in the lift. "I'll get help," he calls, only to see there's no need—no reason to do anything but wait, however anxiously. The display that resembled an obscure sign has recombined its fragments into a number. That lift is ascending, and the other one is coming down.

Luke is clenching his fists and opening them wide by the time the doors part in front of him. As he darts into the large grey metal box he's imitated by a duplicate in the mirror on the back wall. When he jabs the button the doors gape at him as though he hasn't touched the control, and he's about to jab it once more when they crawl shut. In a moment the lift sets about lumbering upwards, but Luke finds he can't breathe until it reaches the first floor.

He's greeted by an ominous inhuman mumble—the ruminations of a glass-fronted cabinet full of soft drinks. A sign opposite the lifts represents the maternity unit with an image of a bird. Luke sprints along a corridor, past windows that show him night has fallen, and lurches into a vestibule that leads to a neonatal facility as well as the maternity ward. Everyone in the vestibule is waiting for him. "Oh, Luke," Freda cries, "you're here at last."

"He'll have come as quick as he could," says Maurice.

"Without question," Ambrose says and glances at the Arnolds. "One of you should be the speaker."

"To offer what one does on such occasions," Delia adds.

Both the Arnolds look bemused. Luke is about to demand what Ambrose meant when Freda's face grows knowing but, Luke thinks, guarded too. In a moment Maurice catches up and steps forward awkwardly, thrusting out a hand. "Congratulations, son."

"It's a little boy," Freda says. "Well, you knew he would be."

"Sophie did her level best to wait for you," says Delia, "but you'll have to take my word and Freda's that there's a limit to how much anyone's able to dictate."

"Well, let's bring an end to the waiting and unite you with your family. Excuse me while I vouch for you," Ambrose adds with an apologetic laugh.

Maurice gives Luke's hand a last vigorous shake and manly squeeze before clapping him on the shoulder to send him after Sophie's father. Luke tries not to let the sight of Ambrose making for the neonatal unit dismay him. Ambrose presses a button next to an intercom and turns to him. "We should reassure you that it isn't as bad as it looks."

Luke wishes he could see at once instead of having to ask "How does it look?"

"He simply means your baby's in an incubator," Delia tells him. "It's standard procedure with a premature birth."

"He looks a lot healthier than you did when—" Maurice gestures as though he's miming vagueness if not beckoning to it, then finds he can be clearer. "When they had you in a display case."

"There's the thing with his hands," says Freda.

Luke is even more reluctant to learn "What thing?"

"You'd think he was trying to make shapes with them like you used to, Luke. He started nearly as soon as he was born."

"It's a positive sign," Delia says. "The doctor said it shows his strength."

The window in the door of the ward has set about resembling a framed portrait of the head and shoulders of a nurse. "My grandson's father is here," Ambrose tells the intercom.

"Luke Arnold," Delia contributes, which appears to prompt Freda to say "Wash your hands, Luke."

"We all have to, son," says Maurice.

The nurse opens the door and indicates a hand gel dispenser on the wall. Once Luke has used it, reflecting that it can't wash away his nature, she says "Follow me, Luke."

The extensive ward is full of incubators and a chorus of wails, mostly feeble and thin. Parents or other visitors are standing by many of the transparent containers with newborn babies inside, but he can't see Sophie. That's yet another excuse for his mouth to grow drier as he's ushered across the ward. He wonders if he can at least be grateful that she isn't near a door or window when he finds her seated beside an incubator.

She looks exhausted and a little tearful, but contented too. "Here he is, Sophie," the nurse says. "Another one delivered safe."

Sophie gives Luke a radiant smile that almost manages not to waver. When he stands by her she puts an arm around his waist, and by the strength of her embrace he knows not to hold her too hard. She rests a hand on his, close to her heart, as she gazes into the incubator. "There's our Maurice," she murmurs.

He seems to be asleep. He has a chubby body and a wizened reddish face, which Luke could imagine is betraying an age far in excess of its few hours. He's lying on his back with his tiny fists loosely clenched. At least this seems normal −other babies are doing so—and Luke is also able to take comfort from observing that the baby has a long nose like Sophie's. The more their child takes after her, the better. He's looking for other similarities when she says "Was he worth coming home for?"

"As much as you are," Luke assures her, and the baby gazes at him.

For a moment he's convinced that their child is about to lift his arms and stretch his fingers wide in the sign of the Folk, but the little body doesn't stir except to swell its chest with a vigorous breath. It expels what Luke could easily take for a contented sigh, and the eyes, which are as blue as Sophie's, close once more. "I think he knows you're here," she says.

She imagines she's being fanciful, but Luke wonders how close she has come to the truth. It's partly to fend off the notion that he says "I wish I had been sooner. I even had to wait when I got here. The lifts had broken down."

"More likely they were locked down. It's part of testing the security system to make sure nobody's baby is stolen. It's worth the trouble if it does that, don't you think?"

Luke hears her believing not just that she and their baby will be kept safe but that everything is normal. He isn't even sure she's right about the lifts, never mind that it was hospital procedure. What kind of voice did he hear behind him in the corridor? Might the voice from the lift have been equally suspect? Perhaps he and the hospital fell for a prank designed to show him how vulnerable they are. The thought has silenced him when Sophie rises to her feet, using him for support. "We'll have to step out for a little while," she says. "They're on their rounds."

A number of consultants are advancing through the ward, examining the monitors above the incubators or reaching through portholes in the plastic to examine the babies more closely. "Don't worry," Sophie murmurs, "it's routine," and Luke supposes he ought to be grateful that she has no idea why he's lingering by the incubator. His reluctance to leave their child alone for even a moment feels like the start of the rest of his life.

36

HE SPEAKS

"FOLK."

"Is that your favourite place now, the park? All right, mummy will take you this afternoon."

"Folk."

"We won't go just yet. Doesn't Maurice want to finish his lunch first? We'll go after we've said goodbye to daddy."

"Folk."

"You don't want daddy to go, do you? You're just saying that's what he has to do. He'll go and pretend to be lots of people and then he'll come home to us tomorrow."

"Folk."

"Home, that's right. Soon we'll have a new one now that daddy's sold his little house, and Maurice will have a garden all of his own."

"Folk."

"Own, yes. That means it's Maurice's for him and his friends to play in."

"Folk."

"And walk about in, absolutely right. Maurice can nearly walk by himself, can't he? What time do you think you'll be home, Luke?"

"Folk."

"Yes, that's daddy's name. Sorry, Luke, what did you say?"

"As soon as I can be. Well before dark."

"Folk."

"Dark, that's when the night comes, but we don't mind even when daddy's not here, do we? So don't go rushing, Luke. Are you going to show daddy you can eat up all your food before he goes, Maurice?"

"Kind Folk."

"That's what it is, your food. Did you hear, Luke? He said it was his food as clear as anything."

"He's coming on all right."

"Does Maurice think that's funny? I wonder if you're going to be a comedian like your daddy. You certainly love to perform. Now are you going to perform eating up a little bit more?"

"Folk."

"No? Oh dear, you've learned that word early, haven't you? I wonder how often I'll be hearing it while you're away, Luke."

"Folk."

"Well, you do like saying your daddy's name. Let's give that face a wipe if you're really sure you've finished and then he can have a goodbye kiss."

"Folk."

"No to that as well? Only to goodbye, I hope, not to a kiss. It just has to be dark and then daddy will come back to us, and you'll forget he was ever away. Now here comes the wipe."

"Kind Folk."

"Your face, that's whose it is and nobody else's. Oh, what a face to make. Daddy wants a nice clean face to kiss."

"Folk."

"You aren't going to say no to everything, Maurice, are you? Ah, what do you want now? You see, he's doing that thing with his hands again, Luke. I know the doctor says he should grow out of it."

"Don't worry about it. I'm sure he will. Look, I'd better be on my way. I want to be there in plenty of time."

"I'll bring him to see you off, then. Are you still after something, Maurice? Don't just reach like that, you'll hurt your fingers. Try and say what you want. I really think the doctor's right and it's frustration, Luke."

"Reaching to grow up, he said."

"Folk."

"Grow, Maurice, yes. That's what you're doing. Do you think he could know, Luke?"

"Folk."

"Know, yes. Maurice is doing so much of that we can hardly keep up. Now are you going to tell us what you want? Juice, of course it is. Silly mummy should have known."

"Folk."

"Known. That's like know when you've done it. What's the matter, Luke?"

"Just, just I really think I need to be off. You're the one who doesn't like me rushing."

"You bring your juice while we wave goodbye to daddy. See, you can say it. You show him you can."

Luke hurries down the corridor ahead of them but has to linger as Sophie leads the toddler after him by the hand. Maurice stumbles a few times, though he's already walking everywhere in the apartment with the support of whatever's convenient. When he and his mother reach the doorway Luke picks him up for a farewell hug.

The boy is plump but lithe and firm. He might never have been in an incubator nearly eight months ago. "Look after mummy," Luke murmurs, at least as much a reassurance to himself as any kind of admonition. Sophie takes the child from him, and Luke embraces her as well, more fiercely than he could risk at the hospital. "I'll call you later," he promises, which is meant to comfort him as well. At the landing he turns to exchange waves with her and their child, and then he hurries downstairs, trying to put some of the sight out of his mind.

It isn't just the suit that covers Maurice from his neck to his toes, leaving only his head and hands free, even though the blue fabric swarms with winged fairies out of a Victorian picture book. Sophie's mother bought it, and Luke couldn't object without making his reason all too clear. Worse, as Maurice waved to him the toddler stretched his fingers unnecessarily wide, and Luke hopes Sophie didn't notice. Perhaps her interpretations of Maurice's words were accurate, all of them, and Luke was only hearing what he was afraid to hear. Perhaps Sophie was right, and the boy kept talking about juice. He didn't really call his father Lucius.

Luke knows it's too easy to be skeptical. It could almost be another trap set by the Folk, to help them go unnoticed until they're ready to make themselves known. While he hasn't seen them since Maurice was born, they feel as imminent as a storm that has loomed over him throughout the winter. It was worst at Christmas, when the fairy that the Arnolds perched on top of their tree became Maurice's first word, which he repeated for hours on end. There's no use in blaming the Arnolds or the Drews, however, or even the Folk. Luke has to acknowledge that the greatest threat to his son may be himself.

He felt bad enough just now, but it's far worse when he's alone with little Maurice. Luke is constantly alert for the child to betray his ancestry, and he's afraid that his very alertness may draw it forth. Maurice's precociousness is a sign of it, and how long before that attracts the Folk to reclaim their prize? It's partly the fear of waiting too long to prevent their intervention that has sent Luke away now. He has to believe he isn't putting Sophie and their child at risk by leaving them on their own; he might endanger them more by lingering. He'll be happy to think those aren't just the echoes of his footsteps that clatter thinly after him down to his car.

As soon as he's out of the city he sees the landscape growing greener. He wants to trust the promise of renewal—to accept the world as it appears to be and relinquish his sense of ancient presences slumbering beneath, dreaming of their own revival. He's far too conscious of one at the heart of the city, deep in the imperfectly drained pool the streets are built on. How can he be unaware that the surface of the world is an illusion when he's pretending himself? He isn't even bound where Sophie thinks he's going; he cancelled the engagement weeks ago. He told the management that he had to attend a funeral, which felt altogether too much like wishing somebody dead. He gave his mobile number in case anyone needed to contact him, but ever since then he has been nervous that they'll call while Sophie can overhear. So long as she believes in him, he could think he's giving his best performance. All the same, he vows that it's the last time he will ever lie to her. He has to achieve his goal tonight, and then there will be no need. The motorways take him south towards the theatre that booked him. Hours later he turns west into Wales. A motorway imitates the meandering of the coast but gives out well before he's in sight of his destination. A more tortuous road stays closer to the cliffs as it winds towards the Celtic Sea. It shows him Hafan Lanwisel between the land and the empty apron of the horizon, and he keeps glimpsing the islet through hedges and tall grass on his way to the closest point. He's hoping to leave the car by the path down to the beach, but the area doesn't look too secure; he can do without returning from his task to find the car broken into or vandalised. He drives to the next village, where he leaves it in a car park overlooked by a Celtic cross, then walks the couple of miles back along the cliff.

The path along the edge keeps Hafan Lanwisel in sight and shows him the causeway that connects it to the stony beach. The tiny island and the equally black trail of glistening rocks that extends from the land put him in mind of a half-buried serpent basking in the April sun. While the name doesn't appear in Terence's journal, Luke wonders if the site could be related to Terence's story of an islet somewhere off the Welsh coast. Anyone who ventured to be marooned on the rock at high tide would be granted a vision if they found the right words to address whatever rose up from the depths around them "at midnight of the full moon". Luke can do without a vision, and he would be happy not to have to wait for midnight. The only words he needs are the ones that will summon the Folk.

The path almost hidden by grass at the edge of the cliff is steep and not too solid. There are no obvious footholds, which suggests that it hasn't been used for some time. Perhaps only the most adventurous would risk the hundred-foot scramble that ends on sharp chunks of rock. Luke slithers almost helplessly down more than one stretch and barely manages to stop short of a viciously pointed rock by grabbing the tough weeds on either side of the path. Someone has abandoned a crooked staff at the bottom, propping it against the cliff, unless it fell there and lodged in a rocky niche. Luke grasps it and picks his way across the beach.

The causeway is natural; at least, it isn't manmade. It's composed of rocks no more regular than the multitude that make up the beach. They're fringed with dripping weeds and encrusted with shells like symptoms of a marine disease. The sea leaps up around them, spattering them darker. Almost as soon as he steps out from the beach the water is too deep for him to sound with the stick. If he doesn't hurry, the causeway will be underwater before he reaches Hafan Lanwisel.

The route is longer than it appeared to be—it's nearly half a mile long. He has to support himself with the stick on the uneven treacherous rocks. Surely the island will reward his efforts, though it's scarcely a hundred yards wide at its lowest visible section, which is taller than he is and glistening with shells and seaweed. Above them it slopes sharply to a flattish grassy summit less than half the width of the base. Luke has to plant the staff among the weeds and lever himself up with both hands on it. He only just locates a foothold on the shells that lets him lurch onto a firmer surface above the weeds. He tramps to the summit and gazes around him.

He can see nothing but cliffs and rocks and restless water. Even the road is out of sight beyond the edge of the cliff. Where may the answer to his summons come from? A depression as wide as a park bench faces a blue horizon that's pretending to be placid. Luke sits in the hollow and lays the staff beside him, and is about to bid his kind to come to him when he thinks of another call he should make. Before he can hesitate he takes out his phone and keys Sophie's number.

"Hello?" She sounds distracted but eager to talk. "Are you nearly ready to go on, Luke?"

"I'm as ready as I'll ever be," Luke says and hears a small voice declare "Folk."

"That's right, it's your daddy. He's going to make lots of people laugh."

This prompts a giggle that lurches closer. Presumably Sophie has switched her mobile to loudspeaker mode. "You like jokes, don't you?" she says.

"Folk."

"Did you hear, Luke? He said joke."

"I don't think we realise how much he knows."

"Maybe he'll surprise me while you're away. I hope you don't miss any important developments. We've been playing and we're just about to have our bath." This seems like a preamble to a goodnight until Sophie says "Is that air conditioning I can hear? It sounds just like the sea."

"That's what it is."

"Well, you give them everything you've got. Just don't catch cold if it's as fierce as it sounds."

"I won't be letting anybody down."

"And be careful how you come back to us tomorrow."

"I'll miss you both till I do."

"But don't let it stop you doing what you're best at. Say goodnight to daddy now, Maurice."

"Bye."

"Not goodbye, only goodnight. He's waving, Luke. You should see him."

Luke can, but hopes he's only imagining the shapes the toddler's hands have taken. He says goodnight and emits kissing noises before he ends the call. Pocketing the mobile, he stares around Hafan Lanwisel. The colour is draining from the sky, sinking below the horizon in pursuit of the sun. While he's been speaking, the sea has risen several inches; some of the rocks of the causeway are already underwater. Apart from the jagged antics of the waves, he can see no signs of life. "I'm ready for you now," he calls. "Let's see you."

He hears a scraping movement below him. It puts him in mind of claws, but it's just the leathery rustle of weeds set in motion by a chill wind across the sea. He zips his padded jacket up to his throat and waits for the flutter of wind in his ears to subside. A solitary car—one of the very few he's heard since reaching the islet—passes on the cliff road, and then there's only the incessant hiss of the sea. "Don't tell me you aren't here," Luke shouts, but is that enough to bring the Folk? "If I'm your kind," he calls in some desperation, "come and prove I am."

Will he have to wait for nightfall? He could take the insidious twilight to be implying as much. A last hint of light expires above the sea, making way for the ancient glitter of stars. A pale thread is creeping across the water towards the horizon; a swollen deformed moon has risen over the cliff. When he turns away from the inland view he feels as if an unfinished face is peering over his shoulder. "You're supposed to be the children of the moon, aren't you?" he protests. "Come out and play, then."

"Girls and boys come out to play, the moon does shine as bright as day... " He seems to recall Terence singing the old nursery rhyme, but is his memory playing a trick or did Terence get some of the lines wrong? "Leave your supper and leave your street, and join your playfellows in your sleep... " Perhaps in his version the playfellows waiting in the moonlight weren't children. However nervous the recollection makes Luke, it doesn't bring him any visitors now, and singing the song aloud fails to do so. "Don't you like my shows any more?" he shouts. "You came to see enough of them. All right then, it's your turn. You put on a show for me."

A misshapen whitish pockmarked face cranes over him. Its glow lets him see that the causeway is all but submerged; just half a dozen rocks protrude above the agitated water. He glimpses the Folk leaping from foothold to foothold, extending their spindly legs to bridge gaps twenty yards wide, their lopsided bulbous pallid heads nodding on flimsy necks above scrawny embryonic bodies. Is this vision the reward Hafan Lanwisel has given him? If it's what he has to invite, he will—and then he has a thought he hopes may be inspired. "Has anybody else like me ever found out what they are?" he wonders aloud and raises his voice. "Am I the first? I'll bet at least there's been nobody else for a very long time. Don't pretend you can stay away from that. You're here."

"Here . . ." Perhaps the almost formless answer is merely a gust of the wind that starts the weeds scratching at the rocks below him. The sea has almost engulfed them now, leaving a band of vegetation less than a foot high to writhe above the water. Even if Luke didn't hear a chorus imitating him somewhere nearby in the dark, he's convinced he has an audience. If the unseen spectators are awaiting more of a performance, he's afraid he knows what their mute request may be. He can't refuse when it may keep Sophie and their child safe. "Here's your sign," he cries and lifts his hands to strain his fingers wide.

They won't stretch far enough. He feels bones creak and hears them too as the muscles begin to ache, but he hasn't even widened his fingers more than an ordinary human being could. Another fierce effort makes his fingers throb so much that he could believe they're being wrenched out of shape, but they don't look as if they are. He lurches to his feet and stumbles to the highest point of the islet, where he brandishes his hands at the glimmering dark all around him. His attempts to produce the magic gesture are too agonising for him to maintain any longer—and then he feels his fingers grow fluid, bending so far apart he doesn't dare to look.

While the pain is excruciating, it's somehow subsumed in his awe at the transformation. He extends his arms on each side of him as though he's preparing to embrace the dark. His hands are indistinct shapes looming at the limit of his vision. He's glad he can't see them, but he isn't seeing any response either. The cliffs tower towards the moon, which shows they're deserted. So is the narrow strip to which the tide has reduced the beach, and the sea is empty except for rags of foam and a few visible fragments of the causeway. He has given in to his own nature at last, and it has brought him no reward.

He's about to close his fists—he's praying that he can—when he's overtaken by a sense of having overlooked some detail. What's wrong with the sea between him and the beach? Has it something to do with the way to Hafan Lanwisel? He peers towards the beach and is just able to distinguish the path down the cliff. At once he sees his mistake, and his fingers twist in a spasm of panic. The rocks protruding from the water near the islet don't follow the line of the causeway, though they're close enough to it to be misperceived as part of it. The lumpy waterlogged objects aren't rocks at all, and as the waves expose what there is of their faces he sees they're watching him.

"I'm here for you," he shouts almost loud enough to lend himself courage. "I'm what you want. I've learned how to be a man and now you can take me back. I'm a man and I'm you as well."

There's only pain in his hands now. His fingers shrink together, and he lowers his shaky arms to clasp his throbbing hands against him. Surely that doesn't matter; he can still see the eyes, which are entirely black, whenever the waves reveal them. He can see that the heads haven't moved. "Take whatever you want of me," he cries, "so long as you leave my son alone. Is it a deal? Haven't I got anything you want?"

He's suddenly afraid that the answer is no, except for little Maurice. The heads are watching him expressionlessly, not least because of lacking any mouths to speak of, and nothing stirs except the waves. He's about to declare that he has no other deal to offer, but then he realises that the shapes crowding through the water towards Hafan Lanwisel aren't just waves after all. Some of the sinuous movements belong to elongated fingers. Without leaving their lairs in the water, the Folk are reaching for him.

The hands scurry like a swarm of crabs up the side of the islet, and the spindly glistening arms extend after them. When dozens of fingers find Luke they feel as cold and boneless as snails. They're more fluid, because they seep into his flesh, reminding how similar he is to them. More than one hand closes around his heart and palpates it, but this doesn't seem to be their goal; perhaps the action may even be meant as some kind of token of kinship. Fingers grope at his lungs and his innards, but most of them are aiming higher. The fingertips that manipulate his eyeballs from within make him feel like a helpless puppet, and so does the finger that invades his tongue from behind. Until they move on he expects them to force him to perform some kind of routine. But they're bound for his brain, and all the fingers cluster on his skull before oozing through the bone into the depths of his mind.

Perhaps once they're at their feast the process takes no longer than a thought, but it seems to last as long as he's lived. When they crawl out of him Luke staggers back and forth, clutching at the air with his agonised hands, almost toppling down the grassy slope into the sea. His eyes are uselessly blurred—he could imagine that a residue of the intrusive fingers has lingered in them—and his tongue is coated with a stagnant taste. Eventually his eyes focus, and his body reverts to not feeling hollowed out from within. The sea between Hafan Lanwisel and the beach is empty apart from the waves, and he knows the Folk have left him. The moon shines down on the cliffs and the seascape, but Luke feels as if the sight is too remote to grasp. He has the impression that a light has gone out of his world.

THE DANCERS

"SO HOW ARE BOTH MY MEN?"

"Replete."

"What do you say, Maurice? Are you full up as well?"

"I'm replete too."

"Be careful saying things like that at school."

"Why, mummy? Don't you want Miss Allenby to say she can't keep up with me again?"

"We don't mind that. She was praising you. We don't want you being bullied, that's all."

"Buthlied, you mean."

"Have you been doing that routine for him, Luke?"

"I must have. When was that, Maurice?"

"When I was very little. I remember, though. And I promise I won't be bullied. I know how to make the others like me."

"Well, that's a talent to add to all the rest. Will you have another story for me to read when I'm home?"

"I'm thinking about one. I've been helping daddy. I can make another pasta sauce now."

"Don't pinch too many of our skills or there'll be nothing left of us. And you're taking care in the kitchen, aren't you?"

"Of course he is, Sophie. I'm making sure."

"I didn't mean you wouldn't. So what's your Sunday treat going to be?"

"Seeing the Arnolds, and then it can be your parents next weekend."

"Hey, Mo, whaddya know?"

"Maurice, stop it. You really do sound like big Maurice, though. All right, I'm laughing, but you need to watch out who you imitate."

"Morry, I do believe you've grown another inch at least. You'll soon be as big as my Maurice."

"Now really, stop it. Freda isn't there, though I don't suppose she'd mind. I could easily believe she was there, all the same. I wonder if you're going to follow us onto the stage."

"I've got some songs in my head I'm trying to make up."

"Honestly, is there anything you aren't going to be able to do? Just don't settle too soon on what you want to do in life. You needn't be like us."

"I want to be, and all my grandparents as well."

"You certainly know what to say to people. You mustn't think I'm saying you don't mean it, though. Now I'd better be going. I'm nearly on. Goodnight till tomorrow, Luke. Goodnight, my favourite six-year-old."

As Luke turns off the mobile, which is lying on the kitchen table that accompanied the family from the apartment downtown, his son says "Dad?"

While his blue eyes are innocently wide, his pinkish lips are playing with a smile, and he's wrinkling his long nose in the way he prefigures a joke. "Go on," says Luke.

"Who's this?" Having hummed a few bars of a jaunty tune, he adopts a patient though faintly aggrieved voice to say "Beethoven."

"It's a good job your mother can't hear you taking off her parents," Luke says, though he thinks Sophie's amusement would be less uneasy than his own. "Now what do you want to do before bedtime?"

"Please may we go for a walk?"

Luke hears him echoing Sophie's parents again, this time with the politeness Delia taught him. "Where do you suggest?"

"Somewhere new."

Luke can't help regretting that he's no longer aware which places may harbour magic. That's just one of the abilities that were taken from him that night on Hafan Lanwisel. By dawn the tide had receded far enough to leave the causeway safe to cross, but the world to which he was returning seemed flat and dull, little better than lifeless despite all the new leaves and blossoms he saw everywhere on his interminable way home.

Only Sophie and their toddler had illuminated it for him. "We'll drive," he risks proposing, "and see what we find."

He opens the front door of the large cottage while Maurice lingers in the hall. The boy is admiring some of the posters with which he insisted his parents should decorate it. Perhaps he'd grown used to the posters in the hallway of the apartment, though the family moved to the cottage before he was a year old. He wasn't much older when he surprised them by reading every poster aloud. More of them are Sophie's, along with her six album covers and her award for a million downloads of *A Song We All Can Sing*, than belong to Luke. To some extent his career has recovered from the series of uninspired performances he gave after his night on Hafan Lanwisel, even if he feels he's simply imitating the shows he used to put on, replicating his own mimicry because he has lost so much of his power of observation. Perhaps now he's too close to human to be able to stand back. "Ready for an adventure?" he calls to his son.

They're in a side street of Woolton, one of the outlying villages of Liverpool. The couple of main streets don't concede too much to progress; tea shops nestle among the bistros and elegant hairdressing salons, and the village cinema stops the film halfway through for tea and cakes. The light of the late June evening gleams on the gate at the end of the path between virtually identical flowerbeds. The wrought-iron image that's central to the gate is borrowing the light in the manner of the moon it represents. One reason the Arnolds made a present of the gate is how fond little Maurice was of it, conveying this before he could even speak. As Luke shuts the front door the boy points at the gate. "That's my story."

"What is, Maurice?"

"They're the hands that made the moon and now they're giving it to us. Maybe it's a song as well."

"I expect your mother would like that," Luke says and feels as if his unease has made him too guarded. "I hope you know we're both proud of you."

"I am of you too."

Or did he say two? Perhaps he meant both; he already knows a good few tricks with language. "We ought to be of mummy, that's for sure," Luke says and heads for the car.

Without her success they wouldn't be able to afford a number of things, not least the double garage. As the boy walks towards it the door rises like a lid somebody is opening from within, but only because he's using Luke's

213

key fob. At least his delight in devices of the kind is childlike. He hands his father the keys once he has wakened the Lexus with the fob, and Luke drives out of the garage. As the door sinks into place he says "Where would you like to go?"

"Shall we go into the country and see what's there?"

"Not too far this late. We don't want to be doing anything we can't tell your mother, do we?" When the boy looks as disappointed as children of his age often do, Luke says "Let's see what we can find that's close. You tell me where you want to stop."

Open countryside is less than half an hour away. Luke wonders if the boy will stay quiet until they reach it, but they're on a road close to the limit of the city when Maurice starts to hum a tune. At first Luke thinks his son is parodying Ambrose again, until he hears how strange the plaintive melody is, not like any he can recall ever having heard. "Is that your song?" he has to ask.

"It's one of them. Can't you see it?"

Luke is trying to imagine what sense Maurice thinks they share—he's afraid to wonder how much it reveals about his son—when the boy points ahead with the fingers of one hand. At least they aren't spread wide, let alone inhumanly wide, and Luke sees Maurice is remembering that Sophie's mother told him it was rude to point. Luke thinks this is true only if you're pointing at someone, implying you're other than them. The boy is indicating a line of telegraph poles, and not too belatedly Luke identifies what he has in mind: the dozens of birds perched on the five wires like notes on a stave. "I can't read music," he admits. "You're the one who's going to be in the choir."

He would happily believe this means the boy takes after his mother more than after Luke, but could it simply demonstrate how good Maurice is at copying her? Luke feels as if tendrils of music are twining into his brain, seeking to revive experiences he can no longer recollect. On the whole he's glad when the avian notation is out of sight and Maurice falls silent, though not before rounding off the wordless song with a phrase that seems somehow to complete it. They pass through a village where only the church spire is over two storeys high, and then just a railway viaduct separates them from an unpeopled landscape.

The viaduct can't help reminding Luke of Terence, though the arches are considerably taller than the one above the Runcorn house. The arch through which the road leads resembles a portal to a different world.

Above fields and clumps of trees the sky has clouded over, suffocating the low sun. As Luke drives through the arch the sun finds a ragged slit in the clouds, and a beam of light wider than the road illuminates a treetop before gliding across a field towards the car. It hasn't reached the roadside when it's engulfed by the clouds. "Shall we go there?" Maurice says, pointing at the field.

"Any reason in particular?"

"Dad." This sounds as impatient as any six-year-old can be with a parent. "Didn't you see?" the boy protests. "It's where we're meant to go."

This too could be a child's idea. Luke drives onto the verge beside the field and lets Maurice out of the car. An ageing stile stands at the nearest corner of the hedge. The rungs look chewed, and they wobble in their sockets as Luke climbs after his son. The boy halts on the thick lush uncultivated grass to wait for him. "Which way now?" Luke finds he's anxious to establish.

"Let's walk to the light." As Luke blinks at the mass of cloud that forms a backdrop to the trees, Maurice says "A bit of it's still there."

Is Luke seeing what he means? The wide swathe of grass that the beam of sunlight traced appears to have retained a silvery glimmer. The faint luminosity puts Luke in mind of the kind of gleam the blades of grass might borrow from the moon. It must be an effect of the evening light— of the secretive glow that seems to be advancing through the trees on the far side of the field. When he steps forward the glint vanishes from the field, and he refrains from asking Maurice if he can still see it. They're about halfway to the trees when the boy lays a hand on his arm and murmurs "Dad."

Luke glances at the hand to be reassured that the fingers aren't excessively wide. "What is it?"

"Look, they're coming to us."

Luke follows his gaze to the trees. A magpie has soared down to the grass, and it isn't the only creature on that side of the field. A squirrel is scurrying down a tree trunk—yes, just a squirrel. As it darts onto the field it startles a rabbit, which stands up on its hind legs next to the squirrel. A mass of blackness clatters out of a treetop, and a crow sails down beside the rabbit. "What are they going to do?" Maurice whispers.

He reminds Luke of a child asking for a show to be put on for him. Luke hasn't thought of a response by the time he grasps that none may have been expected of him. The magpie nods its head and claps its wings, and then the crow does. The squirrel darts forward between the birds, and the rabbit follows suit. Four pairs of black eyes gleam across the field at Maurice and his father. "It's like a story, isn't it?" Maurice says. "One of the fairy tales Grandma Drew read me when I was little."

Perhaps he means how the creatures are arranged in a line with equal spaces between them. Surely he couldn't anticipate how they start to behave, ducking out of sight one after the other and then reappearing in order from the grass. Then the crow twirls slowly all the way around three times, and its companions take it in turn to perform the action. It seems to enliven or even to delight them, because the crow and the magpie soar up in unison before resuming their positions, and then the squirrel and the rabbit leap considerably higher than Luke has ever seen such creatures jump. Or perhaps he did once before, and he's starting to remember when Maurice says "That's how I feel."

He could mean it's how the spectacle affects him. Perhaps he even thinks he does, but Luke knows better. He doesn't need the boy to ask "Have you ever seen anything like that, dad?"

Luke takes a breath he might use to keep his words in, but he has the impression that his son already senses the answer. "When I was your age I did."

At last he understands Terence's words, both in the journal and the ones he said to Luke. **GRACES FIELD**—not, Luke thinks, the one he and Maurice are in, but then it could have been anywhere in the world— **LUKE SHOWED ANIMALS**. He had thought Terence meant he'd shown them to Luke, but it was the other way around and more than that. "See what you did," Terence said as the animals ran away, but he wasn't saying Luke had scared them off. He meant that Luke had caused them to enact a little of his secret power without even knowing he had.

Luke doesn't know whether his son is aware of producing the spectacle, and he can't ask. Will he ever have to help Maurice confront his own nature? If Luke was capable of living most of his life without having to acknowledge what he was, surely Maurice needn't be forced to know. At least Luke doesn't think the Folk are anywhere near, unless he was robbed on Hafan Lanwisel of the ability to sense them. Just now he can't help feeling wistfully relieved that there's still magic in the world. Perhaps that's a last trace of his nature if not a feeble revival of it. He knows how Terence felt about his secret; he feels very much like that now—he could imagine that, having imitated Terence, he's turning into him. He holds his son's hand as they watch the dance of the creatures of the field and woods grow more elaborate and mysterious while the night settles over the countryside. At last the creatures withdraw into the dark. The field is quiet beneath a rising incomplete moon, which follows Luke and his son all the way home.

ACKNOWLEDGMENTS

Jenny read it first, as always—not this version but the unedited work in progress. I needed her encouragement, believe me. John Llewellyn Probert advised on a usage. Gert Jan Bekenkamp kept me supplied with several sorts of culture, and Keith Ravenscroft did with horror films even I had hardly heard of.

The book was written and rewritten mostly here at my desk, but it did spend a few days at the delightful Hotel Da Bruno near the Rialto Bridge in Venice.